Tenth Year in the Sun

by

M.L. Wonder

20% of the proceeds from the sale of this book will be donated to Malaria No More.

Design and Layout: MJ Schwader
Editor: MJ Schwader

BlissLife Press

ISBN: 978-0-9977392-5-1

Dedication

To the dreamers, the believers, and the doers...
and to those whose stories have yet to be told.

Acknowledgments

To my family and friends, too numerous to mention here, who provide loving support and hold the vision of my success; you have my deepest gratitude. Specifically to those who contributed to *Tenth Year in the Sun* by taking the time to read it and add thoughtful comments and insight, thank you: Ama, Michelle, Lanetra. And, though some parts of the novel seem to have written themselves, others are as captivating as they are through the guidance of MJ who helped me hone my art. I would like to thank him, my other coaches, and Bliss Life Press for their encouragement, direction, and illumination of my path.

Contents

PART III

Prologue

The Promise

As Adoma approached the harbor, she realized their promise had come true. An off-handed comment during a girls' night in their twenties sparked a remarkable proposal. Adoma suggested that ten years from that evening they drop everything they were doing and reunite somewhere in the world.

Adoma recalled spinning the large globe, trying to focus her alcohol-laden eyes on the orb as it revolved beneath her finger; wherever it landed would be their destination. She lightly pressed the surface as oceans and land masses spun past, wondering what they would do if her finger landed in Siberia or some other remote destination. As friction caused the globe to stop, the four best friends leaned in to see their destination.

"Ladies," Adoma exclaimed, peering at a small dot off the east coast of Africa, "ten years from this date we meet in the Seychelles!" Giggling like teenagers, they clapped in a drunken stupor. In time and distance, it had all seemed so far away, and in the back of her mind, Adoma questioned where they'd be and what they'd be doing in a decade. Or whether any of them would even remember their promise. Ten years later, they had.

When the driver pulled the car to a stop, Adoma looked up at the sleek yacht and realized how much her life had changed in those years. Chirping seagulls greeted her as she stepped onto the shiny redwood deck. Entering the cabin, Adoma smiled in gratitude. After years as a struggling songwriter, she finally made it when Sasha Pierce, one of the biggest stars in music, released her song, "Drop It." The sexy lyrics had not pleased her devout father, but the song provided financial freedom, with the means to maintain the luxury boat she now inspected before her friends' arrival. At present, she had everything she'd always wanted, a booming career, a loving husband, and plans to have children.

While Adoma continued to prepare, she wondered, with her friends' busy schedules and with each of them arriving from different destinations around the world, who would be the first to arrive, Casey, Mya, or Genna? Each of the women was distinctly different. She marveled at how they had become friends, and even more amazing, how they remained so close. In the passing years, life hadn't stood still for any of them.

As she thought about each of the women, she chuckled at how wild Casey used to be. Then, the incoming sea breeze reminded Adoma of a beautiful spring day many years ago in Mya's convertible…

Mya

"I got a pocket full of sunshine" roared through the speakers of Mya's convertible as she and Adoma drove to the shopping mall on a gorgeous spring day. The new leaves shimmered under puffy clouds that hung lazily in the azure sky. The song that Mya loved so much and played repeatedly reflected her personality to a 't.' 'Being around Mya feels like being in the sunshine,' Adoma thought. 'She makes you feel so warm and so loved.'

Mya had that effect on everyone, especially men. 'Why wouldn't the men like her?' Adoma often thought as she observed both men and women stare at her strikingly beautiful friend. But Mya was affectionate with *everyone*, giving kisses on the cheek, and generous hugs for greetings.

"Isn't it such a lovely day?" Mya asked in her soft, melodic voice as she lightly brushed her wind-blown scarf from her flushed burnt-sienna-colored cheeks. Mya's mannerisms and regal disposition suggested former privilege, reminding Adoma of her mother. But Adoma knew little of Mya's family, which she spoke of elusively and with reservation.

In general, other than at the onset of their friendship, Mya rarely discussed her past. So, Adoma had to construct Mya's former life in her imagination, building from pieces of information shared during wine, when each sip loosened Mya's reserve. In those moments, Adoma received glimpses into her friend's past. What Adoma had determined was that while Mya had escaped her former world, she had not healed from its scars.

Adoma met Mya after Genna and Casey but instantly shared a deep kinship with her. Mya, like Adoma, had been born in Africa, but in East Africa, thousands of miles apart in physical and cultural distance from Adoma's West African roots. And though their ancestral lands differed greatly, between them was an inexplicable closeness as African women in a world that often felt unkind toward their heritage.

With time, Adoma and Mya's connection grew and, as such, so did their affection. In turn, Mya disclosed more of her past.

"Adoma," Mya murmured one evening.

"Yes?" Adoma responded gingerly, sensing Mya wished to share something profound.

"I don't look *exactly* like other women 'down there'," Mya revealed.

Adoma, never at a loss for words, gulped and stared at Mya with widening eyes.

Mya, suddenly hesitant to clarify, decided against sharing her secret. To Adoma's relief, she stood up from the sofa and pretended to check her phone. The tears brimming in Mya's eyes indicated an intensely painful memory, one that Adoma did not feel prepared to hear.

That moment of near-revelation gave Adoma another hint of their difference in upbringing. The more Adoma learned of Mya's past, the more she marveled at how Mya, who had been through so much, remained so full of love. Mya never seemed bitter, but rather, acted with generosity and affection toward everyone, friends and strangers alike.

Adoma smiled as she thought of her beautiful friend, and looked forward to being engulfed in her hug.

Casey

Most women enjoy decadent food, good wine, and physical intimacy. Casey enjoyed them all too – in no particular order, sometimes all at once, and definitely to the point of compulsion. While she sought intimate contact, in reality, she reveled in all physical pleasures.

Adoma hadn't been bothered by Casey's addictive behavior or her self-proclaimed 'nympho' status. She loved that Casey was so fun to spend time with, and their friendship that originated in high school developed further in college.

Then, during school breaks, the two of them would take girls' trips to the nearest party destination, New Orleans. They loved the city, not for its historical and cultural significance, but for the French Quarter and its lewd energy. Adoma likened their city playground to 'a whore' because people traveled from around the world to trash it, use it, and then go home to their 'normal and respectable' lives, with their memories submerged as fuzzy recollections. For the same reasons, she and Casey loved it.

She had many memories of their times there, but a legendary one, in particular, sprang to mind. That night they met two Creoles, who invited them to a party in their hotel suite. Casey ensnared the cuter of the two men with her innocent-looking face, doe-like sable eyes, and copper-toned skin. She didn't hesitate to use her appearance to her advantage, possessing just the right mix of beauty and mystery to enchant the men she met. Her suggestive overtures raised their hopes to the possibility that more could be in store.

That night, Casey and her date clung to each other to avoid falling as they stumbled into the adjoining bedroom. Within moments, the other partygoers in the suite glanced at each other in discomfort as the sounds from the activity behind the door filtered through the walls. Adoma felt like disappearing, embarrassed for herself and Casey.

Within minutes Casey and her beau stumbled out of the room. As Adoma, humiliated, gathered their belongings to escape the judgmental stares, Casey looked around the room at the disdainful faces. "Whatever…" she said as she shrugged her shoulders and sneered at them. "It's New Orleans! Why are they so surprised?" she said to Adoma as they collected their purses and slipped out the door.

Casey might have been free and loose in the evenings while on exploits, but come morning, she would never discuss the previous night. That's when her classy alter ego would emerge. Both sides of Casey would fight for attention. However, the salacious personality usually won that battle, causing her to have impulsive sex and overdrink when she would never appear to do those things during the day.

Together, Casey and Adoma always partnered in crime, but Casey always took things up a notch; and Adoma, entertained by Casey's antics, loved it.

Eventually, Casey's behavior impacted her grades, inflicted a great deal of emotional pain, and alienated her from people who judged her for her actions. And Casey, as she shared with Adoma, hated to be judged.

Genna

"I am sooo sick of these people wearing all of those dumb t-shirts with that face on it!" Genna blurted out after the bearded hipster with the dark-blue jeans and the popular red and black t-shirt of the times passed their table. Genna continued to gulp her coffee as her eyes swelled with tears.

"They have no idea what he stood for, and worse, all of the people he killed or had killed."

Adoma never gave a thought to the t-shirts, but felt terribly sorry for her friend who became so upset by the shirt that she almost wept in her coffee.

Genna didn't expound much on why she cried out that day, but from the strong emotions the t-shirt evoked, Adoma guessed that it involved memories from before her arrival to the U.S., after she and her family fled their country.

That day in the trendy coffee shop provided a rare scene – Genna crying or exhibiting any emotional vulnerability at all. Usually stoic, she hardly let anyone know what went on in her head. Her sepia-colored eyes were blank and void of emotion most of the time, even when she was excited. Sometimes, though, and only just sometimes, you could see her smile when discussing certain topics that touched her heart, like the simple childhood memories of growing up in her native country.

Genna met Adoma shortly after Adoma's arrival; they were the new kids in school. As recent immigrants, they were both old enough to keep more than a slight accent from their home countries. Therefore, they stood out terribly in an unpopular way, leading to many taunts and teases, and had befriended each other as a means of childhood survival.

Adoma, coming from an English-speaking country, managed

communication more quickly, and grammatically spoke English as well as the other children in the neighborhood.

"Adoma, please teach me good English," Genna had begged, "They will keep teasing us until we look and sound as much like them as we can."

Adoma agreed with Genna's astute observation. Since that childhood day they were best friends, even after Adoma's family moved to a better neighborhood. However, despite their connection, after high school, their phone calls to each other decreased.

Part I

Chapter 1
An Unexpected Find

More than ten years before the harbor and a month prior to introducing Genna, Casey, and Mya to each other, Adoma drove, against the sun, from her midtown loft to the suburbs. Having missed the previous month's visit, she arrived a couple of hours early to make up the time with her mother and father before the festivities.

Adoma, in a black cocktail dress, arrived for her parents' anniversary dinner lacking a vital accessory. "My earring just broke," Adoma bemoaned, turning to her mother as she tried to adjoin the small metal loops of her dangly earrings. The concern for her freshly manicured nails hindered the tedious task. "Mom, can I borrow a pair of yours?" Adoma asked.

"Sure… I'm in the middle of giving your Aunty directions to the house. I don't want her to get lost again and make us late, so I am staying on the phone with her," Adoma's mother said as she looked at the clock. "You know where I keep my expensive jewelry. Feel free to look and pick whichever pair you like."

Before Adoma could thank her, her mother returned to her conversation as if Adoma had already disappeared. Adoma shrugged, and then climbed the stairs and turned into the large master suite. In the right-hand corner of the room, her mother's closet – the size of a small bedroom – suddenly overwhelmed her.

"Mom, which drawer is it in?" she yelled out. "I don't see it!"

Her mother responded inaudibly from below. Adoma sighed and unsuccessfully searched the first and second drawers of the large closet. In frustration, she slammed the top two drawers and then reluctantly knelt down to access the lower one.

'Surely she wouldn't keep earrings here,' Adoma thought to herself, but desperately continued the hunt, hastily moving her hands through the drawers and lifting random pieces of undergarments. Minutes later, a pair of earrings still eluded her. Determined, Adoma dug her hand farther back, wiggling her fingers in a final attempt to feel anything metallic. Instead of metal, her index finger touched a crisp, papery edge, the texture of gift wrap.

'A package that's hidden in closet drawers? Huh,' she thought to herself and immediately retracted her hand from the drawer. Adoma paused momentarily and weighed her reluctance to intrude on her mother's privacy with her sense of curiosity. She pushed the drawer closed. Then, Adoma succumbed and pulled the handle toward her, reaching back into the depths of the lower drawer. She pulled the object out and, while still hearing her mother's voice on the phone, proceeded with her investigation.

The bundle was light in weight and had been wrapped loosely in golden wrapping tissue. Adoma unwrapped the paper, unveiling a piece of fabric, very faded and frayed on the edges. Though the fabric appeared aged – due to its faint symbols – and worn at some point, it looked carefully preserved.

Adoma cautiously brought the fabric, an adinkra cloth, up to her nose as if to get some clues from its smell. 'Yes, it's been worn, and the stains on it look like the red clay from back home,' she observed. 'But, if this cloth is so special to save, why must my mother hide it, and why don't I recognize its symbol?' The wheels in Adoma's brain turned. 'This adinkra emblem isn't our family symbol. We have another family cloth.'

Adoma snapped her head to her mother's raised voice. "Yes, that's the house. I'm walking to the door now." Her mother ended the phone call.

'This quest is over,' Adoma said mentally and returned

the fabric. Now more concerned with a family mystery than earrings, she decided to forego her search for accessories.

At dinner, Adoma's mother noticed her bare earlobes. "What do you mean you couldn't find the jewelry box? You were up there forever," her mother asked sardonically.

"I changed my mind about wearing earrings," Adoma replied in a soft voice.

"Umph, you should always have something on your ears and on your lips." Her mom abruptly ended the short exchange by turning to her sister-in-law.

Over the years, Adoma tried not to wonder about her mother's distance or occasional shortness toward her. She also ignored her parents' reticence to discuss life pre-immigration. Their family dynamics and secrecy fostered a sterile feel inside of the home and Adoma, feeling this lack of tenderness, compensated for it with an outgoing, affable personality.

Subconsciously, she would soak up the affection of those who responded to her gregarious nature. That's why Adoma bonded well with Mya and others like her and fully absorbed their adoration in hopes to comfort herself. In turn, Adoma lovingly returned the warmth by bestowing her magnetic charm.

Adoma prided herself on the composure and diplomacy that the English translation of her name – Grace – commanded. In fact, Adoma used this ability to unite her motley group of friends, three women who would have never met, much less stay life-long friends if not for Adoma. With Adoma binding the friendship together, the women formed a sisterhood. None had sisters of their own and Mya, Genna and Casey gave Adoma the affection she lacked from her family. Adoma needed and adored them more than she realized.

She appreciated her three best friends for different reasons: Casey possessed a voracious sense of adventure and fun; Mya exemplified compassion and connection, and then there was Genna. Genna and Adoma had a comfortable, but complicated friendship, which started years before the others in the old neighborhood. Adoma's family had prospered, leaving Genna and her family behind. That was nearly two decades ago; Adoma had changed since then, but Genna had changed much more.

Chapter 2
The Trifecta

At 4:32 am, the next day, Genna slipped into her stylish workout gear, strapped on her shoes and ran. She ran briefly, but forcefully, as she did every morning before her new husband, Fred, woke up. Her long, highlighted ponytail swung as her feet pounded the pavement like she had pounded her way through poverty working for everything she wanted.

Genna ran every morning before dawn, even in light rain. And when she couldn't run outside, she did so on her treadmill. She believed excelling physically and taking one's body to its limits in return sharpened one's actions and mind. As an associate, Genna needed to stay sharp to keep rising in the ranks of her international law firm.

On her run, Genna looked around at her surroundings. She and Fred lived in an exclusive area, with corporate executives, doctors, lawyers, and professional athletes as neighbors. She worked hard to afford her home, selling her portion of the family business and saving aggressively for the down payment. Her top priority was buying a home in *this* neighborhood, where rumor had it if you became an embarrassment to the community, they'd ask you to leave.

This environment differed greatly from Genna's humble beginnings in the old neighborhood, as she and Adoma affectionately called it. Family background mattered here. To compensate for Genna's lack of legacy and pedigree, she made herself look as close as possible to the other women in her neighborhood – to fit in just as she had learned to do before, when maintaining social and physical appearance became important to her.

Genna took pride in her looks and preserving her athletic, yet shapely figure. Also, at all times she must have her hair, nails, and make-up done to perfection – always. Rarely did Genna emerge in a professional or social environment without this trifecta *and* high heels.

Image was so important to Genna that she only let her guard down with her parents – and Adoma. She kept up her facade ten hours a day during work, and it remained on after hours while at home. There, she would change out of comfortable clothes as soon as she heard the garage door begin to open. If Genna were doing something around the house wearing a ponytail and no lipstick and sweats, she would undo her hair, freshen up her face, and quickly put on sexier clothes in time for Fred's return. In fact, Fred had never seen Genna without make-up in their years of living together.

As Genna finished her run, she looked down at her phone. Adoma had just texted her to invite her to dinner the following month. Genna decided to attend since Adoma had been trying for a while to have Genna meet her other friends, Mya and Casey. 'Yes' Genna replied as she tiptoed back into the house, trying to avoid waking Fred before she could reach the bathroom to get ready for work.

Genna splashed her face and head with water and let the warm suds run down her hair and glistening décolletage. She smiled happily that she and Adoma had rekindled their childhood friendship.

The moisture made Genna's naturally curly hair, thickened and lengthened by extensions, start to wave up, kindling a recollection of her last conversation with Adoma when she confessed that she had never let Fred see her entirely natural. She had explained that she would wash, straighten, and style her hair, and only allow Fred to see the finished product.

"What?" Adoma had exclaimed, "I don't see how it is even possible for a husband to never see his wife's natural hair. But then again, anything is possible with you, Genna."

"Noooope," Genna reaffirmed as she shook her head slowly left to right for effect. "You know as soon as water hits my head you wouldn't even recognize me. I look completely different.

I don't want to freak Fred out; he has never seen me like that. Girl, sometimes I wake up hours earlier to get my run in and do my hair and make-up before he wakes up."

"Are you kidding me?!" Adoma nearly spat out her drink at Genna's confession. "I cannot believe anyone would be so uncomfortable with their natural state that they'd rarely let it see the light of day. It must be so tiring to maintain an image of perfection all the time," Adoma, not one to mince words, expressed. "To be 'on' all of the time and unable to relax even while at home? Damn, it must be exhausting to be you, Genna."

Chapter 3
Syrupy Serum

Adoma carefully flicked the mascara onto her eyelashes, paying extra attention to avoid poking herself in the eye like before. "Aargh," she cursed herself for forgetting to curl her lashes before application. Unlike her mother, Adoma needed the extra curl to offset her diminutive eyes. But, nothing could stop her confidence tonight. She looked in the mirror and blew herself a kiss; make-up transformed her from cute to gorgeous. After putting a bit of bronzer on her cheek, she thought, 'There. *Now* I'm ready,' and left her loft to attend her mother's fiftieth birthday celebration.

Adoma danced all night and smiled at seeing her mother and father laughing and holding each other in the lively party atmosphere. 'Everyone's going to pay for this tomorrow at church,' she imagined.

Her presentiment proved correct, as the next day the family, along with her aunties and cousins, sauntered somberly into the church, all of them wearing traditional adinkra attire for the ceremony. Adoma's immediate family had on their respective pattern and sat as a unit to attend the service and witness her mother's fiftieth birthday blessing.

As her mother in her queenly attire walked to the altar to receive the blessing, Adoma's thoughts returned to when she had searched for the pair of earrings in her mother's drawers and found the *other* adinkra cloth hidden in the drawer. Adoma still hadn't discovered why her mother had that old, hidden fabric. Surrounded by her mother's sisters, she knew she could ask one of them and get the answers she needed. Adoma plotted to sit next to her most loquacious aunt at brunch to ask questions.

"Can I pour you another drink aunty?" Adoma asked her oldest aunt.

"Just a little bit," she replied. Adoma filled the flute to the brim and waited for her aunt to take a generous swallow. When her aunt reached in the opposite direction for bread, Adoma refilled the glass to the top and waited. Forgetting she had just finished the glass, her aunt quickly gulped down the refreshed flute. Adoma seized her opportunity.

"Aunty, that ceremony today was lovely wasn't it?"

"Yes, it was," her Aunty exclaimed and drank more.

"Mom looked great didn't she?" Her aunt nodded. "Her dress suited her. And we all looked so beautiful in our matching adinkra, didn't we?" Her aunt nodded in agreement. This time her blinking slowed and Adoma knew the fruity serum was taking effect. So Adoma, never subtle, went to the point.

"It's hard to imagine Mom in any other adinkra. She truly embodies our family symbol." This time her aunt acknowledged the statement with the raising of her eyebrows and a slight pursing of her lips.

"But there *was* a time when she wore another pattern, right? Even after she got married, that's so strange, isn't it?"

Her aunt nodded and said casually, "It changed after the coup."

"The *coup* aunty? What does that mean?" Adoma asked before a pregnant silence.

"The coup, you know, the c—" Her aunt began to explain, then quickly covered her mouth with a napkin. Her cheeks ballooned and Adoma's aunt, unable to contain herself, spewed her mouth's contents into her serviette. Embarrassed, she slipped away to the restroom.

After brunch, Adoma, though confused and disappointed by the information received, had no time to dwell on it. 'The adinkra cloth, the coup - none of it makes sense. Yes, our family arrived in America after the coup, but what does that have to do with a swath of fabric tucked away in my mother's drawer?' She would have to put the pieces together another time. Later that night, she planned to have a great dinner with her best friends for a very special occasion - their first time meeting each other.

Even with Adoma's facilitation, the meal began with moments of awkward silence. The women, all from different backgrounds, tried uncomfortably to relate; and, since they had all met and known Adoma at various points of her life, Adoma had difficulty integrating them. Then Casey, agitated with boredom, took over the conversation.

"I had a *super hot date* last night," Casey said, then continued to describe the specific details of her dinner date's closing ceremony while twirling her thick, raven hair. Genna rolled her long-lashed eyes as Mya's protruded in disbelief.

Genna interjected, "My law firm just won a huge civil case." But, in a passive-aggressive power struggle, Casey ignored her and redirected the conversation back to the story of her date. Then, the conversation veered to politics, so naturally, the temperature and voices rose.

"Genna, how could you and your husband help elect that congressman? He does nothing for his constituents, and now he's making the district worse!" Casey argued, rejecting Genna's political stance.

"No, he isn't, and Fred works for his office now, so watch what you're saying!"

"Or what?" Casey responded to Genna.

"Ladies," Mya, the peacemaker, interjected before the conversation exploded. After a pause, she completely changed the topic. "I plan to start my own accounting practice."

Genna stopped her argument with Casey to congratulate Mya, appearing extremely interested in her motivation to leave a stable job to venture out on her own.

Casey, disinterested with such a mundane topic, changed the subject again. "Adoma, how's it going with the new guy you're seeing?"

Adoma indulged Casey's curiosity. "I can deal with the fact that I have to remain completely hairless and bathed in perfume – even though I'm allergic – but I can't get over the fact that he avoids eye contact when we are..." Adoma cleared her throat, "...intimate." Adoma sighed, annoyed by her current suitor.

"Maybe he thinks it's creepy just to stare at you while he's, like, trying to concentrate?" Casey quipped.

"What? Why does that concern you? Do you think he's cheating because of it?" Mya inquired.

"I certainly think it's odd," Adoma responded. "It's like he's hiding something. I don't know."

"Well, all men cheat if that's what you think it is," Casey said, repeating the well-known adage.

"I don't think that's true," Mya disagreed.

"It isn't true. My husband certainly would *not* cheat. Fred knows better than to cheat on me," Genna added. "And why would he want to? I. Am. Amazing. I have it all - the looks, the brains – plus I cook, and can decorate like Martha Stewart – all in heels, might I add. And, he knows how great I am. I created the entire life he is living right now. In a sense, I practically own him," Genna added flippantly, then defiantly continued. "*No* man is stupid enough to mess that up, *especially* with someone who would never be as good as me." Genna spoke so convincingly no one dared contradict her.

"So," Mya quickly said in a light-hearted tone, "let's talk about something else!"

"Sure, let's," Genna added. "How did you two meet Adoma?" she asked as she pointed at Casey and Mya. "Casey, you and Adoma met in college right?"

"No," Casey explained. "We met in high school but grew closer in college after we were put on an assignment together in a communications class. I was relieved because I could tell that Adoma took the class much more seriously than I did," Casey said, laughing. "I was more interested in flirting with the cute track runner in the class." Casey smirked at the memory. "So, Adoma and I bonded in college during that class project, and we were soon hanging out together. We took a lot of girls' trips together too during that time. Adoma knows where all of the bodies are buried!"

"Umm hmm, I sure do," Adoma joked, and then added, "One day I just might blackmail you! Just kidding!"

"Please," Casey huffed. "I'd have to be ashamed for extortion to work. I had a great time back then, and at least I got it all out of my system – I think. No, not really, I still have some more left in my system." The table exploded in laughter.

Adoma, recalling Casey's college days, laughed (and cringed) at the thought that she may *not* have gotten her explorative days behind her. The Casey that Adoma met in high school came from a hands-on family and behaved much differently.

However, away from home and in college, Casey's party invitations flowed abundantly, and she enjoyed social popularity. Her awareness of her attractiveness reinforced her self-esteem and meteorically boosted her self-confidence to the point she became completely self-assured, even as a student in approaching men, knowing that her advances would be welcomed.

On campus, unlike at their high school, Casey's socio-economic status didn't matter, and she gained a sense of belonging from her affiliation with high profile men such as the athletes and fraternity guys. But those students also talked the most, and through her involvement with them, Casey's reputation grew in correlation.

"Well, as Casey mentioned, we got to know each other in college," Adoma started to elaborate on what Casey said earlier. "Though her social life hindered her studying and attendance in our 8 am communications class. But I had her back. I didn't mind covering for her."

"But geez," Adoma turned to Casey, "you could have helped temper the raging rumors spreading about you instead of fueling them by openly discussing your exploits."

"I guess you're right," Casey conceded.

"Picture this," Adoma began to recount, "Casey, telling a story or two to a captive audience of big-eyed students right in the middle of the cafeteria of our large all girls dormitory," Adoma illustrated to the table. "Usually the tale would begin at breakfast after Casey would saunter in with reddish colored eyes, which confirmed her extreme exhaustion. Then someone would sarcastically ask, 'Casey, you look tired, what did *you* do last night?' Then Casey would proceed to say, 'Well about last night…' and begin. Casey would have the audience of our dormitory rapt with every detail of her previous evening."

"You know," Casey leaned in to add, "they probably loved to hear my stories and live vicariously through me, wanting the same type of attention I received, but they knew in their minds that they would never get the attention of the men that liked *me*. Ha, ha. They just didn't have whatever I had. And, I *still* have the touch," Casey said in a self-congratulatory manner.

What Adoma knew, but Casey didn't – or knew but didn't care to acknowledge – was that after each tale the women would whisper, snicker, and joke about what they thought of Casey. They would count up the number of men she spoke about and make bets on how long it would take her to get through all the XY chromosomes by graduation.

Adoma, a sociology major, had diagnosed that Casey acted as such because of what had happened to her family – the accident and the events afterward. But that didn't explain *all* of it, and Adoma wasn't quite sure what made Casey over-act the way she did. Most of the time Adoma would be entertained when spending time with Casey; other times, Adoma would cringe at their capers or Casey's salacious accounts of her private ones.

Adoma thought that after graduation Casey would have outgrown the escapades. But they continued, though Adoma joined her for fewer of them. When Adoma couldn't travel or go clubbing with Casey, Casey would recount the events and shock Adoma with the more egregious details. 'Casey *does* take things up a notch,' Adoma thought. But maybe Adoma would have too if she knew no one would find out.

Most of the time, Adoma secretly judged Casey a whole lot more than she should have. After all, Adoma was no angel herself. They both had done their dirt; Adoma just never told anyone.

"Enough about me. Genna," Casey turned her head to face her, "you and Adoma met at your law firm right?"

"No, actually we met growing up in the old neighborhood. I'm surprised Adoma never mentioned me. We were both the outcast immigrant kids. Adoma's family left the old neighborhood, and we lost touch for a while. But, we did indeed reconnect just recently when Adoma temped at my law firm," Genna explained.

"Yeah, I temped there after college to figure out my next move. I despised that job," Adoma interjected.

"Why?" asked Mya.

"One, because I was filing and indexing legal documents in a file room, though I was a college graduate. However, after school, I just needed a break, so I took the job to give me some insight on whether or not I would like working at a law firm, and well, I didn't."

"Yeah, you hated it," Genna concurred.

"Right," Adoma added, "but after you and I bumped into each other and started hanging out again, it did get better. Listening to your drama-filled love life kept my mind away from the tediousness of my job. I recall that you'd just begun dating Fred after meeting him at a political fundraiser, correct?"

"Yes, that's correct," Genna concurred. "We had a rocky beginning, and thanks for listening to me vent. It helped me get it out of my system and stay focused on the work. I had to do well as an intern so I could land a junior associate position. You know I couldn't believe they had me working my butt off like that on that high-profile meat industry case as an intern. If they hadn't hired me after I nearly killed myself on that case, there would have been an issue!" Genna exclaimed.

"Oh yeah, that case. It even made the national news and everything," Adoma recalled.

"Yup, that was one of the highlights of your time there," Genna recalled. "So Adoma, it wasn't all bad, right?"

"No, I guess not," Adoma agreed. "Also, I was happy that the law firm won that case. All of my work in the file room wasn't in vain! And, I met Mya shortly after." Adoma looked over to Mya. "Oh, maybe we should talk about that later," Adoma observed.

"Yeah," Mya said shyly, "we met in the strangest way."

"Well, are one of you going tell us?" Casey quipped.

"Go ahead Adoma, it's okay," Mya acquiesced. "I can handle it."

"Ok. Well, one day I accompanied one of the associates to a client's business in an office complex," Adoma continued. "That afternoon, I just needed a break. So I walked to the outdoor seating area and kept walking toward the creek behind the buildings, hoping to find a quiet spot to clear my mind and assess the state of my career. I'd grown tired of the constant politicking at the firm."

Adoma sighed before she continued. "The associates even tried to pull the plebes at my level into the gossip, and that just seemed so unprofessional. And, the arrogance of some of the attorneys – give me a break! Oh, and all of the paper I dealt with daily, filing and reviewing, it had become too mundane, but I didn't know what to do. So, I needed to breathe, and I just kept walking, and soon the metallic-colored building complex felt far enough away that I could inhale. I sat down on the nearest bench and gazed at the surroundings – a hotel, restaurants, and townhomes all lay ahead on the opposite side of the creek. I still saw buildings. So, I got up again and wandered farther to clear my mind. This time I looked ahead and saw birds perched on the bridge ahead. I even saw turtles and paused to take a picture." Adoma took a breath and recalled her surroundings that day, the huge white clouds, especially fluffy and pearly that had peppered the cobalt colored sky. A slight breeze had further calmed her.

Adoma always heeded the wind, which she believed carried heavenly whispers. Most of the time, the wind portended serenity and peace. However, when the wind would suddenly gust, Adoma took notice. This day's wind blew gently, and she enjoyed its touch to her skin and gazed above at the clouds, imagining celestial shapes.

"Then a rustling from behind," Adoma continued, "made me turn around toward the wooded area. The sound was Mya, carefully wandering through the trees that were heavy with leaves, toward the creek. Even from a distance, her demeanor appeared troubled, and as she approached me, her red puffy eyes and nose became apparent. When she noticed me, I asked 'Are you okay?'"

"Excuse me," the waiter interrupted Adoma's story. "Ladies, can I get you some dessert or coffee?"

"Yes," Genna said. "I'll take a tiramisu and an Earl Grey tea."

The rest of the table followed her lead and ordered dessert and after-dinner beverages.

"Where was I?" Adoma wondered.

"You were at the part where we met, and I assured you that I felt fine," Mya helped. "Right before I started to bluster about what had me so upset."

"Oh yeah. And then—"

"Oh, I can take it from here." And Mya began narrating.

"So, I told Adoma what bothered me that day. I had been worried sick about my husband."

"You're married?" Casey asked in surprise.

"Just wait, I'll get to that," Mya answered. "My mother and father, with the help of relatives back home, arranged my marriage to the son of a local family friend in a neighboring town. Since I had already reached U.S. asylum before the arrangement, I had never met him and could not return home at the time to do so. It just wasn't safe. So, oddly, the marriage rites had to be conducted over the phone. I didn't even know what he looked like except through old photographs, but to make up for what we lacked in physical connection, we maintained frequent contact, talking as much as possible whenever possible." Mya's further description of her husband painted a gentle soul who wrote Mya sweet letters helping to develop their very close relationship.

"I was surprised to see how close we became without having met in person. And although distance and time zones separated us, he was as much of a husband as he could be from afar. He would check on my relatives back home for me, and made sure the money I sent back made it to everyone. And, I remained faithful and devoted as well.

"Given that he stayed in our home country during such a dangerous and turbulent time, I felt obligated to remain home in case he called, as I knew access to phones was a luxury for him. In my mind, he had the tough part of staying behind and not knowing if I, his wife, remained faithful and pure, as my relatives had promised during the marriage negotiations. It was vital that this was proven true the day of our consummation. With both joy and stress, I anticipated the day I could prove my love and fidelity, but I tried to put those thoughts behind me. I was more concerned with his safety and just wanted to be with him.

"So, I worked very hard to obtain a visa for him to come here. And I believed I was getting very close, but for one complication. Due to the turbulent situation, there was no consulate back home to issue the visa. Therefore, we had to arrange a time for him to travel to a neighboring country to get the crucial document.

"This was a problem. I imagined that leaving the country would be difficult because fighters were around most of the borders; they rarely let people leave, especially young men who they wished to enlist for their movement. Luckily, for years, he avoided recruitment because he was a top student and his parents and teachers pooled money together to pay the soldiers to leave him alone. That worked for a time, but the payments stopped once I found a broker to secure transportation across the border.

"And then, the day of his appointment arrived, and I didn't hear from him afterward, and then one day of silence turned into two." Mya skipped to the end of the story leaving out the details she had told Adoma; the frantic phone calls back home, and the door-to-door searches. "No one back home knew anything, and no one could help. Not a single person claimed to have known what happened. And that was it. So, Casey, no, I am no longer married."

"Oh my gosh, Mya!" Casey cried out as Mya ended her story. "I'm so sorry. That was intense; I had no idea you had been through that."

Through misty eyes, the others chimed in to comfort Mya, who was visibly upset from sharing the emotional story about her former marriage.

Before too long, the light atmosphere and banter returned, buoyed by their newly found connection. Having enjoyed their first meeting, the women promised to make their dinners a frequent affair – same time, same place.

Mya's triumph over hardship impressed Casey and Genna, and Adoma was so happy they could see the angel in Mya that she did. Now, she finally had her friends together. Hopefully, they could all love each other the way Adoma loved each of them.

Chapter 4
Allow Me to Introduce Myself

"Adoma," Mya said into the phone a few weeks after the dinner, "when are we getting together again? It was great meeting your friends."

"I don't know, but they liked you too," Adoma replied.

"That night, talking to them, you know, the part, umm, about my former marriage. It felt cathartic. I think I let go of a lot that I was holding on to from then. And, uh, I think that sharing that story gave me a sense of peace about it all." Mya paused, then added enthusiastically, "I think I'm ready to… at least get out and socialize. Umm, I might not be ready to date, but just getting out and flirting could be just what I need to feel like; like there's hope, you know? Like, I could find love again."

"Yeah, I understand Mya."

"But don't get me wrong," Mya urgently added, "I want to *ease* my way into it. I don't want to dive in *too* deep."

"I understand. I know the perfect spot; it's very low-key. Should I ask Casey and Genna to join us?"

"Hmmmm, maybe next time. Going out is a big step for me, so let's just keep it to the two of us. I don't need the added pressure."

"Okay, I'll pick you up at, let's say nine?" Adoma hung up in excitement, happy that after months of urging, Mya finally agreed to meet new people.

"Adoma, I can't believe we're about to do this," Mya said hours later as Adoma picked her up.

"Yeah, I'm excited. And you?" Adoma asked as she drove to the swanky lounge.

"Well, a little bit. I'm also scared too. What if no one likes me?"

"Come on Mya. You know you're gorgeous. If you wanted to, I bet you could get a date, or at least a number, in no time tonight." Adoma turned to Mya to encourage her. "Any guy would be lucky to meet you because it's rare to meet someone beautiful on the inside as well out. On top of that, you exude love, right from your heart – despite all you've endured. So, you're so easy to love in return."

Adoma knew that like many others, Mya needed love, not just any love, but committed love, the 'all in' type of love. As it turned out, Roger, whom Mya met later that night, was all in – at first.

Adoma vividly remembered Roger and Mya meeting. Something about him, even then, did not sit well with her. Roger, the type of guy Adoma avoided – the overly confident 'all the women want me' type who expected women to chase him, just did not appeal to Adoma. True, he was a handsome security contractor, who stayed in shape, and had a great complexion and a chiseled jaw. In fact, his only physically unattractive qualities were the veins that popped out of his temples, even when he smiled – that, and the rage that smoldered behind his eyes, even when he laughed. It all made her uncomfortable. 'Oh, Roger,' Adoma thought to herself whenever she recalled him.

But that night at the lounge, Mya didn't notice the veins or the subtle hints of anger behind his smiles; she only saw the veneer, his 'hotness.' So, when Adoma observed Roger staring at Mya while she chair-danced to the latest Beyoncé hit, Adoma predicted Mya would notice him too, and Adoma out of protectiveness silently prayed their universes wouldn't collide. But, Adoma's silent wishes went unanswered.

When Mya excused herself to the restroom, Roger, sensing an opportunity, walked toward her and waited by the restroom door, pretending to look at his phone. Just as Mya exited the restroom, Roger 'accidentally' bumped into her.

"I'm so sorry," he apologized profusely while deftly stealing the chance to touch her arm.

"That's quite okay," Mya responded politely before exchanging pleasantries, followed by phone numbers.

After that evening, Mya and Roger dated frequently and ravishingly. Their emotional connection strengthened, but couldn't compete with the physical attraction that made their love flourish. They quickly moved in together, and an engagement, Roger's first, soon followed.

Chapter 5
Let the Good Times Roll

"Congratulations on the wedding," Genna said. "Sorry I couldn't go or even congratulate you sooner; I have been so busy with the trial."

"It was practically a shotgun wedding," Casey jested about Mya's rushed nuptials.

"Well, still... Congratulations," Genna remarked, then flipped through the menu, wishing they would switch up the location of their dinners.

"Thank you," Mya responded. "I know it was sudden, just six months after we met, but we love each other deeply. So what were we waiting for? I want a family; he wants one too. So, now we are trying to start one as soon as possible," Mya explained, hoping that saying it out loud would speak it into existence. She and Roger had grown anxious after receiving two negative pregnancy test results.

"Yeah, Fred and I think it's time too," Genna chimed in.

"I hope it happens soon," Mya added, ignoring Genna's usual attempt to refocus attention. "Roger has started acting a bit strange at home now, yelling at the television, slamming down the phone. It's stressful. Maybe a baby will calm him down."

"Said no one ever," Casey retorted, rolling her eyes. "I've seen behavior like that before from some of the guys at the gym and work. It sounds strange, suspicious even that small things are throwing him off. Sounds like steroids to me."

"What are steroids?" Mya innocently asked. Adoma began to explain, but Genna interrupted.

"Mya, don't stress about it. You both are just getting used to each other. Welcome to marriage. Everyone knows there are ups and downs and compromises. Like me, I hate when Fred leaves clothes on the floor or sleeps in so late, but it's marriage," Genna bemoaned.

"Genna, sleeping after 8 o'clock means sleeping in *only* to you," Adoma quipped, stunned that Genna equated Mya's concern with mild annoyances like sleeping late and laundry habits.

"That's true." Genna smiled.

Truth be told, Genna liked the idea of being married more than she disliked Fred's habits. In her eyes, she believed it added status in her world, like a badge stating, 'I'm stable, I can handle responsibility, and someone wants me.' It didn't matter that in her world, the law firm and the country club, half the people weren't committed at all, some having affairs with each other. It just looked good to Genna to be married, and she liked looking good.

"What's new with you Adoma?" Genna asked.

"Nothing new to report other than I'm pretty close to getting that dream job overseas I told you all about." Adoma smiled. "But, regarding the love life, I'm once again 'in between boyfriends.'"

"Adoma you're always in between boyfriends!" Casey laughed. "You haven't liked anyone the way you felt for Kev back in high school."

"You're right," Adoma replied, as her mind drifted to her first boyfriend, her first love. They shared a sweet, devoted, but secret romance, shortened by Adoma's parents, who disapproved of his background. Adoma grieved the loss of the relationship, but her heart wept more for her future, which may never again see a love so great. Adoma knew she was fortunate to have been cherished like that and only wished her subsequent boyfriends had loved her so dearly, and that they too had adored and treasured her as much as her first one did.

Adoma reveled in her first boyfriend's ghost until Casey's forlorn expression as she shuffled food on her plate snapped Adoma back to the moment.

"Are you okay, Casey?" Adoma asked. Casey seemed irritable, barely speaking this dinner and uncharacteristically relinquishing control of the conversation to Genna.

"Yes, I'm fine. I'm just thinking of my dad. He isn't adjusting well to his new medications, so I am going to see him this weekend."

"Oh, I'm sorry to hear that," Adoma said, as a picture of Casey's towering father flashed through her head. She hadn't known Casey very well back then, but her father's accident had made the local news. "I remember hearing in high school how awesome your parents were," Adoma said to Casey.

"Yeah, before the accident, they were quite the pair. Always the loudest cheerleaders at my brothers' basketball games," Casey replied. Adoma noticed the flicker of a smile as Casey recalled her mother, a popular high school counselor, and her father at school events.

"My folks were the best – hands-on, family-oriented, and very much in love. I wish my dad and mom were still together so that he could have someone to help take care of him," Casey said. In response, Adoma rubbed Casey's back in comfort. Adoma shuddered at the thought of Casey's father tethered to a machine and living alone.

"Is everything okay?" Mya inquired after she and Genna noticed the two friends in somber conversation.

"Oh yes," Casey replied sharply, attempting to avoid more attention.

"So, I have an idea," Mya interjected to lighten the mood. "Why don't we all take a girls' trip together? We know that soon Adoma could be going overseas when she hears about her job. And," she looked over to Casey, "it sounds like we could all use a break anyway. So, maybe it will be fun to do something together like a girls' trip, right?"

'Not a bad idea,' Adoma thought to herself, remembering the ones she and Casey used to take all the time.

"Sure, gals, let's do it. Why not?" Genna responded. She looked forward to spending her first weekend away from Fred. "But where should we go? There are only a few places we can go to let our hair down. Umm, actually, really just two if we limit ourselves to the continental U.S.," Genna commented.

"Where?" asked Mya.

"Those two places, of course, are either Las Vegas or New Orleans," Genna explained. "And you know, there are advantages and disadvantages to both."

"I've never been to either," Mya mulled over the two options. "But I do like the idea of seeing some shows."

"Vegas is fine with me. I've been to New Orleans, but I've never been to Vegas," Genna replied.

"Neither have I," Adoma agreed.

"I vote for Vegas," Casey emphatically interjected. "Adoma and I have had many – too many – trips to New Orleans. We used to take trips there all of the time, and frankly I'm tired of the Big Easy." She faked a yawn and an exaggerated sigh of exhaustion. "How about we go to Vegas this year and have a lot of fun in Sin City. Vegas rules apply – of course. Then next time we can go to New Orleans. It's close by, and we can always go there. It's not going anywhere."

"Well," retorted Adoma, "I know you are tired of New Orleans but it *is* just a drive away, and Vegas costs a plane ticket. Economically speaking, New Orleans just makes more sense. Plus, Mardi Gras is coming up."

"Oh, I've heard about Mardi Gras," Mya worried. "I don't know about all of that."

"Come on Mya. Live a little. You only live once!" Adoma urged.

"Why don't we take a vote?" Genna said, attempting a democratic solution.

They voted 3-1 for the Crescent City.

Chapter 6
Beignets and Bourbon Street

"It's great to be back!" exclaimed Adoma as she, Mya, Genna, and Casey entered the city limits. "I can hear the live music and taste the Cajun food already. First stop, beignets!" They were soon people-watching in the famous Cafe du Monde, enjoying delicious coffee and hot fried dough as they dipped in and out of conversation.

Two hours passed as they sipped coffee, chatted freely, and plotted the weekend's activities. There were a few parades on Canal Street, the calmer street, and they planned to attend those when they needed a break from the epicenter, Bourbon Street, which swelled as the Mardi Gras tourists poured in.

"Genna," Adoma began as she shook her beignet in the paper bag to smother it in powdered sugar, "do you remember Mama Sylvia, the fortune teller you went to the last time you visited here?" Adoma smiled as white powder stuck to her gloss-coated bottom lip. Adoma licked the remaining sugar from her lips as she thought of the entertaining story Genna was about to recount.

"Ugh," Genna replied, "yes. You just *had* to bring it up. But how could I forget?" She turned to Casey and Mya to fill them in. "I was so desperate for Fred to commit that I went to a fortune teller, like a Miss Cleo, 'to help' you know. Why, you ask? I'll tell you why. Since Fred and I had lived together for such a long time, I became slightly self-conscious about the fact we hadn't married. I even started wearing a ring to avoid the looks we received when we attended firm functions as a couple. I never complained to Fred, because that's just not me, but I got frustrated with our situation. So, imagine my relief in seeing

Mama Sylvia's shop as we toured the riverfront. 'I specialize in fixing relationships' the sign read."

"All the psychic signs say that Genna!" Casey mocked and gulped more of her extra-Irish coffee.

"Yeah, Genna," Mya butted in, "and, I'm afraid to hear where this story goes next. That is weird. I can't believe you went to a palm reader. That doesn't seem like you."

"Hey! Stop judging!" Genna, laughing at herself, continued. "As I was *saying*, I was relieved when I saw the sign. So, since Fred always sleeps in and I always run in the mornings, the next morning I ran from our hotel to Mama Sylvia's shop, entered, and told her about my situation. Mama Sylvia promised she could help. But before she could, I had to give her a 200 hundred dollar down payment. She would not start without that, of course."

"Of course," Casey snarked.

"Of course," Adoma echoed. "But she didn't help, remember?"

Genna recalled, "No she didn't. So, when I didn't get my promised results, I called her, frustrated. I told her that I did everything she told me to do as planned, but I still didn't have the ring. "'My child, my child,'" Genna said, mocking Mama Sylvia's voice, "'did you draw the scenes of your future life with the feather pen?' I replied yes and told her that I had everything I drew, except the ring, the engagement, and, you know, the husband I complained about." Genna continued her impersonation, "'My dear when you put the pictures together, did you put them in order?' It was at that moment I realized what I did wrong," Genna said to the group. "I *never* put the pictures in the 'right' order, so of *course*, the marriage didn't come before our house and cars, duh!"

"Duh!" they all chimed in and laughed.

"We've all had those, 'I can't believe I was *that* girl' moments," Adoma laughed with the others and turned to Genna. "And, you didn't have to wait *too* much longer to get your money's worth. A year after your psychic encounter, Fred overcame his fear of marriage, and now you're a happy wife."

"Yes, it's perfect," Genna said smugly as they continued to

reminisce and enjoy the light atmosphere filled with stories, laughter, and bonding.

Adoma cherished the closer connection developing between them with each moment they shared in the French Quarter. 'Would our friendships stay intact after I move?' Adoma thought to herself. She didn't know, but this trip wasn't for speculating on the group's fate.

When Adoma took her last sip of coffee, she stood up in her chair. "Remember ladies, this girls' trip needs to be epic! We have so much to celebrate. I'm thankful that I may have an exciting job offer for a position half-way around the world!" she said overly exuberantly from the mixture of caffeine and alcohol. "Come on ladies, no more sitting," she pressed on, "and no more sipping and staring." Adoma stepped down and pulled Mya up by the arm, who then grabbed Genna, who in turn snatched Casey. As they all stood shoulder-to-shoulder, she shouted, "Laissez le bons temps rouler! Let the good times roll!"

Chapter 7
The Rolling Good Times

Bourbon Street took less than five minutes to proffer a bare behind. The owner of the buns hopped on one foot in a circle, pants to his ankles for an audience of hysterically laughing women. Displayed body parts, familiar during Mardi Gras, helped Bourbon Street live up to its reputation. However, the same street had a charm during quieter times. The buildings that peppered the famous street retained their French-style architecture and vivid hues of burnt orange and bright gold, with elaborately designed wrought-iron balconies. Later that evening, these balconies would brim with partially nude revelers leaning over and throwing beads to people shouting, "Throw me something!"

The Mardi Gras beads facilitated the debauchery. One could trade a bounty of them for a peek of something or another. Both men and women flashed each other for the cheap plastic, which varied in design and ornateness. Although the bigger, the better, whatever the design or size, people bartered the beads like they were gold during Mardi Gras. Those who collected the most or best beads strutted like proud peacocks during the festivities. Then the same beads that had made men and women do almost anything, promptly entered trashcans by Ash Wednesday.

The group averaged five beads around their necks as they casually strolled farther down the street.

"Mya," Casey scolded. "We told you not to wear open-toed shoes. There's no point in having our feet look cute on these dirty streets filled with garbage and urine. Look at me. I have on tennis shoes, ok? And see – my party is all on top. That's all the guys care about anyway. No one is looking at your feet."

Everyone laughed at Casey.

"Speaking of feet; let's go to the next bar to rest ours," Genna suggested. "I could use some hydration and a semi-clean restroom."

With frozen hurricanes in hand, they bee-lined to the next flashing sign, almost reaching its entrance when four young men intercepted them. After introductions, the men and ladies naturally paired off in conversation – except for Adoma and her intended match.

He, also of West African descent, ignored Adoma's body language and immediately asked, "Can I kiss you?" Expecting a 'yes' he leaned forward. In New Orleans, more so during Mardi Gras, going a step further than flirting was acceptable and often expected.

"Can I at least have your name?" Adoma asked, dodging his pillowy lips.

"Duke," he replied confidently and straightened slightly for the introduction. Duke and his diverse group of buddies were soon-to-be graduates from a prestigious law school. They were attractive, not so much in the physical sense, but as in the whole package. Their looks averaged a seven, but their projected incomes made them more appealing. The ladies surmised that they were worth getting to know, and remained in their presence.

"Well, Duke, I know it's Mardi Gras and people everywhere are kissing in the middle of the street like it's no big deal. But, although there is smooching every where I turn, I'm sorry, but I just can't kiss you. I don't know you and frankly am not drunk enough to randomly make out with a stranger," Adoma chided.

"Why nooooot," he slurred.

"Because, as I said, I don't *know* you," Adoma rebuked. But truthfully, familiarity wasn't the needed prerequisite; only an hour earlier Adoma had kissed a stranger herself.

Duke taunted, "If you don't kiss me, I bet one of your friends will," he said, turning his blurred gaze to Casey, who danced alone in the middle of the bar while Duke's friend had gone to get drinks. He abruptly left Adoma and walked toward Casey.

Duke joined Casey's rhythm, and as they swayed side-to-side, he pulled her into him. Then it happened. He didn't even have to ask. In less than fifteen minutes, Duke went from having a conversation with Adoma and begging to kiss her to making out with one of her best friends right in front of her eyes.

Adoma calmly sipped her hurricane and watched him in disbelief. Duke looked her directly in the eyes as a smug 'I told you so' smile crossed his face.

Chapter 8
The First Year in the Sun

Adoma, Mya, Casey and Genna stumbled past the other bars and nightclubs on Bourbon Street, and at 9 am tumbled into a cab en route to their hotel. While in the taxi, Adoma's hand stroked the beads that Duke gave her as they departed the bar. Adoma decided there was something about him, and regardless of his spiteful kiss of one her best friends, he stayed on her mind. She pulled out his business card and ran her fingers across his name.

The friends rapidly packed their clothes and checked out of the hotel. On the long car ride home, they chatted about the beignets, the gumbo, the hurricanes, and the rest of the fun they'd begrudgingly had to bid adieu. They were exhausted from the long nights but planned on using car tunes and conversation to keep their energy up for the return leg of the trip.

"Every second was fun, ladies! Thank you for my first girls' trip. We had a good time and met some cool people, especially last night. I wonder what happens next? Do you think we'll keep in touch with everyone, especially those Ivy Leaguers?" Mya asked, about thirty minutes into the ride.

"I doubt it; most of the time people don't keep in touch. And, those guy from last night, I'm sure they just went to Mardi Gras to sew their oats before returning to their high-class lives and girlfriends, who I doubt would even dream of being at Mardi Gras unless it were to attend one of those debutante balls or something," Genna sardonically added. "Casey, it looked like *you* had a great time last night. Who were you kissing on the dance floor? I couldn't see you too well through the crowd, but I saw *that*."

"What do you mean?" Casey grumbled through her malaise.

"The guy at the beginning, you know on the dance floor? Or, did you smooch so many that you can't even remember?" Mya clarified as Casey, managing to recall, curled her lips upward.

"Oh yes, *that* guy," she responded. "Adoma knows. Now can you stop asking me questions so I can enjoy this ride home in peace? Do you ladies realize we got back to the hotel at 9:30 in the morning? Like, that means that we got home when most people have already arrived at work, had their first cup of coffee, checked their emails, made a few phone calls, and perhaps just finished a meeting or two. And we staggered back to the room at that time. That is like slightly unnatural." She yawned. "I am so tired, and I need sleep on this ride back. Good night, err, I mean day!"

"So Casey, you're just going to go to sleep and not help drive?" Adoma asked pragmatically. Casey kept her eyes closed pretending not to hear. "His name is Duke," Adoma answered for Casey.

"Whose name is Duke?" Genna had already forgotten the topic.

"The guy she kissed on the dance floor; his name is Duke," Adoma repeated. "He is a nice guy, in his last year of law school like his friends. He's studying international law with a focus on international commerce."

"Oh, that's nice, and how do *you* know?" Mya interjected.

Adoma responded, "Because we were talking before he decided to leave our conversation and get better acquainted with Casey."

"Casey, you kissed Adoma's man!?" Genna yelled out in fake horror. Casey just smirked, while keeping her eyes closed.

"Well," Adoma continued, "I think I like him and I'll just pretend that didn't happen. He's going to graduate soon, and I'm sure he already has a job lined up at one of the top firms. I think I can overlook something like kissing strangers during Mardi Gras." Mya stared incredulously in response to Adoma's statement, but Genna nodded in understanding.

"Besides," Adoma added, "we continued to speak afterward, and he isn't into the party and Mardi Gras scene. He has a good head on his shoulders. I found out as we got to know each other better. He gave me his card and I think I'll keep in touch. He seems like good people," Adoma said casually, unaware of the significance Duke would later play in her life. With that said, Adoma's attention returned to the road. "Only four hours to go!"

The friends filled the remaining time with more of their typical conversation. Mya discussed trying to get pregnant again and Genna mentioned that she and Fred decided to wait a few years longer due to their hectic schedules.

Then, naturally, the conversation veered off to work. Other than Adoma, they all had begun stable careers: Genna as an associate, Casey as a contract manager, and Mya as an accountant. Adoma still worked as a "temp" and looked forward to leaving job instability behind for a position with a multinational energy company.

After a series of aptitude tests, a background investigation, and a drug test, a meeting with executives at the company headquarters remained the final step. Every candidate who made it that far practically had the position; as long as Adoma didn't say anything offensive, an offer letter was expected shortly after that. Adoma coveted this opportunity because she knew that attaining this job would take her into an international life with the chance to rub shoulders with affluential people.

"Adoma, did you say that after getting the offer you would have to relocate in as soon as three months?"

"Yeah, after a one-year process, when I finally get the offer, I will need to be ready to go rather quickly." Adoma raised her eyebrows. She couldn't believe that her world would completely change in three months. "I don't even know where they'll send me first, but rumor has it that it might be South America," she said, filling them all in.

"How exciting sis," Mya sweetly added. Mya had shared with Adoma that she felt excitement for Adoma's new opportunity, although it meant losing frequent contact with her closest friend. Mya, so sweet, had such a good heart and always wished the best for her friends and those she loved. And in turn, they always wanted the best for her too.

The long ride back afforded the friends the chance to

converse more than they had on their way to New Orleans and during Mardi Gras combined. They opened up further about their pasts, the present, and the bright futures they hoped lay ahead. However, after a couple more hours, they succumbed to their sleep deprivation, and the lively conversation became sporadic, with only occasional bursts here and there. Then, a heavier silence blanketed the car as a familiar guitar riff blasted through its speakers.

Adoma instinctively did what she had done growing up when the song played ubiquitously on the radio stations, playfully knocking her hands on the car dashboard in the familiar rhythm. She could mimic the beat of the song by rocking the bottom of her palms and knuckles back and forth. Then Adoma accompanied her impromptu beat by singing Prince's famous verse about his mother and father. After Adoma's voice had built to a crescendo during the two-line solo, Casey, Mya and Genna helped her finish the chorus to "When Doves Cry".

They reached the city limits as the song ended. Unwilling to part when the trip ended, they agreed to relax a bit and unwind with one final drink, which led to two and then three cosmopolitans more.

"Ladies, our trip wasn't just a good time; it was the genesis of deeper, more meaningful friendship between us," Adoma noted. Their connections felt emboldened; now they'd truly become best friends.

And then the ten-year reunion plot hatched. "To the Seychelles!" Adoma toasted as she raised her glass.

"To the Seychelles!" Genna, Mya, and Casey saluted in response.

As she sipped her cosmo, Adoma giggled and whispered under her breath with pride, "I love these women."

Part II

Chapter 9
Shimmering Reflections

Waves gently rocked the anchored boat causing Adoma to lightly brace the small countertop as she sampled from the cheese plate she had picked up on her way to the harbor. On her third nibble, she recognized a familiar voice from the dock below and waved to her boat's captain.

"Hi, Captain, we're still set to sail tomorrow. See you at 10, okay?!"

"Aye, madahm," the wind-burned captain confirmed.

'Great, but I must remind him to stop calling me madam. I could be his daughter,' she thought and began to chill the bottles of wine she brought for their reunion.

Adoma finished her inspection, ensuring all appeared in order for her best friends' arrivals. 'Yup, everything looks good. Now I just need my girls.' A smile plumped the bulbs of her cheeks.

Adoma walked onto the ship's deck as a lovely sea breeze caressed her skin, causing her to cover her shoulders. She looked toward the horizon and soaked in her surroundings. The seagulls harked, and the waves sparkled in unison. The curling water hypnotized her. 'Today is a blessed day; this is the best, and life is so blissful right now,' she reflected in gratitude.

A yellow butterfly flew by as Adoma stepped back inside and contemplated a brief nap. 'They'll be here soon, but I still have time to rest.' She closed her eyes in exhaustion and let the memories of the years leading up to their reunion dance in her head.

It had been years into Adoma's dream position before the doubts began. The tedious work, the disenchantment, and the lost connection with her loved ones made her long for home. With the excitement of her new position fading, she thought about missed birthdays and celebrations even more.

Her parents visited her once, but to her surprise, neither Mya, Adoma, or Casey had visited. She assumed they would all be excited to see her and have a free place to vacation, but they always had a reason to delay.

Mya became preoccupied with her troubles with Roger; Casey actively moved up the career ladder; and Genna precariously balanced work and social events, as she and Fred, a rising political aide, became the local power couple.

Everyone seemed too busy for each other those days. Even their promised reunion had seemed in jeopardy, but this uncertainty began long before. Shortly after their New Orleans trip, Genna had made her doubts known at Adoma's good-bye dinner.

"Do you really think that we can stick to a plan to reunite in ten years?" Genna had asked. "I think it's a stretch, and I don't think it will happen."

"I agree with Genna," Casey added. "Ten years is a lengthy amount of time to commit to something. Some marriages don't even last that long. That's a decade. Who knows where we will be, who we'll be, or with whom we'll be?"

Genna continued with her cynicism. "The idea seemed fun and definitely possible when we got back from the girls' trip, but now – under the umbrella of sobriety…"

"What incentive do we have to keep the promise? Would we really care about seeing each other as a group in ten years? Our lives will certainly change – look, it already has. Adoma is leaving us to live in another country," Casey continued.

"Wait, guys. The point is that we *will* care. Just look at how much, even in the last months, our friendships have grown. In a few years we could be closer, who knows - maybe more like sisters. I don't have sisters of my own, so I consider you all my sisters, and this, my sisterhood. Sisters don't stop knowing each other and forget about each other after ten years. I know we can do it, ladies," Mya optimistically responded.

"Agreed. None of us have sisters of our own. And, I always wished I had one. So, I cherish you all… I think we can prove to ourselves that our friendships – our sisterhood – will span the test of time. After Mardi Gras that's fair to hope, right?" Adoma argued.

"Yeah, nothing like three days of all-out debauchery to bond a group," Casey sarcastically added.

"Speak for yourself," Mya teased and poked Casey in the rib.

"I know we were all buzzed when we made the promise, but it can happen. I *know* it can." Adoma paused for a moment in thought. "Okay, I have an idea to solidify our promise - something to look forward to and anchor our commitment, since we're already wavering," she said as she grabbed a piece of paper and began to tear it into pieces. "Let's write down two things. One – a dream we hope to fulfill by the reunion; and two – a deep secret we want to put behind us. Fold up each piece of paper, put your name on the outside, and here, put it in…" Adoma looked around for something she could place everything. "Here, in this brown bag."

"Adoma, in your doggy bag?" Casey smirked.

"Yes, Casey, it is indeed my takeaway, but I promise I won't throw the sheets out, and more importantly, I promise not to look. Once we put the paper away, we are not to think about it again until ten years from now. We won't open it, and it will not see the light of day until we are all in the Seychelles. I'm sure by then we will have forgotten what we wrote anyway, and when we open it up, it will be like surprises. Okay?"

"Okay, that works for me, but since you relocate next week for your job, won't it get lost?" Casey asked Adoma.

"No, I will hide them in my closet at my parent's house, and tuck them away in one of my many shoe boxes."

The other three ladies nodded in agreement and

ceremoniously wrote on their pieces of paper. Adoma watched Casey scribble and wondered who between herself and Casey would have the bigger secret.

Chapter 10
Who Has It All Anyway?

'Happy Birthday!' Adoma read the messages from Casey, Mya, and Genna. Although the ladies hadn't visited her, they kept in contact via written communication and never missed a birthday.

Birthdays never meant much to Adoma either way, but as she read her 30th birthday messages alone, eating room service in a foreign country, instead of being surrounded by family and friends, she contemplated, 'Would it always be this way?'

Lately, that pesky question seeped through the cracks of her mind. It would creep in often, but she pushed it away. 'Who has it all anyway?' The louder declaration would then take the smaller insecurity's place. Adoma silenced both thoughts by immersing herself into work, where she succeeded – as evidenced by her promotions and the size of her homes, office spaces, and expense accounts. They grew in correlation to her professional achievements. However, the bigger homes just drew attention to the accumulated shoes and purses that occupied the extra bedrooms. The inanimate objects, collected on various adventures, no longer substituted for the love and connection she had wished filled her home. 'Would it always be this way?' The pesky question popped in again.

Adoma just ignored it, shoved it back, and continued working hard. When tired of excessive work, she distracted herself with exotic trips, fancy dinners, and casual flings. The brief romances at times turned into flickers of a relationship, but nothing more. Her love life, already in need of rehabilitation, suffered more in her new environment, prompting Adoma to think often of her first boyfriend, her first love, her first everything. Her disapproving parents had unfortunately curtailed that, her only happy relationship. Hollow times like these caused Adoma to worry that she'd never love like that again.

Adoma never thought that a chance encounter in New Orleans would lead to more, but she and Duke had something special and remained in close contact throughout Adoma's career transitions and relocations. Even with his transfer to Germany and Adoma's heavy travel schedule, they stayed in touch. He made arrangements to see Adoma all of the time, but only succeeded when the location suited him, and it suited him to meet Adoma in Argentina during her work conference.

A romance bloomed on their first night in Buenos Aires while in a plaza square. Duke wiped the water from a fountain's spray from Adoma's cheek, and he enveloped her in a hug and gazed into her ebony eyes with his own. When their eyes locked, Adoma smiled invitingly and Duke bent down slowly for their first kiss.

By this time in their lives, Duke had become very successful, a business titan in the making, accustomed to the control he wielded in his professional world and by extension into all aspects of his life. Duke always received a 'yes'. And, on the rare occasion he received a 'no' he could turn it into a 'maybe' and then eventually the 'maybe' into a 'yes'. On their next visit with each other, Duke asked Adoma to stay with him that night. She said 'maybe'.

After that evening, their relationship begged acknowledgment, which Duke hesitated to validate. Confusingly, Duke proclaimed he wanted to marry Adoma, but simultaneously backtracked, subtly blaming Adoma's career ambition as the reason why the two of them would never work. Yet, the frequent visits continued, and when they met in Miami for dinner one evening, Adoma expected, finally, a commitment. Instead, she received a confession.

"I'm engaged," Duke admitted. Adoma dropped her jaw and then her fork as he explained that he recently promised himself to another. He also admitted that he didn't want to get married. Duke said that he knew he was marrying the wrong woman, and that he had always wanted to be with Adoma and wished he could instead, but he had no choice. He had to marry the woman who was carrying his child, an accident after their casual fling. He claimed to be miserable, but that he had no choice.

He droned on and on and even discussed the past. "Adoma I tried to show you my love before, but my attempts went unnoticed. You could never see what I tried to offer you, and now it's too late." Duke kept speaking about what could have been. He professed to care for Adoma and that he still wanted to be with her, but he had to do the right thing. He asserted a lot of things, but Adoma no longer believed him.

After that evening, Adoma cut off all communication with Duke. Just like that, Duke, who orbited her life like the moon, became equally as unattainable. His upcoming marriage meant no more wondering, hoping, or fantasizing about what they could have become.

It took a while to heal from the loss of Duke in her life, but finally, the dead weight on her heart lifted. And when it did, Adoma looked at all of the other areas in her life that had felt unfulfilled. Adoma wanted to fix those too. The new clarity in her love life led to seeking the same lightness in the rest of her world.

So, Adoma reevaluated all of the things and people in her world and realized the exotic trips, the beautiful homes, the lavish dinners were all just distractions, temporary highs, none leading to a life of permanent fulfillment. True, she reached her dream of having a job with great travel, but what about her trajectory? She often thought, 'Ten years from now would these same things fulfill me?'

'I doubt it,' Adoma answered her own question. 'But, I don't know what to do. Do I want a change from this lifestyle that I wanted for years and have loved?' Adoma smiled at her memories. 'Do I really just want to throw it all away? I worked so hard to be here.' Adoma struggled with opposing thoughts. 'No one ever leaves a job like this. Am I crazy? It took me nearly two years to land this job, and it made my parents and me so proud to get it. I can't just walk away.' Adoma's heart tightened as fear paralyzed her into indecision. 'I've had some amazing experiences, made some awesome friends, and met well-known people, even some celebrities. Seriously, I'm crazy for thinking about leaving! My company pays well; I get a free car and house. Do I really want to walk away from all of this for the unknown?'

'Yes,' Adoma decided, and she just quit – without a real plan. She. Just. Quit. And, it felt… liberating.

Chapter 11
Wide Awake

The smell of home-cooked jollof rice wafting in the air welcomed Adoma back home. She ate her favorite comfort food, savoring its tomato-based flavor and the company of her mother and father. When she finished, she walked upstairs, crawled into her childhood bed, and then slept – for days.

She hadn't shed a tear since announcing her resignation. She didn't cry when saying goodbye to her coworkers, nor did she cry when the movers put the last few years of her life into boxes and crates. So when she returned home, she processed all of the good-byes and the recent changes in her life in her own way. She slept. She slept for days. Even when she was awake, she was sleeping. She slept for more days. The tears she could not shed while awake, poured from her heart while she was asleep. Then on the third week, when her soul had adequately purged, she emerged from her womb of self-protection.

Adoma woke up refreshed and with a melody playing in her head. So, she threw off the bedcovers, walked to her closet, and rummaged through her stuff. She shoveled through old clothes, shoes, and scrapbooks. She glanced at her faded journal, and beside it found her songbook.

She opened it and saw the first song she had ever written, a love song about a broken heart. Not a terribly bitter one, just a song explaining sadness over a broken relationship, but gratitude for its good times. Adoma flipped the pages. The next song in her book was a tearjerker – about the same guy! 'How schizo,' Adoma thought to herself. 'Funny how I could feel so heart-broken over men who seem insignificant now.'

"Where Are You Now?" Adoma repeated the title of the song.

'Ha, I could really care less where Troy is now,' she mumbled.

She kept flipping. 'Oh, *another* sad love song,' Adoma muttered, this time as she looked down at the tune "Something More Than Love" and sang its lyrics out loud.

There's gotta be
Something, something more than love for me
'cause when I'm thinkin'
Thinkin' I'm loving
I'm wrong – oh so wrong.

Then eager to move past her previous emotional pain, she quickly flipped to the next blank page to record the lyrics of the song she woke up singing that wanted a home outside of her head. Satisfied with what she'd written she smiled and thought, 'I like this. I want to write happy songs now, uplifting songs, not just those about confusion, loss, or heartbreak. The catharsis is nice, but there is so much more to life and so much more to write about.'

It pleased Adoma to discover her recently inspired creation was about the hope she now felt for love and in her life in general. She titled it "Freedom".

The new song reminded her of the song "Unwritten" she used to play, which made her think about her life's path and the life she could have. Similar to that song, she imagined she was the screenwriter of her life. And filled with new hope, Adoma said to herself, 'Every day I could write a new page and create who I am and who I will be. Feel life, drink it in, take chances, do it all. I know it doesn't mean that I won't feel some pain. Letting go in a changing life can feel uneasy and uncomfortable, but as the 'captain of my soul' I decide what I do and who I will be,' Adoma jotted in the journal that she found lying next to her songbook.

Adoma's self-revelations made her heart sing – until she noticed her disheveled closet. She got up and carefully refolded her clothes, strewn on the floor while she looked for her songbook. As she neatly organized everything, Adoma couldn't help but think about the preserved fabric she discovered years ago in her mother's drawer. 'I'm curious if my father knows about the cloth?' Adoma wondered, as the questions and doubts about her family's past returned.

She shelved those thoughts along with her songbook – for the moment. She placed the book high in her closet next to the shoebox with her dreams and secrets, and those of Genna, Casey, and Mya waiting to be re-opened at the reunion.

Chapter 12
Decisions, Decisions

For months afterward, Adoma passed the time writing lyrics and studying the craft of songwriting. She wrote copiously, soon filling a notebook with her creations. She sang her new songs to any available ear, but mostly cajoled Genna, Mya, or Casey to listen when they met for dinners.

When perfected, Adoma shared her latest song "Freedom" at their most recent meal. Casey, who loved music, surprised her, saying, "That's really good. I remember you always talking about being a songwriter our freshman year in school."

"Oh yeah. I did," Adoma said. The statement hit her with mixed emotions. She was happy that musically knowledgeable Casey validated her talent and remembered their frequent college discussions of what they'd do in life if money didn't matter. But, Adoma also felt saddened that for many years she suppressed this childhood dream and ventured onto another path, an all-encompassing one, leaving little room for creativity.

"You know, had I not returned home, I probably would not have realized that," Adoma surmised.

"I'm sure your return has availed you the opportunity to reconnect with family, friends, and most important, the root of your being," Mya added.

True, Adoma had received the answers she needed by coming home, and her creative spirit burgeoned, flying again as she rediscovered her life's calling. To properly summon it, Adoma felt that she needed to fearlessly delve into her life's journey by braving the unknown.

"Y'all, what if I'm not meant to stay here?"

"Are you seriously considering leaving again?" Casey lowered her fork and raised an eyebrow to Adoma's question.

"You're seriously thinking of leaving to pursue *songwriting*? You sure are brave," Genna added.

'Bravery,' Adoma thought to herself. Yes, Adoma left the States to go off to a fancy job overseas, and before that, she convinced her friends to reunite in a foreign place. She was never afraid to venture off into the unknown, but this time would be a real test of faith. Leaving to pursue a dream, something not yet real, seemed so much harder to do. Yet, she *had to* try.

"Yes, I think I am, chicas. I don't think I can make it in songwriting if I stay here," Adoma explained. "And I am starting to feel as if I am being urged to take action. I feel like I am missing out on some parallel life that has already begun without me. I need to be in a creative place in a city with those types of opportunities."

"Where does an aspiring songwriter go?" Mya asked.

"Well, it's either New York or Los Angeles, I think," Adoma nodded shyly, but continued as if in consolation, "Wherever it is, I will still come back often to visit!"

"What?" Mya ignored the last phrase. "Those places are far, and you just got back!" Mya's head and shoulders slumped as she spoke. Mya had recently begun to rely heavily on Adoma's emotional support.

"I know," Adoma said. She paused for a moment to squeeze Mya's hand, as she knew that she had been struggling a lot with Roger. "I just have this feeling that I need to go and see if songwriting could work out. I don't think I can do that here." She added, "Wherever I go, we will see each other again before we know it," she said in a high-pitched, overly exaggerated positive tone. "We will always remain in contact, so, I know, the distance between us will not affect the quality of our friendships, which will always connect us no matter where we are. I am sooo grateful for you ladies and know that I am blessed to call you my friends," Adoma said, sharing with her friends the appreciation for their support, which began to fill her heart as she reflected on it during the dinner.

"I don't know, Adoma, it's a very unstable career choice to put all of your faith into," Genna said, as she bit into her salmon.

"Like really, who does that? Buuuut…" Genna began to change her tone, as she sensed Adoma's disappointment in what she just said. "If anyone can do it, you can."

"Adoma, just do it. You have been writing songs since college. It's in you," encouraged Casey.

"Yeah, I agree with Casey. Just follow your dreams and see where they lead you," Mya concurred, attempting to be positive.

"Whoop, whoop," Genna said with sarcasm as she raised her glass and swooned a bit in her chair. No one knew what was going on with her that night, but they ignored her sarcastic calls for attention.

"But," Adoma continued, "I just kind of need help deciding where to go to pursue this. Should it be Los Angeles or New York? There are disadvantages and advantages to both, you know." Having family in both locations made the decision harder for her, but Adoma leaned toward the Los Angeles weather and its palm trees and nearby ocean. The sunshine of Los Angeles better matched Adoma's cheerful disposition, but she acknowledged that she might need the ambitious entrepreneurial energy of New York to get her into gear. Adoma could not decide.

"Doesn't Duke frequent New York?" Casey chided.

Before Adoma could respond, ensuring Casey that she had not spoken to Duke in about a year and had no plans to reconnect, Mya interrupted.

"Wait, I have an idea to help you decide!" said Mya, thinking that it would be a good idea to employ a trick she had learned in marriage counseling. "Ok, just close your eyes and imagine. Imagine you are walking down a street, and you look around. What do see around you? Describe it to yourself. Where do you see yourself?" She paused for a moment. "That is where you should go."

Adoma giggled. "Ok wait, let's do this again, and this time, I'm going to take it seriously." Adoma closed her eyes and to add to the drama grabbed Mya's hand to her left, and Casey's to her right. Then they took Genna's hand. Adoma swayed a little bit and smiled with closed eyes. Then she stopped, fluttered her eyes open and said, "I know where to go. Thank you; that helped so much."

Adoma exhaled in relief. "You know, friends can either encourage or discourage your dreams, and I'm so blessed to have friends that support mine. Aaand…" she added to lighten the mood, "…we can't get rid of each other yet. We still have our reunion. I totally love you, ladies." And with that, she held up her glass, the others held up what little remained in theirs, and she toasted with the familiar three-word phrase, "To the reunion!"

"To the reunion!" Mya, Genna, and Casey replied in unison.

Chapter 13
A Warm Welcome

"My darling Adoma, you look fantastic!" Adoma's cousin, a long time New Yorker and daughter of her mother's loquacious older sister, said as she greeted her, hugging Adoma tightly.

"I'm so happy to see you Cuz! It's been way too long! And for real, I'm so grateful to you for having me, and I promise to get out of your hair as soon as I get grounded and on my feet. I'll figure out my next move soon," Adoma extended her thanks.

"Nonsense," Adoma's cousin countered sternly. "And please don't bring up paying me rent for my extra room again. The apartment is rent-controlled anyway, so I'm more than fine. Plus, there is no way I would accept money from you; you are family, and it's our job to help each other out when we need it. That and my mother would kill me if I ever took a dime from you after your parents helped us out so much. Plus, I'm happy to have you."

"Thank you for saying that. I appreciate it, really, but it's so expensive here, and you would probably be renting out the room if it weren't for me." Adoma wouldn't let the subject go.

"No, not really. After the last experience, I'm done with renters. Some of them aren't worth the trouble, and I'm too old for it now. I like my privacy too much, and with the last renter, who turned bat-crazy, I had to sleep with one eye open. Believe me, having you around is a welcome relief after that experience." She grabbed Adoma's luggage and helped roll it through the airport toward the parking lot.

"So, I spoke with my mom. What's this about you becoming a songwriter? You didn't tell me that part," she smiled at Adoma, hinting a bit of disbelief. Adoma smiled in return.

"It's true. I just want to give it a shot and not have any regrets later on when I look back at my life. I hope it works out, but if it doesn't, I have nothing to lose. With my skill set I could always go back to working corporate. But, I'm going to give this a real chance. Got any ideas of where I go to be seen and start making contacts?" She asked, seizing the potential networking opportunity.

"Ha, ha, not even thirty minutes here and you're already ready to get out there. You never go for the low hanging fruit. Geez. Songwriting?" She laughed, then added, "Well you know it's tough; everybody wants to be discovered here in the 'City of Dreams.' So many people come to New York to try to make it. I heard a statistic that, like, 40,000 people a year come here for a new life, you know, to try to be an actor or a singer or something creative like that, and by the end-of-the-year, 90% of them are gone. That isn't to say things won't work out, but not everyone gets lucky like Madonna famously did. But I hear that is the story all of the hopefuls tell themselves when they want encouragement."

"I hear you Cuz," Adoma interrupted. "I'm not naïve, but I do want to give this a shot. You never know unless you try. Besides, in New York, you never know who you might meet, and connections are everything."

"True. Like you said Adoma, 'you never know'; plus sometimes knowing the right people is worth more than talent." Adoma could see her cousin thinking for a moment as she shut her car door and put the key into the ignition.

Suddenly her cousin turned to Adoma. "I *do* have a cool younger coworker who dates the brother of a very hot celebrity."

"Oh really?" Adoma took her eyes away from the window and snapped her head to the left. She couldn't believe what fate may be handing her so soon. "Which one?" she inquired with squinted eyes.

"Well, I would tell you dahling, but I don't want you to get too excited."

"Oooh, tell me the naaaaame," Adoma begged.

"No way! You might get your hopes up, and it may not mean anything. But I will give you a hint. It's a female celebrity, one of the hottest at the moment, and my coworker dates her brother. But you know young people these days; they are constantly dating new folks and 'hooking up' as they call it. Buuuuut," she thought about it some more and paused. Adoma clenched in anticipation, noticing her cousin's change in demeanor. "Since my coworker is a sweetheart and absolutely gorgeous, it's more likely that she could be hanging around for a while – ha ha. You know, he might be quite enamored with her. Hopefully, enamored enough to do anything to impress her, maybe to even accept a song from her and possibly give it to Sa - I mean the hot celebrity who shall not be named. Like you said Adoma, you never know…" Her cousin smiled knowingly as the wheels appeared to turn in her head. Adoma didn't relent, but her cousin never succumbed to her interrogation.

So Adoma's cousin switched topics. "Are you going to work or just continue to write while you're here until you get a break?"

"Ummm," Adoma contemplated, still undecided about conventional employment.

"I know it's not what you went to school for," Adoma's cousin started, "but there is a receptionist position at my company's front desk, and I think you should apply for it."

"Not a bad idea," Adoma responded with a yawn. Exhausted with travel, she closed her eyes, opening them again when they reached her cousin's brownstone a few moments later.

Her cousin opened the door to her apartment, unable to keep her large puppy, a labradoodle with humongous paws, from jumping on Adoma. The dog already reached her shoulders as he stood. Adoma leaned back, but his contagious affection soon made her hug him back.

"Oh," she cooed to the puppy, "nice to see you too." 'What a loving, but heavy, dog' she thought, 'but there's no better welcome to my new world that I'd want to have.'

The next day her cousin, to better acquaint her with the surroundings, guided Adoma through the neighborhood.

"My, this neighborhood has changed," Adoma observed.

"Yes, it has," responded her cousin, while pulling her braids back into a ponytail. "When I first moved here there were nothing but dealers and prostitutes walking the streets at night, and sometimes even in broad daylight. And now... well, you see hipsters and their baby strollers. Time changes things."

"Yup, that's so true. Time does change things. Look at me? I would have never thought that I would be living in New York City. I've always been a southern girl. I don't like the snow. I hate the subway; I like to drive my car. I still can't believe I'm here!" Adoma looked around again. "Well," Adoma added, "the neighborhood has lost some of its vibe. So many cultural things started in this part of Brooklyn, but you'd never be able to tell now. Oh well, you can't stop the world from changing, and at least it's safer. That's the most important thing; I see more security around now. Funny, where were they before? Back then is when they needed to be here," Adoma laughed.

"Yup funny," Adoma's cousin responded with snark.

"Cuz, how is your mom doing?" Adoma asked. "I haven't spoken to Aunty in a while. In fact, the last time I did, I think, was at my mom's birthday brunch." Adoma scratched her head. "Oh yeah, that was it."

"Yeah, you're right. My mom was pretty embarrassed about that day. She didn't mean to cause a scene. She hardly drinks and told me that she didn't remember ordering that much mimosa," said Adoma's cousin, grimacing at the memory of her mother's episode.

"It's okay; things happen. Everyone was toasty that day. I don't think anyone, but you and I noticed," Adoma lied to make her cousin feel better. "I only wish that she could've finished telling me what she started to say that day."

"And what was that?"

"Well, I wanted some information. One day I saw something odd. Upstairs in my mother's drawers, I found a white fabric – an adinkra pattern. It was an emblem that I have rarely seen – not our family's – you know?"

"Okay... That is odd." Adoma's cousin scratched her forehead in confusion. "The white cloth, hmm... Isn't that used for church? The last time we wore our white fabric was for the day after a funeral."

"Exactly Cuz! So... who died and from what family? Because it isn't a relative of ours – I don't recognize the pattern at all. And then, why would my mom tuck it away – like really hide it?"

"Hmm. Your guess is as good as mine, Adoma. I don't know the answer to that one."

"Well, your mom seems to know. Before she left the table, she was going to tell me, but all she could get out was the word 'coup.'"

"Hmm," Adoma's cousin responded.

"I don't know what she meant by that, Cuz."

"What do you mean? Didn't your parents tell you what happened during the coup?" Adoma's cousin raised her eyebrows in surprise.

"No, not really. My dad hardly ever talks about home. Well, what happened? Are you going to tell me?" Adoma pressed.

"I dunno. I think you should let your parents tell you."

"Well Cuz, obviously that isn't going to happen. And you seem to know. I am sure Aunty must have told you something."

"I don't know Adoma..."

"Please," Adoma begged, "just tell me. For my sake, please let me know. I need to know more about our family history. My parents never speak about the past, and I wish they weren't so secretive about it. This is starting to drive me crazy."

"Maybe it's just too painful, Adoma. Did you ever think about that?"

"*What's* too painful?"

"What happened."

"Well, what happened? What do you mean?" Adoma's voice rose a bit higher.

"You know, your father's disappearance."

"His *what*?!"

"Adoma, you mean your parents never told you what happened during the military coup?"

"Told me what? Can you just say it, puhlease?"

"I don't know, Adoma, why don't you ask your parents?"

"Because I know they won't tell me. I need to know this. Please tell me," Adoma implored.

"Here sit down." Adoma's cousin nodded to a bench on the sidewalk. "Okay Adoma, I will tell you, but please, do not bring this up to your parents. I will tell you what I know.

"Obviously, things are fine now back home, democratic elections, all that good stuff, but as you know, it wasn't always that way. Before the last coup, Uncle – I mean your dad – worked for the old regime. But, when the military coup happened, the country fell into turmoil. People disappeared – and worse. No one heard from your father for days. He was presumed dead I suppose, as was the fate of many of the other former government officials. But the family prayers worked – Amen – and your father resurfaced two days later. He was alive!

"It turns out the new regime decided to keep him. Who knows, maybe since he handled the purses for the prior administration, they figured that he had a skill set that they needed, I guess. So he stayed and worked for the new government until you all came to America."

"What? Oh my gosh! Really? Is that true? That's what happened to my father? That is terrifying! No wonder he never speaks of it," Adoma responded to the shocking news.

"Yeah. I imagine your father wishes to keep it all behind him in the past. Who knows what unspeakable things he has seen?"

"My poor dad. Well, if he stayed and was okay, I wonder then what brought him here to America?"

"I can't imagine that he felt completely safe," Adoma's cousin continued. "He may have always thought of himself as an outsider; that his days could be numbered. Also, just imagine how he felt working with people who turned his world upside down? I suppose he lost friends, you know, to the same people he worked for."

"Oh my gosh," Adoma's hands began to shake. "I'm in shock. But," Adoma thought for a second, "that still doesn't explain my mother's secret."

"I don't know the answer to that one Adoma. But I told you everything that I know about your dad and why my mother could have said 'coup.' There is nothing more that I know and nothing more that I can tell you."

"Okay. Well, thank you for letting me know."

"You're welcome." She reached over to embrace Adoma. "There's no point in dwelling on it. That happened eons ago, you know? Things are so different now. Home is a different place. No more military rule like before. It is fun, vibrant - the gateway to Africa, they say. So don't stress about it." Adoma's cousin rubbed Adoma's shoulder. "Your dad came here and started a new life. He doesn't seem to think about it at all, so you shouldn't either."

"You're right, Cuz. I won't dwell on it. Some things are best left in the past."

"Exactly," her cousin said as she hugged her tighter.

Chapter 14
All That Glitters

The icy cold shook Adoma to the core, and she grimaced at the thought of taking her glove off to find her MetroCard. Her hand shivered in the blistering weather as she struggled to slide the card into the receiver with an ungloved hand. Finally, on the third attempt, the green light blinked, and she could pass. 'Fickle machines,' she thought to herself. 'These cards are so flimsy. Why can't they make sturdier ones for the thousands of people who travel the trains every day?'

She plopped herself between the sleeping businessman and the elderly woman holding tightly to her handbag; they avoided eye contact. The subway door closed after the beep and warning, and the train commenced its soporific clickety-clack for the twenty-minute ride to her job.

This day marked her second month as a receptionist for her cousin's company. The rigmarole Adoma performed to get through each day made her doubt the value of going to work at all. She struggled to wake up in the mornings to face the harsh climate and the walk to the subway, the subway itself, and her job answering phones, where her coworkers, assuming she was uneducated, treated her like a second-class citizen.

As Adoma tromped four additional blocks from the station to her office building, she wondered why she left it all behind and moved to New York. Things had been going okay in her life. She had traveled the world in her old job while staying in contact with her family and best friends.

'Why *did* I just uproot my life and leave it behind – and for this?' Adoma asked herself and blew her nose. 'Now I'm completely starting over, changing careers, starting from the bottom, and practically walking in a large freezer to get to work. I bet everyone thinks I'm crazy. And now, *I* think I'm crazy, too. Yes, I *do* think I'm crazy. Why didn't anyone stop me? What have I just done with my life? I just effed up my perfectly good life. And why?' Adoma almost screamed her thoughts out loud.

Then she remembered why. Adoma could no longer ignore her creative side and the heightened sense of urgency gnawing at her to be expressed. No one but Adoma could understand what that felt like inside.

And then came that day when she woke up with a beautiful song and realized that she had to follow her passion instead of leaving it in the background of her life. After that, the songs flowed effortlessly, almost automatically, practically writing themselves as they called to her in her dreams at night. So writing music became the thing that she could not not do, and she knew that her soul would continue to dream of songs while she slept until she could birth them to life.

"This has to pay off soon," Adoma mumbled as she slipped on her headset. While Adoma worked as a receptionist, she continued writing songs and going to industry events in the evenings, but she didn't get any traction. She still kept writing. She wrote about anything and everything, and one day even wrote a song about a lizard. "Friend or Foe" was inspired by a baby lizard that would scurry away as Adoma tried to save its life.

Then, in Adoma's ninth month at the job, her cousin surprised her by asking, "Adoma, would you like to go to an industry party with me?"

Adoma put on her nicest outfit and accompanied her cousin to the birthday party of a co-worker, which took place at the opening of the latest club. And although Adoma hated nightclubs, especially the pretentious ones in the New York club scene, she agreed to go and potentially network.

Adoma and her cousin walked past the other women – who all looked very similar: sharply dressed with hair to their waist, not so natural-looking eyelash extensions, and perfect studio make-up – and through the velvet ropes. They sat down in the VIP room next to the birthday girl. Adoma surveyed the room filled with well-known faces and identified a gossip columnist, a pro basketball player, and a familiar-looking man Adoma noticed from other music industry events.

"Aren't you the receptionist?" the coworker asked.

"Oh Ana, I am sorry," Adoma's cousin interjected. "This is my cousin, Adoma. She is living with me for now. She came to New York a few months ago."

"Oh yeah? What brings you here?"

"I write songs. You know the kinds that make the whole world sing, the kinds of love and special things. I want to make it as a songwriter."

"Oh, that's so cute. Everyone comes here to make it big," she said in a dramatic tone, without realizing Adoma's facetiousness.

"No, but she has talent," Adoma's cousin advocated.

"Oh really? Well, hmmm… Today may be your lucky day. It's my birthday, and I'm in a good mood." She flipped her hair and turned around. "See my boyfriend over there?" She pointed to the bar toward the familiar looking man dressed in stylish jeans pulling out his wallet to pay for drinks. "You know who Sasha Pierce is right?"

"Of course. Who doesn't?"

"Well, that guy, my boyfriend, is her brother and assistant." She grabbed Adoma's arm. "If you can hold his attention for more than fifteen seconds and pitch him, you *may* have a shot. Come with me." Ana walked Adoma to the bar and introduced her to her boyfriend.

Sasha Pierce's brother focused more on balancing his drinks than conversing with Adoma. But, he paused mid-stride and set down the cocktails when she passionately stated she could bring back what's lacking in the art of today's music – poetry.

"Really? That's a bold claim. My interest is piqued. Here's my card," he replied with curious suspicion.

The next day, Adoma pulled out "Freedom," then quickly changed her mind as she remembered Sasha Pierce just released something similar. Instead, she retrieved "I Love You So," a melodic love tune intended to be sung over a dance beat.

As soft as the wind blows
As light as the twilight glows
As bright as the ocean on a sunny day
Take my hand
And walk with me
And don't let go - oh no
I love you so
I love you so
I love you so
Just want you to know
I love you so…

Adoma pressed 'send' as she hummed the melody. Then she closed her eyes in quick prayer.

Chapter 15
Uncoupling

Mya's tailored suit hung loosely on her delicate frame. Already slender, she now appeared frail from the pressure of her upcoming divorce from Roger. The stress also caused her to start losing her thick curly hair, which had stopped growing when her marriage problems began. However, her beauty remained intact, and that morning she pulled every tendril of hair into a tight bun, one so tight it hurt and made her eyes squint at the corners. She didn't mind the pain. In fact, she wanted to feel it; she needed to prepare because, in her mind, this was war.

Mya tried, but could barely walk up the courthouse steps with confidence. The last time she walked the same steps, Roger accompanied her to retrieve their marriage certificate before their beautiful ceremony. They wed traditionally for cultural reasons, surrounded by family and friends. And right before the ceremony, for the nuptials to be recognized in her culture, Roger, a Christian, converted, an act he did gladly out of his deep love for Mya.

After the ceremony, they stepped out of the building with huge gleaming smiles and in a side embrace so close that they appeared attached. Mya glowed in her ornate gold gown, and Roger appeared natural in the traditional clothing of Mya's heritage, hand-sewn by her cousins. They replaced their embrace with tightly clasped hands, and with faces glistening in the sun, said goodbye to their guests. They departed appearing to be the perfect couple, with a brilliant future ahead. The memory of that day remained one of the few good ones of them as a couple, and she let that recollection remain sacred, unsullied by the divorce.

Now, with a broken spirit from having lost love again, she felt wounded from the many accusations Roger made in his paperwork. Their marriage failed because *Roger*, not Mya, refused to make it work. But he managed to twist the situation around and blame her.

So, they had come to this point. So in love before, but now possible enemies for life; their life and intimate moments to be put on display, judged, and a matter of public record. Today would be a tough one, but the months before took the heaviest toll on her emotionally. Attempts at mediation or an amicable divorce failed miserably, and soon the meetings grew so contentious both parties left more frustrated and sometimes furious.

So Mya reluctantly walked toward the doors to the courthouse, ready to hold tightly onto the life she created and to keep everything that she had earned. Her phone buzzed, and she looked down to check the message. 'Keep your head up. Thinking of you,' Adoma had texted. She looked at it and used her shaky finger to turn off her phone.

Mya raised her head and saw her attorney standing in front of her, waiting at the ornate doors of the grand courthouse entrance. As she approached, he smiled, and then extended his hand to support her. She grasped it and held on tightly.

Chapter 16
Bent, Not Broken

"How are you feeling Mya?" Christian, her divorce attorney, asked.

"I'm okay. I just want this day to be over," Mya responded, as they spoke outside of the doors to the courtroom.

"Well, we have a challenging day ahead of us. Your soon to be ex-husband Roger is unemployed, wounded, and wants it all. With nothing to lose, he is going to go after you, Mya, with gusto."

"Yes, I know. I can tell by all of the untrue things he's claiming happened. I'm so frustrated with all of his lies. How can I feel this way about someone I used to love so much? I wouldn't wish what I am going through on my worst enemy." Mya sighed before continuing. "He, a full-grown, able-bodied man, standing over 6 feet tall; he can work, but he wants me to pay him alimony. Seriously? I can't even fathom the idea. Where I come from, the men are supposed to work, take pride in working, and do everything possible to keep working and be providers – not the other way around!" she exclaimed. "The idea that even after our divorce, after my emancipation, he could still be living off me, and that I would be writing him a check for him to live just doesn't sit well with me. In no lifetime do I see a scenario where my hard-earned money goes toward the happiness of one of the worst mistakes of my life!"

"I know, Mya," Christian responded. "We're going to work hard to be sure that doesn't happen," he assured her. "Be ready for surprises, though. As I said earlier, he is desperate, with nothing to lose. I just got wind that his attorney uses someone I know as a private investigator. This guy is good. I couldn't find out much, but I found out they hired him for this case before you filed, so that gives me a hint Roger started looking into things long before we realized. I think he had this planned for a while. Be prepared that he may have looked into your finances, like your separate bank accounts and your business revenue. Don't be surprised if he doesn't just stop at the house and cars. His attorney is savvy, and Roger may try to go after the business that you started while you were married."

"Noo. That can't be. Everything I have, my possessions and my business, I built from scratch without his help or even his input. My family and I arrived here without jobs and hardly any material items. But we all worked, and I put myself through community college and then started my accounting firm. He can't have a cent from my business," Mya, now a shrewd businesswoman, said curtly.

"Trust me, Mya. I have your back. Now, let's take our seats."

A moment later, the opposing attorney wasted no time addressing the biggest issue of the proceedings.

"Is it true that at the time of your marriage to my client, you were aware of his desire to have children, and you *knew* that you could *not* conceive. And..."

"Objection your honor. Can she answer the question?" Mya's attorney exclaimed.

"Sustained," the judge said quickly. "Counselor, please.... Ask her a question – one at a time. And then, give her a chance to answer the questions."

"Yes, your honor. Pardon me. And," the opposing counsel continued with a stern tone, "that you hid this fact?"

"That's absolutely untrue," Mya testified. "I had no idea that I could not have children until we had tried several times unsuccessfully. Even then, it was just one doctor's opinion. I, even today, still hold onto the possibility that I may still conceive naturally. And although I was wrong to have kept the information from Roger when I first found out, I eventually told Roger about it. There are also other ways to conceive and Roger..."

"That's enough. Thank you," the opposing attorney interrupted.

"And Roger opposed them – all of them. I even suggested adoption, and Roger refused even to consider it," Mya defiantly finished her sentence.

"Your honor, I ask that the last sentence is stricken from the record," the opposing attorney addressed the judge.

"Overruled. Counselor, please continue." He then turned to Mya's attorney. "And Counsel please instruct your client only to answer the question asked."

The opposing counsel returned to Mya in mock tenderness. "Ma'am, please describe the day of your diagnosis."

"Objection your honor! Relevance?" Mya's attorney interjected.

"Your Honor, this goes to the state of mind," argued the opposing counsel.

"Overruled. She may proceed," said the judge.

Mya, holding back tears, began, "I remember the day well. I was confused as to why we, who tried all the time in the early days of our marriage, could not get pregnant. Reluctantly, I sought medical help to understand why our frequent intercourse – whenever, wherever, and whichever way possible, had not resulted in pregnancy. We both wanted to have children. So, I visited a gynecologist referred by my friend Adoma, who accompanied me to the physician's office." Mya continued to testify and felt herself drifting back into the memory of that day.

Mya had waited in the doctor's office with sweaty palms and upper lip, tapping her toes together in the examination room in anticipation of her test results. Abruptly, without knocking, the doctor walked in and continued to study the ultrasound with a furrowed brow, concentrating intently on the images before him. He only paused to shake her hand as a perfunctory greeting and then walked briskly to the computer to review the ultrasound notes. Then, his eyes crinkled and darted from the computer to the images in his folder. He compared the notes the radiologist had made to what he observed written down. The wheels in his mind appeared to turn as he tried to comprehend the images. Once he did, he gulped and prepared to explain the diagnosis to Mya compassionately.

"Mya," her eyes widened as she listened, "the diagnosis is…"

Then his voice sounded muffled to her ears as though he spoke through a pillow. Mya tuned everything out at the point he gave her the ultimate bad news. When the doctor finished speaking, he gave her a copy of the report.

Mya's eyes watered too much to read it, and she left the office unaware of the severity of her diagnosis or its cause. Stunned by the news, she wandered aimlessly out of the doctor's office into the hallway to the waiting area, where Adoma stood by patiently. She sat down in the empty chair next to Adoma and immediately began to sob.

Without speaking, Mya handed Adoma the report, which she instinctively read to Mya out loud. Adoma closed her eyes afterward, acknowledging the devastating news, then hugged Mya tighter and more compassionately than she had ever done before.

"Not me Adoma," Mya said as Adoma held the paper. "I've always wanted to be a mother. I've dreamt about it forever." The tears welled in Adoma's eyes in response to Mya's pain. "To find out that I may never be able to have children is devastating. What will Roger think?" Mya wailed, her bosom heaving up and down in Adoma's arms.

"Mya, I am so sorry." And then they both cried for Mya's pain.

Like a scratched record, the opposing attorney's voice pierced through Mya's ears and pulled her back into the courtroom.

"Your honor, we have a copy of the medical report that I would like to submit into evidence. "The attorney showed the sheet of paper to the judge, who put on her glasses to read it and then nodded her head as she handed the evidence to the law clerk.

The opposing attorney put on her glasses as well and began to recite the information from the doctor's diagnosis.

Mya sobbed at the unfolding humiliation.

"...caused by obstructive damage to the vaginal canal, the uterus' failure to completely shed uterine lining during monthly menstruation has caused chronic infections that have resulted in a fragile uterine environment. The side effect is a hyperactive uterine defense system and fragile uterine environment that may treat any foreign object as a pathogen and attack it. Due to the noted, it appears the uterus may be unable to sustain life and hold a fetus to term. Any pregnancy would be a risk to an unborn fetus and the mother…"

Mya's shoulders slumped, and she lowered her head. She felt defeated and exposed at having her medical records read out loud during the trial. She directed her gaze upon Roger, who remained emotionless and icy.

Then his lips curled up slightly, and he possessed the slightest smirk as he watched Mya's suffering. Mya, with swollen eyes, turned to her attorney, eyes begging for respite.

"Judge, may I ask for a recess?" Mya's attorney asked.

"Let's recess," the judge agreed, "and reconvene in an hour."

Mya and her attorney stepped out to discuss the proceedings.

"How the hell did he get that?" Mya asked.

"They subpoenaed your doctor's records. Try not to worry. You're doing okay Mya, but I'm afraid you don't appear present to the jurors. You also look so fragile on the stand; I'm afraid for you – like you are going to break."

"That's because I am," she responded.

"No, you aren't, you are going to be just fine. You got this, Mya." He paused, then continued, "And also…" he placed his hand on hers, "…I'm here for you."

"You're right. I got this, and you have been here for me. Thank you so much."

Mya, with an improved stride and new resolve, returned to the witness stand to finish her testimony.

"Didn't you know about your inability to conceive a child before you got married? You tricked him into marrying you, didn't you – even though you knew you could not give him a child? You knew how much he wanted kids and you stole that from him didn't you? You robbed my client of his ability to marry someone who could carry on his family name." The opposing counsel forcefully asked.

"Your honor, objection! Counsel is clearly badgering the witness!"

"Sustained," the judge dryly replied.

Mya inhaled and spoke calmly. "No. That's not true at all. I, too, wanted children and did not learn about my condition until after that doctor's appointment. I would never trick anyone into marrying me. He's the liar – not me."

On the outside, she appeared emotionally intact and in control, even after Roger swore on a Bible and ignored his oath during his testimony. On the inside, she brimmed with anger that grew the more he spoke. She continually wrung her hands under her desk, to calm herself amidst the venomous lies Roger spewed to the jury. His salacious untruths, along with his theatrics, feigned grievances, and spectacular displays kept the jurors rapt in attention. When he finished, he then honed his chestnut-colored eyes on Mya, expecting her to buckle under his gaze. But she didn't, she wouldn't, she had this.

As Roger left the stand, he strutted in front of Mya, swaggering as if to remind her of what she would be missing. But she no longer cared; he now disgusted her. Mya didn't want Roger to see that, though. The emotions brewed inside of her, bubbling to the brim, but she suppressed them, jotted notes to her attorney, and moved on – for the moment.

Then during a brief recess as the lawyers prepared for closing arguments, she observed Roger and his attorney conferring. The slightest of acts, a dismissive hand motion, reminded Mya of the times he dismissed her in their marriage, and it triggered her. Back then, every time she needed something, materially, physically, or emotionally, he ignored her. 'I gave Roger my all to be a good wife and he didn't care, he treated me the same way he just motioned his hands,' Mya thought to herself.

'I got this. I got this.' Mya repeated the mantra to calm herself, but her hand still shook as she wrote notes to her attorney. The extra pressure Mya placed on the pencil almost broke it, but Mya still continued to write. And then she leaned over to her attorney and spoke in her pleasant, reserved voice, crackling in the moment as if a stronger person inside it wished to break through.

At first, Mya eeked a few words under her breath, "Everything was done to me. I have been a victim of other people's will since childhood," Mya gazed at her attorney as if begging him to understand. "I have done nothing to deserve this and I have suffered far too long." And then Mya and her voice gathered more strength in response to the irritation she felt from her environment. She continued, "Since my birth, things – unfair, terrible things – have happened to me, have been done to me without my permission, even when I was an innocent child." Mya paused before continuing, unable to stop. "I was cut in my most delicate area when I was young, not even old enough to know it was against my will because I didn't know what will was. I even had to flee my country, and I have lost what I have loved – including my first husband. Bad things have happened that I have had no voice in; bad things were done – terrible things." Then Mya's voice grew stronger – loud enough for the opposing counsel and Roger to hear her.

"I have almost lost hope, and I have cried so many times for my losses. I have cried for my past loss, my present loss, and as you all have heard, for my future loss. I have been told that I cannot have children. It wasn't supposed to be this way and wouldn't have been if it weren't for what happened to me when I was a girl. If one of my first and only dreams was to be a mother, have a child of my own, what hope is there for me to cling on to now?"

Mya turned her attention to Roger and spoke defiantly, "Do you think you are the only one with nothing to lose? So you think you have the power, that you can hurt me because you want to take everything that I have worked for?" she asked incredulously. Then she stopped for a moment. "Well," Mya said before frenetically reaching into her purse. "Have it all!" Mya pulled out a handful of twenty-dollar bills mixed with some tens and threw all the money she had in her purse forcefully, yet aimlessly toward Roger. "Here!" she exclaimed, "Have it aaaall!" she yelled at Roger, a deep cry from within the deepest part of her – her womb; a scream that would make anyone stop and shudder. "Take all of this money! Wait," she paused and kicked some bills over to his direction, "you dropped some! Here! Pick it up from the floor like the dirty little dog you are. Do you want my money? You can have it!"

"Mya pl…" her attorney grabbed her wrist to pull her back in the chair, but her force was too great.

"I will *not* stop! I always stop! I always do what's right! I always put other's needs first, in front of my own, and I am *tired*! I am so, so *tired* and I have had *enough*!" she tromped rapidly toward Roger with spurned purpose. The bailiff, already heading her way to intercept contact, could not reach Mya in time to stop her. Mya scooped some of the money off the floor and at about a foot away from him, attempted to stuff the bills into Roger's mouth. "If he wants my money, he can have it. How about that?!" Roger raised his muscular arms bulging with veins in the sign of an X and blocked Mya's contact. So Mya scooped up the money again and started dealing the bills into the air showering him with the money as a customer does a stripper, until the bailiff yanked her away.

The red-faced judge spit furiously, "Order! Counselor get a hold of your client or she will be in contempt right this moment!"

"He doesn't deserve one penny of *my* earnings, and I will no longer let him control me. Enough!" Mya continued as the bailiff dragged her to her attorney, who gently tugged on her arm and coaxed her back into her seat.

But, Mya said in an even louder voice, "He can have it all you know?" nodding her head as she spoke, then she changed her tone to an exaggerated nonchalant manner. "It's just money; he needs it more than I do, which makes him weak. So he can have the money. Believe me, he won't break me, he won't break my bank, he won't break my spirit, he won't break me. I have my brain; I have my work ethic. I can rebuild!" she huffed and huffed and then, finally – she rested.

Chapter 17
After the Gold

Exactly a month after Adoma sent the email, Sasha Pierce's brother contacted her. He asked for more music, and when he heard "Friend or Foe" it confirmed his opinion that Adoma had writing talent. Word spread fast about her, and Adoma, with the help of her newest proponent, landed a rare meeting with executives at Joy Records.

Adoma headed there on a brisk fall New York day that never left her memory. As she walked to her meeting, she stopped for a moment, looking at her surroundings and taking in the majesty of the tall buildings around her. Her expanding lungs slowly breathed in the crisp morning air while Adoma closed her eyes and caught a strong realization about New York City, her new home. 'If you already feel lonely,' she thought, 'New York makes you feel more lonely. If confident, New York makes you feel more confident. If powerful, well hell New York makes you feel as if you rule the world!' New York amplified everything, and this morning Adoma felt confident.

Adoma maneuvered through the bustling sidewalks of Manhattan with a confident stride and feeling of comfort, loving the city that was allowing her to accomplish her dreams against all the odds. Adoma, contrary to New York custom, smiled at the passersby. Adoma's smile, beautiful and inviting, put people at ease. When she spoke, her voice was full of clarity and authority, without being overpowering. Whatever sense of intimidation one may have felt, quickly gave way to her smiling, glistening eyes. Adoma stood at 5′2″, but appeared taller, probably because she always donned heels, but most likely because of the sense of assuredness she projected. Ironically, she rarely employed assertiveness; her gift of persuasion assuaged others into gladly complying with her requests.

Although validation of Adoma's talent boosted Adoma's self-confidence, she still needed to be at optimal capacity for the meeting at Joy Records. Keeping command of herself and thoroughly explaining her skills were essential. Everything depended on this meeting – her success in New York and her future both lay in the balance. If Adoma failed, she didn't know how she could continue to have faith.

Adoma looked around once more to receive invigoration from the stately surroundings. The skyscrapers all around her seemed to impart a bit of their majesty and elevation to her. Recently, she stopped asking herself, 'Why did I leave it all behind again?' Now, as she walked the buzzing sidewalks of New York, exuding the confidence of a native New Yorker, self-assured and no longer feeling lost in the anonymity of the complicated city, she felt great about her decision to leave her former world. Adoma teetered on the cusp of reaching one of her childhood goals, becoming a songwriter. On her way to a miraculously manifested meeting with Joy Record executives, she thought to herself, 'New York isn't so bad after all.'

Chapter 18
Lives Diverged

Adoma inched closer to the goal of making a living doing what she loved, professional songwriting. Her work life gained traction, and therefore, it took a moment for Adoma to notice the absence of communication from her best friends.

While her world formed into her dreams in the making, all of her friends, even Mya, were conspicuously silent. Usually, Mya, Genna, and Casey championed her accomplishments, but when Adoma sent them a text about getting one of her songs into Sasha Pierce's hands, Adoma thought she'd receive celebratory phone calls or texts in return, but she hadn't.

Adoma contacted Mya again and received no answer. Adoma also texted Genna a time or two and likewise received no response. Adoma only received a reply from Casey who texted, 'Congratulations!' a day later. So, Adoma texted Casey to find out what was going on with her two other best friends back home.

Adoma: Hey Casey, what's up? How are you?

Casey: Not much Chica. And you? How is New York?

Adoma: NYC is good - - hey can you talk?

Casey: Sure when? I'm getting a pedicure, so in like 30 minutes, is that okay with you?

Adoma: Yup talk then. One quick question.

Casey: ????

Adoma: Have you spoken to Mya or Genna? I'm scratching my head as to why I haven't heard from them.

Casey: Yup, coffee with Mya. She's still in shock and adjusting. Also, I think I heard something...

Adoma: About Genna or Mya?

Casey: Genna

Adoma: Do tell…
Casey: Will call you in 30 minutes :)
Adoma: K

Adoma urgently wished to find out what was going on. This had been the longest period she had gone without hearing from Mya or Genna. In fact, they communicated with each other more when Adoma had lived overseas.

While Adoma waited on Casey's call, she flipped through pictures of all of them. 'Such lovely memories,' she thought. In some pictures, Mya had her arms around Adoma or lovingly touched her face. Genna posed for most of the pictures with her legs crossed, regardless of if she were sitting or standing, and though she barely had a hint of a smile on her face, she always seemed to look gorgeous. Casey would often have a beautiful, carefree expression and some overly exaggerated pose in the pictures.

They each brought their unique style to the images and the group, and it worked. Somehow their union, though oddly assembled, created a beautiful medley, like a patchwork quilt. Each patch being different, but when combined, the unity of the pieces formed a greater beauty.

Adoma continued to flip through the pictures, passing quite a few that were taken at their favorite restaurant, talking about or celebrating one thing or another. Then Adoma stopped at a funny photo from New Orleans. 'What a cute picture,' she observed. 'We all look so happy and fun-loving there.' She gazed at that photo, remembering the highlight of the trip, the promise to meet again, and sighed. When she noticed the time, her phone rang. It was Casey, punctual as always.

"Hey girl," Casey said in her usual relaxed tone. "Congrats again! Such great news about your successful meeting and everything. What a break. How else are things going?"

"Well, it's a bit overwhelming, but things are going as well as they could be, considering that I moved here without a plan. I'm super excited to have been discovered."

"Yes, you should be. It's close to a miracle. Most people never accomplish what you have," Casey replied.

"Casey, you're so right. Won't He do it!?"

"Ha, ha, yes He will! Remember, though, that you've always wanted this and that you've always written songs. It's been in you."

"Yeah, I remember. Thank you, Casey. But enough about me, what is going on with you ladies? Like really, are things falling apart over there without me? I haven't heard from Genna or Mya in ages. Is everything okay?"

"I think so. Why?"

"Okay, well, I've tried to get in touch with them and neither have even bothered returning my texts or calls. Usually, they are so supportive..."

"Well, Adoma, I'm sure they both have a lot going on, just like you do – Mya especially, you know with the divorce and all. Though I do think it's weird that you haven't heard from them. Not even a 'congrats' is a bit odd... But, you can't take it personally, and you can't put holding our friendships together all on your shoulders. We're grown women, and we need to take responsibility for our part in tending to our relationships, and if we don't stay friends, that is not on you; it's on us."

"Well I don't know where that is coming from but, yes, I know."

"Good, and speaking of Mya, her divorce was very messy from what she confessed. So terrible."

"Uh. How bad did it get? I never liked Roger," Adoma commented.

"Yeah, I know. You always remind me of that. Well, Roger claimed that Mya coerced him to convert religions and that he suffered undue emotional stress later at work because of his conversion. You know he worked for a security contractor, right? So, he claimed his employer, after finding out that he converted from Christianity, discriminated against him relentlessly. Supposedly, he did well at work before, but after the marriage, time after time his immediate supervisor overlooked him for promotion – always finding a reason to delay. He also claimed he had been denied career advancing assignments that he witnessed go to less experienced co-workers. Then, as if it could not get worse, soon after, he said his male colleagues began to harass him. Geez... and that all of this resulted in mental and physical abuse so psychologically traumatic he no longer felt comfortable going to work… and that is why he eventually quit. Shortly after that, he claimed to be shut out of jobs in his profession, and therefore unable to get another job."

"Oh my gosh really? Well, all of that sounds like a discrimination issue with his employer. I can't believe he would blame all of that on Mya. I guess you can't stop someone from claiming what they want to claim, no matter how ridiculous it is… And seriously, he was huge. I don't see anyone getting away with physically harassing him. Ugh! That…"

"Then," Casey continued with the news, "the worst part is – and you know this is what started the messy part of the proceedings from what I heard – he twisted the situation around as if Mya led him to marry her under pretense, that she knew she couldn't have children before they married, but didn't disclose it and pretended that she could in order to get him to marry her." Casey laughed. "Can you believe he claimed fraud as one of the reasons for divorce? They even read Mya's medical report. She broke down."

"Oh my gosh, poor Mya!"

"Oh, don't worry; Mya got him good in the end. That was the best part. I am sure she will tell you about it. She will be okay. She is a softy, but she is also a fighter."

"You're right, she is. She has to be. She had to be. I am glad she and Roger are finally over. She needed to let that loser go," Adoma added. "His erratic behavior and mood swings were troubling – and he always played the victim, blaming it all on the stress. Whatever. Mya wanted a baby too, and she felt awful for not being able to have one. I know she did. And I resent the fact that he had no sympathy for her and never, not once, tried to understand the way she felt. He was such a coward. Mya had no idea during their engagement that she was unable to have kids. She got the bad news at the doctor's office. I was there! But even after the diagnosis she remained optimistic that she could heal, and have a baby," Adoma said with frustration she wished she could direct at Roger.

"Calm down, Adoma."

"I can't, Casey! He could have helped the situation, but

instead he made it worse!"

"Some things are just out of our control, like other people's relationships..."

"I know."

"...and the reunion. I know you keep stressing out about it, but we planned that years ago, Adoma, and things change. What if we aren't even friends anymore on that date?"

"Well, that's the point. Genuine friendships span distance and time. We are true friends, aren't we? If we are – we are."

"Adoma, but on the flip side, if we are authentic friends nothing can change that. Not a reunion, not anything. Things happen Adoma, just accept that."

"I can't accept that Casey. I'm a woman who keeps her word, and I take that seriously. Word is bond, Casey, and we promised. Honoring commitments means the world to me. Now, stop trying to depress me, and let's talk about something else. You said you might have heard something about Genna. What did you hear? Now that you mention it, she hasn't forwarded pictures of Fred and her in the local publications in a while. I guess they don't go out as much now. And you know, lately she has been low key about Fred's job at the congressional office," Adoma reported.

"Yeah, but you know what else? It's what I meant to tell you. I'm not sure if it's true, but the guys at my job were gossiping. You know men gossip more than we do. And, they were all just standing around talking, and then, well... in the break room, they mentioned a possible congressional office investigation. I couldn't quite make out everything, but it sounded bad, like possible charges, but I couldn't really get what the charges could be. I didn't want to seem that apparent eavesdropping, so I kept fixing my coffee, but slowly, you know, so I could hear as much of what was happening as possible. So, I'm not sure if that is why Genna has been so quiet; but from what I could hear, it's entirely possible that it's the congressman Fred works for and that there could be some ethics violation. I don't know the details of who else may be involved or at what level, but I did hear that it could be big, like huge."

"Oh, my gosh Casey, really?"

"Yes, girl. So, that could be the reason why we haven't heard from Genna. And if Fred is involved, she's probably advising him, or..." Casey paused, "if it is anything that could tarnish her image, she may be trying to protect herself. Genna is smart. There is no way she would let herself look bad professionally."

"Yeah, we know that Genna doesn't play around, and I so hope Fred isn't involved. Ugh, that is terrible Casey. Well, if you see them or speak to either of them before I do, let Mya and Genna both know that I'm thinking about them. All of this has got to be tough. I want to reach out to Genna, but I probably need to let her reach out to me when she has a chance. If it's something like what you heard, she is going to need a lot of support. I hope it isn't, and I hope that if it is, it doesn't involve Fred. I wouldn't wish that on my worst enemy."

"Yes, Fred's involvement would be the worst possible outcome. Lahwd, let's hope that none of that has anything to do with him. You know, I think I will try to organize something to see them. This way I can find out for myself what is going on with Genna," devised Casey.

"Yeah, Casey that is a good idea. But, don't hold your breath, though; you know Genna can be flaky when it comes to getting together and right now, with so much going on in both of their lives... let's hope they *both* show up!"

"Yup, let's hope." Casey paused. "Well, I just caught the time, and I'm running behind. It was great catching up, finally. Keep me posted on everything going on for you with your music. I can't believe everything fell into place so quickly. That is amazing!"

"Okay, my dear, thank you. And thank you for catching me up on what is going on with the rest of the crew. I was beginning to worry about them, and about what was happening to us. We can't start falling apart right when the reunion is getting closer!" Adoma joked, but actually, she was serious.

"True, true. Well... I gotta run, my friend. I have a meeting."

"On a *Saturday*? Where ya goin'?" Adoma asked curiously, wondering if Casey had a date.

"Goodbye!" Casey ended the questioning.

"Bye!"

Adoma tried to digest everything Casey said in the call. 'Medical reports? Potential investigation?' she thought. 'Ethics violations? Whoa!'

After Casey and Adoma had caught up, Adoma knew that she needed to get in touch with Mya soon, as she feared that Mya would crumble without her support. She just couldn't risk the wait and hope that Mya would reach out; Mya was a friend in need.

Adoma sighed. It also appeared their sisterhood was fraying. 'I should return,' Adoma thought. 'I don't want to lose them. They are the only sisters I have.'

Before, in times of need, they could call on each other for strength. If someone needed a hug, they had a choice of arms in which to seek comfort. Valentine's Day need not be lonely for any of them, single or married; on each holiday they reached out to remind each other they were completely loved and adored.

They all cried together and weathered the storms together. The opposite also proved true. Whenever one of them laughed, they all laughed together. Through the years and the tears, both happy and sad, the teardrops always had a shoulder or a bosom-filled embrace to land. They even joked about growing old with each other.

Each friend complemented the rest… Mya's huge heart and softness balanced the group, who, including Adoma, were type A, career-driven and ambitious women. Without Mya in their lives, they would not have seen the beauty in so many situations.

But all of their personalities bore gifts. Casey reminded everyone to enjoy life, to live it, and that they were all human. "Life is for the living, breathe it in and experience its pleasures," she would say. Genna kept things polished, refined, and professional. Finally, Adoma, the group's glue, reminded them that everything and anything was possible. "We are here to create, and we all can create anything," she would often say.

'Would there even be a reunion at this point?' Adoma began to doubt the event's certainty. The reunion was only a short time away, and now no one seemed interested in attending it anymore.

As Adoma looked down again, her pictures reminded her

of the fact that they remained friends despite distance or time, helped each other through their most challenging experiences, and planned to be there for each other in the future. She could not let the idea they conjured go.

Adoma prepared to pen them a letter in hopes that they would all remember the great memories they shared as friends. Adoma freed her feelings from her heart and unto the paper.

Dear Genna, Casey, and Mya,

We seem to be going our separate ways. This is a mistake, and let me tell you why. Through the years we have shared heartaches, laughs, tragedies, and triumphs. I could never imagine my life without you all as my support system – often when I had no other. And though we are all different and unique on our own; when we come together, it's beautiful, a friendship filled with magical moments that can never be forgotten. These moments have inspired and transformed me, and I hope that they have inspired each of you. We have all grown so much through the years together. Imagine where we will be in the next years? Let's not forget about each other and let's not forget our promise. I hope to speak with and see you all soon. I love you all.

Lylas, Adoma

Chapter 19
Mr. Nice Smile

Adoma finished the letter she wrote to Casey, Mya, and Genna, thought about its contents, folded the paper, and placed it in an envelope. She gave up on mailing it when she couldn't find a stamp and prepared to leave her place instead. She walked despondently toward the bar across the street to try to socialize and sip her favorite beverage.

When Adoma reached for the door handle, a gentleman pulled it open before she could. She looked up and thanked him. He smiled back with straight, pearly, glistening teeth, the hallmarks of a beautiful smile.

'Nice smile,' Adoma observed. 'Don't let him also have nice shoes too.' She almost drooled at the thought.

Adoma tilted her head down to his feet while they both walked toward the bar. 'Yes, lawd!' she thought. 'Mr. Nice Smile' donned soft brown leather shoes without a scuff mark in sight. They were loafers, comfortable and masculine looking. 'Without buckles,' Adoma chuckled. 'I hate men's shoes with buckles. A man with buckles on his shoes should never bother to approach me – ever ever ever, especially if they are the fake buckles that only serve for decorative purposes. I really can't stand that,' she thought, not knowing from where her disdain for shoe buckles arose. Of all the topics she and her friends discussed, men's shoes were never one of them.

'Conversely,' Adoma wondered, 'is it a turn off for men to see a woman with unattractive shoes, too?' As much as she cared about polished shoes on men, she was a lot more lax with her shoes, which often had scuff marks of their own, especially on the heels – the result of stepping into sidewalk cracks. 'Ugh, cracks in sidewalks are kryptonite to expensive pumps. Every woman knows about that.'

But yes, the gentleman at the door, Mr. Nice Smile *and* Shoes, definitely intrigued Adoma. 'Yup, a gentleman he is,' she thought because in New York she rarely would see a guy open the door for a woman to let her go through. This was more commonly observed down south, no matter who the man or woman was. So, this small, but chivalrous act by 'Mr. Nice Smile and Shoes' was a noteworthy act of kindness she welcomed, a feeling she hadn't felt since she began to be homesick.

In hopes of striking up a conversation, Adoma strategically sat next to him at the bar. When she ordered her drink, he took notice. He sipped a Scotch too and turned to her to say, "So you like that brand? Wow," he continued. "I am impressed. I haven't seen too many women sip that one. It's aged 16 years, very fragrant and *very* strong, but smooth." Adoma got a bit excited at the way he spoke about her drink as if he may have been describing himself. Again, she was quite intrigued.

"Yes, a guy friend, a banker, introduced me to this brand," she smiled coyly, "and it introduced me to a whole new world. One of the appreciations of the finer things," she said with very little subtlety to her statement.

"Oh really?" he smiled.

"Yes, really." Adoma smiled even wider, and they both laughed at the game they played. Then he got serious.

"Well, my name is Mark." He stretched his hand to shake her hers.

"And, I'm Adoma." She received his hand and noticed its clean nails – softness with an absence of callouses – because nothing disgusted her more than a scratchy touch to her face. But, she also didn't like a man's hands to be *too* soft like he had never seen a day of manual labor in his life. 'Was that too much to ask? A man with nice teeth and shoes, soft, but not too soft, hands?' Adoma said to herself. But she didn't think so, and 'Mr. Nice Smile, Shoes, *and* Hands' was looking very attractive to her at the moment.

Until he asked, "What do you?"

"I'm a songwriter," She responded. 'Why do men ask that?'

she thought herself. 'For years they've complained that women always wanted to know this, and now it's the first question men ask these days.'

"Cool, what kind of songs do you write" he responded, without offering what he did.

"All types." She added, "And yes, I am a bit of that NYC cliché; I moved here to make it big."

"And how is that going?" he asked before taking another sip of Scotch.

Adoma tilted her head to the side and responded coyly, "We will soon see."

Chapter 20
Perfectville

Genna couldn't pin point the reason for Fred's silence around the house. Lately, she noticed he had been more self-absorbed than he'd ever been, even more so than in the initial stages of their courtship when Genna first noticed his egotistical personality traits. Genna ignored that, and they lived together for a while. And still, flaws and all, she married him – quietly, in a courthouse.

Genna always wanted a big wedding, but when Fred finally proposed, they tied the knot discreetly to avoid bringing attention to the fact that they had not been married. Her colleagues at the firm, and most other people believed they were already husband and wife while they cohabited. They probably assumed this because Genna wore a ring on her fourth finger, purposefully leading them to this conclusion.

In the world of political galas and fancy fundraising events she attended professionally, married women encircled her, and she wanted them to assume she was one of them. Before she wore the band, some of the attorneys' wives acted as if she were 'beneath' them. 'As if they were the ones to have worked their butts off to attend a top law school and then be one of the few minorities to have graduated that year from said school. What have they accomplished on their own? Why do they think that being *married* gives them some status over me? Please!' Genna had thought contemptuously.

Genna felt this way about women whom *she* thought hadn't had to work as hard as she did. But, there were some women – just a few – whom Genna felt worthy of her admiration. This type of woman slightly intimidated her, though Genna would never admit it. The women in her neighborhood, those from the established families – the women with pedigree or with family legacy – *they* awed her. She dreamt of a day when her last name would carry weight like theirs, or that there would be some scholarship or cause created in Genna and Fred's honor. 'Maybe that could happen with Fred's growing political influence?' Genna dreamed. 'As long as nothing messes that up,' she concluded to herself.

Then, Genna would think about her original family – her mother and father and how much she loved them, and instantly became embarrassed that she felt ashamed of them. Her parents had been through a lot and had done so much to build a great life for Genna in the US. And although Genna gave them the money to start the family business through a bank loan she had received, they never asked for anything more. Genna came from a hard-working family, and she worked hard, too. She had paid her way through school by working full time. Instead of being proud of that fact, she felt insecure that her parents were not footing the bill like a lot of the students' parents she knew of back then.

Coming from a poor family made Genna feel self-conscious. So when she met Fred, she thought it would be the end to those insecure feelings; with Fred, they appeared to have it all.

Genna and Fred made such an attractive couple. She was beautiful and had an inner self-confidence, a goddess-like quality that made people look at her and think, 'she's gorgeous.' She truly held this belief about herself as well. One could see it in the swagger of her walk, and especially in the extra swagger that she added to her sway when she walked with her man, Fred. That is when she *knew* she had it all. She wanted to keep it that way too. She felt a sense of power when she observed single women looking at her and Fred walking together hand-in-hand and imagined that she knew what they were thinking. And that they thought that maybe they wanted to have Genna's life – her great body, her beauty, her hair, and her man. So Genna held on tightly to these things that she thought made her 'her.' Whatever the cost, she held on, grasping tightly, even while her relationship with Fred had its moments of doubt.

Earlier, in the years when they lived together, Fred helped create her insecurity when he lacked the desire to commit fully to her. Although Genna knew that she was a desirable woman, Fred's reticence to marry deeply affected her self-esteem. Genna wondered what she lacked that made her unworthy of his vows. They shared a home, a life – and almost a child – together.

The previous pregnancy she thought would bring them closer added salt to her wounds. Back then, Genna, new to the firm, was not ready to be a mother, or moreover, to have Fred's child out of wedlock. And, even though she sent her parents money, her devoutly Catholic father would disapprove of an unwed pregnancy. These same religious beliefs also kept Genna from considering the alternative. So she devised a crazy plan.

"Fred, what if I hid the pregnancy, then left town to give birth, and let my parents raise the child? I would only tell a few people about our secret baby, like Adoma, Casey, and Mya and everything would be okay until we got married and I got more settled at work and then – we could 'adopt' and then finally reunite and have our child back," Genna had fantasized.

Fred looked at her, then her stomach, then simply said, "Ok."

"Ok!" Genna yelled "Really???? What kind of man have I gotten involved with?!"

"This was *your* idea, Genna!"

"But I didn't want you to think it's okay! You should have said 'Absolutely not! I will marry you, and we will be fine and raise our family together'!" Genna had stormed out, never to discuss it with Fred again. But that day, her feelings of inadequacy began to creep in. So when Genna had miscarried later that month, she felt sad but mostly relieved.

Her hard feelings toward Fred metastasized deep in her subconscious but were made readily available when she pounced on him in a flurry of words when given the chance. However, on the surface, she appeared ecstatically happy in their relationship. She currently had what a lot of women wanted – beauty, a high-powered job, a handsome husband on her arm, and an excellent reputation.

Genna and Fred didn't have the perfect relationship, but it looked that way, and it worked, and she planned on it working out very well for her in the future. Not just a marriage, but a partnership as a future local power couple. However, something had Fred shaken up, and Genna needed to know what it was.

Chapter 21
Hot Potato

A month after their phone conversation, the water cooler rumor Casey divulged to Adoma had proven correct. The congressional office Genna's husband worked for was indeed under scrutiny for possible ethics violations. The scope, or the extent of Fred's potential involvement, remained unknown. Genna, an established attorney, would need to tread carefully and insulate herself so that her husband's potential legal problems would not become her own.

Unfortunately, Casey was no longer in a position to find out more information from her workplace rumor mill. As Casey walked the hallways of her office building and greeted her coworkers as usual, most averted their eyes or mumbled 'hello' beneath their breath. Casey also had noticed strange behavior amongst her colleagues earlier that month; their congeniality and respect had lessened toward her. Instead of the usual professionalism, some also started to tease her, mocking her voice, or playing anonymous small pranks. Even her supervisor hardly looked her in the eyes when they spoke.

Casey, one of a few women in her position, became concerned at the change in office behavior toward her. Unwilling to complain officially, she wished to reach out to the other women in the office and see if any of them knew what had suddenly changed their work climate. But she couldn't. She had no female alliances, as Casey tended to keep her distance, always paranoid she was seen as a threat. Her assumption that other women were always jealous alienated her, and outside of Adoma, Mya, and Genna, Casey had no other female friends.

Though Casey felt uncomfortable with this new professional insecurity, instead of cowering, when the next proposal meeting required her input, Casey prepared her portion day and night in hopes to impress her boss. And, in hopes that whatever had everyone behaving so strangely would disappear with their awareness that Casey, an outstanding employee, actually excelled at her job.

At 7:30 am, Casey surveyed the boardroom for an empty chair at the executive table and sat down near her colleagues. But, her buddies remained distant and intentionally leaned away from her, snickering amongst themselves. Then their supervisor paddled in.

Unlike the other former military personnel at her job who walked with confident strides, her boss's big beer belly threw off his balance. This initially made him hard to take seriously, but his booming voice commanded attention and made up for what he lacked in authoritative gait.

When he called Casey to the front, Casey made her presentation and answered all questions precisely. Not one surprised her. She looked at her boss, who remained grim. She wanted to ask, 'Is everything ok?' but feared the response. 'No news is good news,' Casey told herself, so she decided against bringing up the issue.

When the meeting adjourned, Casey gathered her papers to leave the room and reached for the door.

"Casey, I need you to stay behind for a moment," her boss's voice bellowed.

Casey gulped and turned back around.

Chapter 22
Listen to the Wind

"Oh, Mark! You didn't have to do this! But, thank you so much!" Adoma smiled from cheek to cheek.

"Of course I did, Adoma. We have a lot to celebrate! You just got an offer for your dream job! You are an in-house songwriter. And you're also moving out of your cousin's place; I can visit you at your own home now." Mark said, giving a sneaky smile.

"Well it's a conditional offer. I still have to pass the probation period, but yes, it's true! We need to celebrate. I can't believe this!"

"And you accomplished all of this in just over a year."

"I did. I can't believe it myself. Thank you for reminding me of that. That is certainly an accomplishment."

"And, you should be proud." He reached over and kissed her.

"Thank you, Mark." Adoma cupped his hand. "You have been incredibly supportive, and I have enjoyed the time we have spent together."

"Me too, Adoma, me too." Mark touched Adoma's hands. "How are your friends? The three famous ladies you speak about all of the time? Let me see if I can remember their names. Kayley; no Casey. She's the wild, adventurous one. And then there's Genna, right? The perfectionist. And Mya, the sweetheart. I can tell how you feel about her. Did I get the names right?"

"Yes," Adoma laughed. "Yes, Mark you did. Well, I finally spoke with Mya and Genna, and I think I am caught up with what was going on."

"And what's that?"

"Well as you know, Mya got divorced. We spoke about that and now she is working on cultivating inner strength, as she says, and letting go of Roger. On another note, I'm so happy that Mya finally saw the light. I never liked Roger, especially when I noticed that he seemed prone to quick anger – though Mya never said that anything physical ever happened."

"Hmm."

"But, I had not been prepared for the news that Genna shared when we finally spoke. It's surprising what's going on with her."

"Genna the attorney, right? And what's happening with her?"

"Yup, the attorney… Well, I'm not surprised Genna is less happy with the behavior of Fred, her husband, these days; but what I can't believe is that she's being open about it and letting me know about her frustrations."

"Maybe Genna is prepared to shatter the whole illusion of perfection you say she and Fred live in and face reality?"

"Maybe, but why now?" Adoma considered. "He must have done something wrong for Genna to take this turn. She always had us believe that everything was great with them – their lifestyle, all the fancy parties, their home. The concept of family is also important to her. In fact, she used to take care of her parents. Now their family business is going well, and they don't need her help. But, she still sends them some money now and then… Wait. It must be that scandal that Casey mentioned. What if Fred *is* involved? Hmm, I guess I'll have to wait to figure it all out on our next call."

"Oh. You think? No… let's not presume. And how is Casey by the way? She seems cool."

"Casey seems well. Last we spoke she told me that her job was going well and it looks like she may get a promotion. You know, she's one of the few women in management at her job, and it's interesting to see Casey excel in such a conservative environment, especially with her views. I wonder what they would say if Casey ever let slip the way she really thought about everything. Not to mention if they ever found out about her 'extra-curricular' activities too, if I'm to be frank. It really shouldn't matter, but you know the double standard. If they knew, she'd be marred professionally." Adoma smirked as she imaged what Casey must look like at work in contrast to when they used to go out on the weekends. "Mark, it seems so odd that free-spirited Casey would thrive in such a stuffy place, but Casey always did have a side to her that liked structure, certainty, and rules."

"Hmm, that's a paradox."

"Yup, Casey is a paradox, but I think we all are aren't we?"

"I suppose you're right about that, my dear."

'He called me 'dear',' Adoma smiled to herself, then at Mark. Adoma felt so blessed to have met him. He began to amaze Adoma with his intellect and compassion.

"Adoma, I'm so glad we met. It was such a coincidence. I'm hardly in town, and when I am, I rarely go to that bar." Mark's work as an international affairs journalist caused him to travel often.

"I know what you mean. Just as I was sad about losing touch with my friends and needed something to cheer me up, you showed up."

"And the conversation between us flowed so naturally, Adoma. And that is why I had to see you so often since then."

"Yes, I enjoy the time we spend together, too."

Mark courted Adoma in the old fashioned way. Since Adoma had spent so much time in-between relationships, being wooed was foreign to her. However, she appreciated Mark, and not just because of their romantic dates and the new places he showed her. She noticed that the best dates with him didn't involve money, fancy restaurants, or shows. They were the simple dates, like getting a cup of coffee, sitting on a park bench, and talking.

Their next date mirrored another simple, yet beautiful, no-frills outing as the day started out serene. The clouds hung still in the sapphire sky, and the sun shone gently on Adoma and Mark as they walked holding hands toward the park across the street. After safely crossing, they both looked up at the blue sky simultaneously and stepped onto the park's well-maintained grass. Adoma squinted; the sun shone brightly even with her sunglasses, so she turned away and laid her head against Mark's shoulder, and they continued to walk together. Their pace slowed at an empty bench alongside an umbrella adequate to shield Adoma from the sun's rays.

They sat down, feeling each other's energy, enjoying their

own company. Then the wind blew softly, caressing Adoma's cheeks. Adoma playfully stood into the wind with outstretched arms, as if receiving gifts of love, contentment, and hope. 'There are secrets and sometimes treasures in the wind,' she remembered reading somewhere. She closed her eyes, savoring this scene in her head. 'What treasures does the wind have for me today?' she inquired with a slight smile.

When Adoma finished imagining herself caught up in the breeze, she laid her head back on Mark's right shoulder and as two birds flew by, placed her hand over his.

"When you were playing in the wind, I had to resist the urge to touch you. I just wanted you to enjoy the moment," Mark said, rubbing Adoma's arm.

Adoma pinched herself, 'Is this all true? I can't believe my life has turned out like this'. Adoma acknowledged her blessings and her growth in her approach to love this time around. Typically, she possessed a semi-impermeable barrier to the interest some men tried to show her. She feared being hurt. That was the primary explanation she gave for the reason true love hadn't come into her life again. More accurate was that Adoma built a life around her that lacked for nothing, and therefore, couldn't recognize love when it approached her in various forms. She rejected anyone's help, so she never became accustomed to receiving. Outside of her circle of friends, most other's love didn't have a place to land.

This time, she forced her heart open and let Mark love her, despite her apprehension. Sometimes she would just stare at him in the mornings in wonder. And now that he entered her life, her initial fear transformed into a sabotaging distress of losing him. 'All good things must come to an end.' Adoma wished she had never heard that phrase because she internalized it, and every time romance had been right, she thought more about its departure instead of her part in keeping the love sustained.

'Will this last? How does it last?' Insecurity gripped Adoma as she worried how long she and Mark would stay smitten. She knew she needed to correct her feelings and stop analyzing everything, but she couldn't help it; she always looked through women's magazines for keys on "making it last."

'There has got to be some trick to this. It's never been this easy before.' But soon, she released those conflicting thoughts and just allowed herself go with the abundant flow of love that was moving into her life. 'Who am I to question and doubt this gift I've received? I deserve love, too.' When she thought about all she had gone through, she changed her perspective, knowing that she deserved it even more.

The rising wind whipped and snapped Adoma out of her brief daydream. The breeze turned sharp, with gusts slapping her hair against her cheek.

"Whoa. Where did that one come from?" Adoma asked Mark.

"Is it too much wind? Are you ready to go back?" He asked, squeezing her shoulders confidently.

"No, not yet, it's too gorgeous here today, and I am enjoying being here. Let's wait here a bit to see if it passes," Adoma responded even while the umbrella next to them began to wobble.

"Okay," Mark agreed in a tone indicating he knew they couldn't stay much longer.

Within five minutes the gusts increased in strength, making it too uncomfortable to remain. They both got up, Adoma more reluctantly than Mark. As soon as they did, the umbrella next to their bench fell over almost hitting them.

"That was close!" Mark exclaimed.

"Yes, it's definitely time to go."

"True, it looks like a storm is rolling in." Mark's eyebrows furrowed as he looked up intently assessing the clouds moving with the wind.

Adoma agreed. The gray above them indicated he could be right.

Chapter 23
What the Wind Blew In

It became official: Adoma passed her probation period at Joy Records. The record label employed her to write songs for Sasha Pierce, and whichever songs Sasha passed on would go to the other female talents the record label discovered throughout the year. Adoma was there to stay. Her goal of making money doing what she loved had come true.

To quickly appease Joy Records during her probation period, Adoma delivered a few of the songs written before they hired her – good songs, but ones she thought would never see the light of day. But, like an insatiable machine that had to be fed with music, Sasha demanded more new material. And, as her mega-success proved, she was a larger-than-life pop figure, whose love of the art and expectation of perfection always remained high.

These pressures and demands were more than Adoma imagined. Being creative came naturally to Adoma; forced creativity did not. As the weeks went by, she seemed to have a bit of a creative block. Adoma didn't know why it started – or from which well to dig to keep creating. She needed time and a way to find her muse to keep producing beautiful music.

Naturally, Adoma questioned whether she was spending too much time with Mark. But, the problem wasn't with the amount of time they spent together – Adoma felt assured that their involvement didn't block her creative juices. In fact, quite the opposite – things were flowing very well between them. Physically and emotionally, fabulously healthy would be the way Adoma would describe her relationship with Mark. They loved sharing with each other, and teaching and learning from each other's backgrounds. Their love unfolded beautifully.

"Mark, why do you like me?" Adoma asked one evening during dessert.

He lifted his head sharply from his ice cream and looked at her incredulously. "I've never been asked that before. Do I have to have a reason?"

"No," Adoma said, although she was disappointed that she didn't receive an answer. She needed to know. There must be a reason – some catch.

"Adoma, I like you because you are you," Mark indulged her curiosity.

Adoma, still unsatisfied, pressed, "But what *about* me, babe, do you like?"

He reached over to her and touched her chin. "I love your cute right cheek with the dimple in it." Then he touched her head. "I love your wit and how smart you are." Then he touched her chest right above her left breast. "I love your big heart, and how honest you are… and your loyalty, I love that. I see the loyalty in the way you are with your friends. I know you are loyal to those you love and that is important to me." Then he rubbed his thumb over her eyebrow. "I see a lot of myself in you too. You are like me, optimistic, idealistic – we can change the world can't we?" He laughed.

Adoma giggled. "But this thing – what we have, how do we keep it the way it is? Do you think it will last? How do we make it last?"

"Babe, there is nothing we need to do to make it last. I will keep on caring for you every day, and you just keep on caring for me every day, and before we know it, the time will have passed, and we will have been together for longer than we are aware. That's how we make it last." He smiled at her and reassuredly pulled her closer.

With a new love life in place, Adoma totally rehabilitated her life – recuperated, nurtured, and strengthened it, bringing it back to vibrancy. She had a new life redesigned and on her terms. She even prepared to move out of her cousin's place into a new apartment the upcoming weekend – a whole new leaf. But, unfortunately, Mark wouldn't be there to help her, as he had to travel overseas for a story.

Mark's upcoming absence disappointed Adoma; times like moving made her appreciate having a man in her life to help with the boxes and furniture. But most importantly, she felt disappointed that he would miss a major event in her life: her move into her own spot in Manhattan, with no roommate, just her. 'Won't He do it?' Adoma chuckled to herself as she repeated the phrase she and Casey would say to each other when things went well.

Adoma put aside her need to have Mark with her and filled with pride because of the work he would leave her to attend. Duty called him, important work that would help uplift women in another area of the world.

Instead of Mark, Adoma's cousin helped her move the few possessions she brought to or accumulated in New York. The move started out as one of her easiest ever. Even easier than the many times she had relocated before for her last position – much easier.

After small talk, Adoma's cousin asked, "So, Adoma, where did you say that Mark went this time?"

"He went to Southeast Asia."

"And what possibly for?"

"To research and write a piece on the increase in violence against women in one of the countries. He planned to expose the local government over their lack of response to the increased statistics."

"And are you afraid for him? Most foreign countries don't like outsiders meddling in their affairs."

"Well, just a little bit, but he knew that it could be dangerous, so he spoke with some private security firms in advance of the trip."

"Okay, that's a bit of relief," Adoma's cousin said, unpacking the last of the boxes. She then surprised Adoma with, "Well, I didn't want to tell you this before, because I didn't want you to think I was getting into your business, but you are not going to believe who is in town and reached out to me."

"Who?" the strange disclaimer piqued Adoma's interest.

"Your old boyfriend… Duke!" she blurted out quickly, almost afraid to get the name out.

"Duke? What?!? What did you speak to him for and why? You *know* how I feel about him. I can barely say his name. He hurt me so much!!" She nearly yelled so loud her cousin cowered her head. Adoma continued, "You *do* know what he did to me, remember? And he didn't even tell me he was married! He *was* you know? And he strung me along for months! Then he told me he was getting engaged, but he had been married the whole time we had been romantic! I had to live with the knowledge of having slept with a married man. Do you know how dirty I feel from that? You *knew* this, yet you still spoke with him! *Why* and how could you betray me like that?" Adoma yelled hysterically.

"Adoma, because and only because, when we spoke, he begged and begged me to at *least* meet with him if I wasn't going to give him your phone number."

"You mean you *met* with him?!!"

"Yes, I did. And," she added, "he is divorced now, and he told me he misses you. That he misses you so much and he wants to explain what happened and why he stayed and he just wants to say that – he is sorry. If anything at all, all he wants is to meet with you and tell you that."

"There is no way I want to meet with Duke – ever. He hurt me so much, more than any man has ever hurt me. I fell in love with him when I didn't have to and at the most inconvenient time in my life… I was fine without him. But I let him in and loved him. And I trusted him, you know when he said he loved me too. And, I loved him so innocently, like a child – and like a child, I believed every word he said. Every picture he painted, every single word he said, I hung on to; every bit of hope he gave me that we would be together forever, I clung to. And he told me lies and untruths, and I was left with trying to figure out the omissions. Lie after lie – and I found out the truth – I found it out through the internet. He never intended to be with me, and he should have told me sooner before we slept together, because I only let it happen because of the promise I felt on his lips when we kissed… But, it was all a farce; he never intended to be mine. And I never expected to be treated like a whore."

"But, Ad…"

"This conversation is over, Cuz. He no longer exists to me."

"But Ad..."

"Please, please, please do not say another word," Adoma warned more than begged in saying 'please,' and her cousin, understanding the tone, acquiesced. So Duke, persona non grata, remained unmentioned for the rest of the move. In fact, the rest of the move was almost silent.

But the damage was done. Adoma's world suddenly felt like a whirlpool. The life she created no longer seemed stable; she felt adrift. Just like that, she questioned the stability that grounded her – her relationship. With just the mention of Duke's name, every moment of time they spent together, all of the feelings they had for each other, even all of the fruitless possibilities came flooding to Adoma's mind. Their time together rushed into her consciousness: the friendship she and he shared during the early years; then in the years shortly after, the small fluttering wanna-be love that turned into lust; then the heartbreak of the years much later.

When she broke things off, she stopped communicating with him altogether. She didn't even respond to his final email to her. Adoma patted herself on the back at how strong she had been, and how she had let the ghost of the empty, but hopeful, idea of ending up with him go. She did the work and released him, and he ceased to haunt her.

And now this? He left her alone for so long; she hadn't given him a moment's thought. And just as she was happy, Duke, this large unwanted presence, attempted to re-enter her life. Adoma knew she couldn't crack that door, for if she did - he would burst right in.

Chapter 24
Situational Awareness

Adoma zealously communicated with Mark, faithfully responding to and sending daily texts to distract herself from the news of Duke. Mark's reliable communication added the most value to their relationship while he traveled; not a day passed without a text or phone call from him, regardless of his location on the trip.

Almost two weeks had passed, and Adoma eagerly anticipated Mark's return and, with that, the return of normalcy into her life. 'Focus on the good,' Adoma told herself as she tried not to think of Duke's visit to New York or if he were still in the city. Adoma tried not to think of Duke at all. He was in her past and Mark in her future. Mark gave her everything emotionally that she needed while Duke did the opposite, draining her down to the reserves. There was no question; if there were a contest for her love, Mark would win. He'd have to win. He deserved to win. He was the one.

The irony is that Duke had never asked to win her love in Adoma's imaginary contest. Despite their previous promise and potential, nothing healthy materialized between them. Yes, years ago he *alluded* that he wanted to be with Adoma, but claimed that Adoma didn't recognize it as such because she was too focused on her career. So, he let her remain focused and never mentioned wanting a commitment with her – ever again. They appeared resigned to being placeholders in each other's lives, occasional companions until their real loves arrived. A flirtatious friendship had seemed fine back then – until Buenos Aires.

Years of seeing Duke off and on made Adoma realize real love couldn't enter her life if she continued to accept Duke's 'crumbs of loving.' However, Adoma had nothing new on the horizon; therefore she had kept the status quo – until Duke unveiled his shocking news.

'So what's made him want to re-enter my life now, and what does it mean?' Adoma considered. 'And, what could he want?' Despite her unwillingness to think about him, there was something she couldn't release. She perused her electronic trash bin for their latest communication in hopes that unopened emails might bring clarity to her questions.

Attached to Duke's last email was a picture of them in Buenos Aires. A mixture of nostalgia and pain accompanied that memory, as it marked the change in dynamics of their relationship – an end to the innocence. That night in Argentina, Adoma fell deeply in love with Duke, which made her want him more. He fell deeper in love too, which made him pull away.

She scanned the email for clues and rushed over most of the words, until she read, "There's no way I would ruin the stability of my life from which my success has sprung. I don't love her as much as you, but she helped me build my career, and without her, the money (and power) I now hold would soon dissipate. Believe me in saying that she would take the money and my family and make me pay. I will never leave her, but I also can't live without you."

'Why did he even send me this?' Adoma thought. 'How was I supposed to answer this piece of rambling trash? Did he think that I would respond to this? That I would be okay with a plan to keep me in the shadows of his life while he kept on? Not in a million years! What kind of woman does he think I am? I have more to offer anyone than illicit meetings in the dark. I'm not a mistress!'

Adoma frantically pressed the delete button about twenty times. She permanently deleted it and then checked her trash bin repeatedly to be sure that it was gone, like Duke, forever.

I landed! Mark texted as soon as the wheels of his plane hit the tarmac and the seatbelt sign switched off. As he got up from his seat, he removed his bag from the bin just before the aisle crowded with passengers also anxious to vacate their seats after the long trip. He reached in and checked to be sure the gift he bought Adoma remained secure and undamaged from the nearly day-long journey back home. 'Yes, and almost home,' he thought to himself. He planned to be gone for only two weeks, but his trip extended an extra week when he received a lead for another story. He couldn't wait to get home.

'Yes, my babe is back!' every cell of Adoma's body exclaimed when the text came through. She flung off the covers and rushed to meet Mark at his place. Knowing he'd be tired from the trip, she bought groceries to greet him with a meal, as he'd been gone for so long.

Adoma gathered her hair into a loose, messy bun and looked down to inspect her toenail polish. 'Yup, just a little bit more,' and she fumbled through her drawer to grab maroon lacquer. She opened the drawer and saw a necklace, one of her favorites, given to her by her mother. She looked at the shiny gold pendant and touched it lovingly. The chain carried her family's adinkra symbol, Funtunfunefu-Denkyemfunefu.

To those who didn't recognize it, the pendant simply looked like a two-headed reptile, but in actuality, it represented a lot more. The two-headed reptile, actually Siamese crocodiles with an adjoined stomach, symbolized that there was no point in the crocodiles fighting over food, as it went to the same place - their shared stomach. Therefore, this symbol commonly represented unity, as it did for Adoma's family.

Her father and mother wore this same symbol on their wedding day and wrapped Adoma in it on the day of her birth. Whenever there was a traditional event, the family wore this adinkra pattern in unison to signify to everyone they were family – a united one. Adoma wore the necklace often to remind her that when she was not with her family, she was still part of them, no matter how far she traveled or lived.

Adoma clasped on the necklace, dabbed perfume behind her ear and lower neck, applied lip gloss, and approached the front door with a huge smile as she prepared to be in the arms of the man she loved.

"I've missed you so much!" Mark caressed Adoma's hair. After they had greeted, he recounted harrowing tales of his assignment. Mark told Adoma the details of how he tried to get a meeting with some of the government officials to speak about the conditions leading up to the increase in crimes against the local women, to no avail. Then Mark talked about the lead he received that led him away from his initial assignment. A tip about some of the women he initially followed brought him to the Canary Islands to report on the vacation destination's underground sex trade.

Adoma caressed Mark's arm and changed the sad topics. "Speaking of islands off the coast of Africa, how *are* the Canary Islands? Do you think they are better than the Seychelles, where my friends and I are going for the reunion? I can't wait to visit. By the way, you should meet them." Adoma paused for a moment as she considered what it meant for Mark to meet her best friends. He placed a finger on his sharp square chin, then with his other hand traced a line around Adoma's full bottom lip and said, "That's a brilliant idea."

"Yeah babe, that would be so great," Adoma continued. "As you know, I have been looking forward to the reunion forever, but now, who knows, we don't even talk much like we used to. Mya, to whom I'm the closest, and I, have barely spoken in forever. I know though that she is going through a hard time settling her affairs after the divorce. I think I mentioned the situation to you when we first met, right?"

"Yeah, I remember you telling me about that – infertility and the crazy courtroom scene."

"I think about what had happened between Mya and Roger the most out of everyone - other than Mya of course. I guess I feel partially responsible for their meeting. But, I never sanctioned the relationship; they fell in love on their own and took it to another level. But, it's over and about time she got rid of him; she held on for too long with that guy. I never liked him from the beginning. He always seemed to be controlling and mentally abusive. I never knew what it was; I could never put my finger on it. He just seemed so wrong," Adoma rambled. "And Mya, sweet Mya. She needed something better, you know? She is such a good person, and she has gone through so much, so much. You know she lost her first husband right?"

"What? No, how?" Mark asked in surprise.

"Yup, she did, it was an arranged marriage, but a good one, and even though they'd never met, she fell in love with him. And then he just disappeared. He disappeared just like that – off the face of the earth. From what Mya could find out, it seemed like rebels may have kidnapped him since her country was in the middle of war and falling apart at the time; but she could never prove that. No one heard a word from him or had seen him at all after his disappearance. Just like that – gone…" Adoma snapped her finger for emphasis and continued, "…into thin air and never heard from or seen again. They searched for him from town to town to no avail. Mya mourned for days. We met around the time she was still holding out hope. She looked like she had seen a ghost the day we met; she was so distraught that she wrung her hands and rocked back and forth as she told me the story. She and her first husband were married for only six months at the time of his disappearance, and it took almost twice that amount of time for Mya to heal and come to terms with the fact that she would never see him again. Yeah, it took time, but she slowly let herself come back to life and back to love. Mya soldiered on for love only to have met the devil – Roger."

"Whoa babe, that is so sad; she *has* been through a lot."

"And that's not it," Adoma continued with her soapbox. "Back to the divorce. It's not even her fault she can't have children. I mean, yes, the doctor thinks it is her body, but the issue is with the fact that she can't have a baby because when she was a little girl she had FGM."

"And that can cause infections et cetera, leaving some women infertile…" Mark added.

"Yes! How did you know that?"

"I covered that issue as well. It's very tragic. It is a worldwide problem, too, affecting tens of millions of little girls and, as usual, no one speaks about it."

"Yeah babe, it's so sad…" Adoma agreed with Mark. "Well, I know you must be exhausted from your trip. I'm going to leave to let you get some real rest."

"Okay babe, thank you for coming by and welcoming me back… and also for the food." He hugged her tightly as they swayed back and forth. Adoma reluctantly released his embrace and headed for the door. As she turned, he grabbed her arm.

"Wait, I want to give you something." Mark scrambled over to his carry-on, shoveled through clothing, and pulled out a gift bag."

"What? What's that?"

"It's for you."

"Oh babe, you shouldn't have." Adoma's eyes swelled with tears. This was the first time any of her boyfriends brought her a gift back from a trip.

"It's no big deal, babe, really, it's just something small, but I was thinking of you, and I wanted you to know." He hugged her again. "Look at it when you get home."

"Thank you, babe." She kissed him again and turned reluctantly toward the door.

As Adoma walked to the subway to get back to her neighborhood, she thought about how much she was falling for Mark. He was so thoughtful, loving, and informed. He cared about issues that she also cared about, and through his work, he knew more details about some of them than she did. It was refreshing for Adoma to meet someone who cared about what was going on in the world. She could see herself being with him forever and had to stop the words 'I love you' from drifting from her lips when they spent time together. And not necessarily the words 'I love you" in a romantic way, but because she didn't want it to seem that way, she wouldn't say it first, so she didn't say it at all.

But Mark *was* someone she loved and would still love no matter what. He was making an impression on her life and changing it for the better. He was different than the men in her past, the men with whom she wasted so much time. Now, she could forget about the two-timers and the non-committers, and focus on Mark, the real deal. Yes, Adoma loved him.

Adoma unlocked her door, walked to her bedroom and sat quietly on her bed. The worthwhile jaunt to see Mark exhausted her, but it was a great way of showing him she cared. She looked at the gift bag and smiled. She had a feeling that his gift would make her teary-eyed, so she didn't open it on the subway.

But now safe in her home, she opened the velvet handles of the fancy gift bag and slowly sifted through the wrapping paper, almost afraid to see what was inside. When the crinkly paper fully parted she reached down to take hold of the item the bag bestowed to her.

'How thoughtful,' she thought when she uncovered the gift. It was a book on the Seychelles, probably one of the nicest in the gift shop. Adoma pushed the gift bag over to the side of her bed and felt another item in it shift, so she looked inside. When she couldn't find it, she turned the gift bag upside down to shake the contents out and discovered a seashell. Inside the seashell appeared her name and a date not that long ago. 'Cute.' Adoma smiled.

Inside, the book contained an inscription: *'I bought this book at a bookstore in the Canary Islands. I don't know why they randomly had a book on the Seychelles, but in case you don't know where to go, I marked some places of interest, places I heard you should check out.'* He had indeed marked about ten pages with lovely handwritten messages on stationary notes. She would read the pages later; she wanted to continue to read the inscription. *'And about the seashell… I got the seashell on the beach in the Canary Islands. I was sitting alone contemplating everything and realized I wished you were by my side. That is when I knew I loved you. I took the seashell I had in my hand at that moment to get glossed and inscribed with your name and that day's date.'* Adoma's eyes swelled, and she pulled the seashell closer to her. *'This is the day that I fell in love with you.'*

'Oh my goodness, he feels the same why I do. This is amazing!' Adoma closed her eyes, then drifted into a dreamy nap.

An hour later the ring of her cell phone jolted her from sweet dreams.

"Hey, what are you up to?" Adoma's cousin asked.

"Oh, nothing," Adoma groggily replied.

"Are you up for a cup of coffee? I know this excellent spot that just opened up in Harlem. It's called Drip. Wanna go? It's a chain; I think there's already one in Burough Hall, but the one in Harlem's new, and the place has a good specialty brew, you know? They mix two blends, Rwandan and another; I think Kenyan. I love Rwandan coffee, and I'm surprised it's so hard to find at a decent price, even here in New York."

"Yeah, I like it too, but Colombian coffee seems to remain my favorite. But, sure, I'll check it out. I'm always up for finding a new coffee spot. Shall I meet you there?"

"Well, I'm not that far away so we could meet at your stop, the C train platform headed uptown," her cousin instructed.

"No problem. I'll meet you at the train station. I'm getting ready now," Adoma said in a slightly muffled voice due to the phone's precarious position between her left cheek and shoulder blade; she started to strap on her tennis shoes.

Adoma's cousin stood on the platform checking her phone when Adoma reached her in the subway station. "Hey," she greeted her cousin with a hug and kiss. "You're looking good Cuz."

"Thanks, Adoma, I just got my braids re-done."

"Nice, it looks good; you need to tell me the place you go to."

"Sure, it's not that far from where we're going now. I got it done yesterday, right before I noticed the new Drip Coffee."

"Cool!" Adoma yelled and nodded over the noise and the 'Please step away from the doors' announcement.

"I'll point it out to you." Her cousin tried to match her pitch over the next 'The doors are now closing' announcement, and they took their seats.

Harlem, somewhat of a trek, took a while to get to, but the vibe and atmosphere always proved worth the long train ride. Something new opened in Harlem all the time, and the latest Drip Coffee shop seemed to be the newest 'it' spot.

They got out of the train station and walked down the avenue past some of the historical churches and other places of significance. On the other side of the street, a saxophonist played for money. He was blowing his heart out for change, his cheeks almost as big as Louis Armstrong's, and at his feet laid a red hat with a yellow feather sticking out of it to collect money.

New York had many artists like this, and it seemed like every neighborhood had its own theme music playing as one strolled. Harlem still had the soul of its renaissance years running through the rhythm of the streets that day.

"Oh I wish I could go across the street and give him some change; I just don't have any!" Adoma often wondered how in the days of credit cards, street musicians made money. There were many a time she wanted to give money and couldn't because she never carried cash.

"Me neither," replied Adoma's cousin. "Maybe they should start having credit card machines, huh?"

"Good idea," and they both laughed.

"But wait, is the store he's playing in front of new?"

"You mean Sankofa? No, it's been there for a while. Why?"

"Do they sell adinkra as the name suggests? I thought about adinkra today. I'm thinking about gifting the ladies adinkra symbols custom picked just for them for the reunion. I just need to match each friend to the right symbol…"

"Well, that's easy; Genna would be 'superiority,' what else?"

"Ha, so true, what else?" Adoma joked.

"You know, of all your close friends she is the one I gel with the least."

"Yeah, I get that, but there is more to her than meets the eye. She is a loyal friend, a hard worker, and she is incredibly generous to her parents and a lot of her other relatives."

"Oh yeah, you told me she took out a loan to start a business for her family to run. Yeah, that was quite generous of her. So, maybe you will have to think of something other than *that* symbol for her." Her cousin smiled. "But yes, that is a shop for all things West African, jewelry, art, fabric, clothing; it's a pretty cool spot. Wanna check it out right now?

Adoma considered going and paused. "Let's go after Drip. I'm totally ready for some coffee now."

"Good, me too," Adoma cousin replied, relieved that Sankofa did not detour them.

'Sankofa,' Adoma said to herself as she looked at the shop sign once more. It means you can always go back and learn from your past. Adoma always personally related more to the Sankofa symbol, in either of its two forms – the bird or the heart-like shape – more than any other.

As she and her cousin continued to walk, Adoma still wondered which emblems would best represent her friends. There were some beautiful adinkra symbols to choose from that Adoma had seen adorning the fabric, jewelry, or homes of her West African homeland. The most familiar symbol, Gye Nyame, representing God's omnipotence, could be seen *everywhere*. The symbols had usage and meaning going back hundreds of years. Since the emblems were a part of Adoma's culture and identity, she wanted to use the symbols to show her friends what they meant to her. 'Which symbol best represents them individually?' Adoma thought again. 'Genna could be the symbol Bese Saka - for affluence; she takes a lot of pride in that. Mya would be Akoma and Casey could be Nsaa."

The sounds of the coffee shop noises of Drip bustling with customers interrupted Adoma's thoughts. The crackling of the coffee-makers and the bubbling sounds of the steamer and espresso machines pleased Adoma's ears. The shop smelled fragrantly of fresh roasted coffee beans.

Coffee made Adoma happy. In her excitement to enter the establishment and put her favorite morning beverage to her lips, Adoma nearly hit a customer with the doorknob as she opened the door.

"Excuse me; I'm so sorry."

"That's okay, sweetie," responded the small-framed older woman with slightly disheveled hair and ill-fitting clothing. She cowered her shoulders then scuttled her petite body outside, and instead of eventually straightening and walking purposefully toward a destination like most New Yorkers do, she slowed and plopped down at a spot that she had already prepared for the day. Adoma wondered what the lady did all day outside of the coffee shop, but lost focus as her cousin spoke.

"It's extra-packed today," her cousin said as she tried to maneuver past the other customers.

"Yep, it is. Is it always like this?"

"Not quite this busy, but yes, it is busy most of the time, actually all the time, but I see a place to sit over there by the corner. Why don't you go sit down while I order? What can I get you? Your usual? Is it still the same? Caramel macchiato with soy milk, right?"

"Yep that's right," Adoma answered, reaching into her purse.

"No, don't worry about it. This one's on me. You get the next time, but hurry up, those people over there are eyeing our spot and starting to move in." She motioned her hand back and forth frantically toward the direction of the empty table.

"Oh yeah, I see. I'm on it." Adoma rushed over to the table, grabbed it just in time, sat down, then pulled out her music while she waited for her cousin. By the looks of the line, she wouldn't have much time to listen. Drip baristas seemed to be working efficiently in making the coffee for the customers. But, Adoma had about five minutes or so to take a quick break from the environment and put on her headphones. She unraveled them and pressed play to hear a song she longed to hear after seeing Mark that morning.

"I Believe in Love" pleased her ears as it played through her headphones and sweetened the busy background noise around her. Before when she longed for love, she played this song constantly.

It seemed back then as if she were trying to convince herself of its words and that maybe she didn't really believe the lyrics when she sang the words before. Now, she did have faith in amazing fairy-tale love and sang the song like a true believer. As the song blasted loudly in her ears, she wanted to sing the words and not care about who heard her. Because, now Adoma finally had the strong, real, lasting love the sweet lyrics described. Yes, Adoma finally believed in love.

And then like that, just as vinyl skips and then scratches on the record player, the music in her head halted, though it continued to play in her ears. Adoma looked at her approaching cousin but gazed through her and over her right shoulder. Adoma's stomach tensed and her mouth dried, and her throat refused to swallow. She blinked her eyes once, and then again, but the image above her cousin's right shoulder remained. And the image along with her cousin approached her. As it came closer, it took shape. Adoma looked at her cousin and then back to the image and then back to her cousin, who smiled with embarrassment.

Her cousin now stood close enough to Adoma to hand her the coffee, but Adoma simply stared, speechless, with mouth ajar. The only word she could eek – 'Unbelievable' – formed on her lips but only sounded in her mind, as she couldn't voice a syllable. Adoma only thought over and over again 'Unbelievable'. She said it again to herself and took a big swallow.

Unsuccessful in her attempts to give Adoma her coffee, her cousin placed the cup on the table. Adoma reached for it, as she now needed it to moisten her parched mouth. She swallowed, then trained her eyes at the apparition next to her cousin.

The tall form, a man, stretched out his hand to touch her arm, but Adoma jerked it back violently before he could reach it. His eyes winced at her reaction, but he remained calm and self-assured, as Adoma stood face-to-face with him.

"Unbelievable," Adoma finally managed to express out loud, and she directed her disbelief verging on ire to her cousin. Adoma looked into her cousin's eyes while simultaneously shaking her head. "Unbelievable," Adoma spat out once more as she left her coffee and her cousin behind.

Adoma weaved her way through customers and pushed her way through the front door.

"Bye, honey," the lady she almost hit with the doorknob earlier shouted from her cushy spot on the sidewalk.

"Bye," Adoma gasped as soon as the wind hit her face. Slowly, the pressure that had built up inside released itself from within her.

She panted loudly, heaving, her breath rushing in and out rapidly through her air passages. She hunched over, placing her hands on her knees. Adoma could no longer walk, and she needed to catch her breath and.to.just.breathe.

Adoma remained still, breathing in and out, now slower, almost meditatively for what seemed like forever, and then she began to rise and compose herself to continue her walk to the train station and away from Drip.

Not a moment after she rose, heat blanketed her back, and strong arms enveloped her from behind. The arms held her so tightly she could not escape, nor did she have the energy to scream or resist. She submitted to her only option and melted into the arms, letting the warm body attached to them speak through its embrace, saying the words she had wished to hear for the longest time: "I'm sorry."

Chapter 25
Gold and Shiny Object

Reluctantly, Adoma's heart softened, and she forgave her cousin for bringing her biggest heartache personified back into her life. After their unsolicited reunion, she and Duke met to reflect on their past together – the good times and all the others.

While Adoma and Duke spoke loquaciously over coffee one afternoon, in between the many hugs and tears, Duke attempted to clear the air. He assured Adoma that he had divorced six months earlier and that he and his ex-wife were separated for about a year before that.

After that, against her better judgment, Adoma would meet with Duke whenever he visited New York. They met without Mark's knowledge, and often when he traveled for assignments. Adoma wondered why she kept the outings with Duke from Mark. She didn't know why, she just did.

On her way to meet Duke for about the fifth time since they reconnected, a subway musician covered a former hit song. She sang behind Adoma as Adoma stood on the platform waiting for the uptown train. 'That's definitely not a good sign. Maybe I *am* being 'a bad, bad girl' and 'careless' like she's singing. Though Mark isn't 'delicate,' he *is* a gentle man who doesn't deserve this. I really should stop,' Adoma's conscience warned. However, Adoma didn't listen to her inner voice, and she and Duke continued to see each other.

After they started meeting again, Adoma reminded Duke about her plan to reunite with Casey, Genna, and Mya, whom he had already met in New Orleans years ago. "Very nice, Adoma," he responded. "I like that you follow through on your ideas."

"Thank you Duke, and you know what adinkra symbols are, right? I think I'm going to give each of them a gift for the reunion – an adinkra pendant representing their essences. Hey, why don't you accompany me to Harlem, so I can go back to Sankofa, the West African store, to shop for the reunion gifts?"

"Sure, let's go."

They weathered the long cab ride to Harlem and entered the store. The Sankofa store clerk wore traditional clothing. A fancy head wrap, usually worn at very formal traditional ceremonies, adorned her hair for no particular reason. 'A nice way to draw in customers,' Adoma thought to herself. "Clever uniform," she added sarcastically to Duke. Other than a high-pitched "Hello! Let me know if I can help!" greeting that was spoken in a valley girl accent as Duke and Adoma walked in, she ignored them and continued folding fabric while they looked around.

The couple traversed the well-stocked store directly toward the gold and shiny objects. The display of adinkra pendants next to the beautiful textiles and the wooden statuettes almost overwhelmed Adoma with options.

A large book of West African history caught her attention from the corner. She flipped through the book's pages and considered buying a similar one to explain the adinkra symbols and their meanings. Another particularly attractive book had a striking black and gold hardcover with an Ashanti stool and the ubiquitous Gye Nyame symbol on it. As she contemplated purchasing it for her coffee table, Duke placed his right hand at the base of Adoma's lower back and applied gentle pressure to move her toward the jewelry counter.

"Oh, yes, look at these. Aren't they gorgeous?" Adoma asked, waving to get the store clerk's attention.

"These gold pendants are lovely; your friends should really like them. Are you excited about the reunion?" Duke questioned as he peered through the glass.

"Yep, I am, though I seem to be the only one excited about it right now. Everyone else has drama in their lives at the moment. Each one of them - Casey, Mya, and Genna – are in various stages and scenarios of life complications. Mya just had a difficult divorce. I think I told you that I never liked her ex-husband from the beginning, but I couldn't say anything to her because she was so enamored with him. She couldn't see what I could from one hundred miles away," Adoma said as the store clerk opened the display case.

"I remember Mya from New Orleans. She was such a sweetheart back then, and I noticed her gentleness."

"Yeah, you're good at reading people. She is sweet, and unfortunately, some people like Roger, her ex, take advantage of that. But she has learned, and now she is getting more cautious of others' intentions. What I admire most about her is that after all she has gone through, she has not given up on making it all work for her. She is rebuilding her life, recommitting to her accounting business, and she still believes in love. If it were me, I would be afraid to love again after losing my first husband the way she did, and then being dragged through the mud by my next husband. But she isn't afraid to get out there again. And she even says she's open to getting remarried."

"Yeah, she sounds remarkable," Duke responded. "You remember I wanted to marry you, right?"

"Duke, please. Let's not rehash that again."

"Did I lose my chance, Adoma? I loved you since the first time I laid eyes on you in New Orleans."

"Duke, stop. There is no point in discussing this anymore. You know that I'm with Mark, and… I am happy with him. I have no reason to question the past. I am happy. I have a wonderful relationship now."

"Adoma, if you are so happy with him, why aren't you completely honest with him? Do you tell him that we spend time together? Do you let him know that an ex-lover of yours sees you every time that he's back in town and that you, without reservation, hang out with him and give him hope that you could be together again?"

"I don't…" Adoma interrupted, but Duke kept speaking.

"Adoma, I told you that I am available now and that I have changed… and that I love you and want to be with you. We were always supposed to be together, and I know I messed it up and got involved with someone else and couldn't get out of it, but I am telling you that you – you are my soulmate. You are the one. Who is this *Mark* who you have hardly known compared to me?" Duke asked derisively.

"Duke, I will tell you who Mark is at another time because right now it is none of your business… And what do you mean you got *involved* with someone else? You did more than just get *involved* with someone else. You know that. So let's not go there again. I am in love with someone new now, Duke. Just leave it alone."

"You see Adoma, I can't take any of the words that you tell me seriously. Not when…" Duke turned to step closer to Adoma and look into her eyes. "…not when you are standing right here next to me. Adoma, I have known you for almost ten years, I know what we have, and I know that we are meant to be together, not later, right now. We have a second chance and the time is now. You know it and even your relatives know it. That is why your cousin helped us get back together.

"But I will give you some space. I will play my position for now, but I will soon tire of it, and you will have to make a choice. Soon you must choose whether you will continue with this sudden new obsession of yours, this shiny new object who temporarily has your attention, and you think is love. Or whether you will come to your senses and return to me."

Adoma pretended not to hear him, and spoke directly to the sales clerk, "I think I will come back another time."

"Ok. Totally awesome," the clerk said while reorganizing the pendants without looking up.

Duke took an important business call on their taxi ride back, and Adoma relaxed her body and reclined her head to the window to lose herself in thought. She replayed the conversation she and Duke had at the jewelry counter. 'He's right,' Adoma thought. 'Why am I spending time with Duke if I am so in love?' Then Adoma justified that Duke's magnetic pull drew her back to him. 'What would Mya say?' Adoma tried to guess what Mya, the recipient of hours of counseling, would suppose. 'Oh, I know. She'd say that I am allowing Duke to court me as a way for him to atone for the hurt he caused me.' Adoma nodded. 'Yes, that's what she'd say. She'd probably be right.'

Adoma should have left the past behind, but she didn't. And

she didn't know why. She took the chance of sabotaging the best thing that had ever happened to her. And she didn't know why. 'Ugh! I feel like an angel sent Mark to me, but I'm not cherishing the blessing like I should.' Adoma sighed. She undeniably loved Mark, who gave her love and adoration. But Duke, Adoma's first mature love, was the first man she had ever imagined herself married to, and he brought an excitement to her life. He wielded power and Adoma felt a sense of affluence through association with him.

Duke hung up from his business call and put his hand on Adoma's knee. She felt a familiar surge enter her body. 'I have something special that he sees, I must be beautiful, because he could have anyone he wants, but he wants me,' Adoma thought. Adoma knew better than this, to feel good or bad about herself because of another's opinion, specifically male judgment, but she let herself fall under his spell. And she didn't know why.

Duke smiled, patted Adoma's thigh, and moved his hand an inch farther up. Mark, though a wonderful man, didn't give Adoma the shaky knees or the butterflies like Duke did. The adrenaline between Adoma and Duke addicted her, but could potentially harm her. 'This situation is untenable and risky. And I need to do something before Mark finds out I spend half the days he's away with another man,' Adoma assessed. However, she doubted she was ready to relinquish Duke's company, and spending so much time with him made Adoma consider that maybe Duke was right for her all along.

The taxi reached Adoma's apartment.

"Adoma, we made it to your place," Duke interrupted her thinking. "Is it the final stop?" Duke asked expectantly.

"Uh…" Adoma started to speak, knowing she had arrived at a crossroads and needed to make a decision.

Chapter 26
We Need to Talk

Adoma made the second trip to Sankofa alone. As she had done before, she automatically walked toward the jewelry counter that held the pendants. Then the vibrant textiles in their brilliant colors called her attention. She pivoted to the fabric and touched one swath of cloth, placing it between her middle finger and thumb to assess its thickness and quality. 'Yes, these are traditional; they even have the waxy smell and right feel to the surface. They are not thin and poorly made like the ones from China that some places, like festivals or markets, have started to sell.' Adoma continued evaluating the product. 'No this is proper, not the kind that will shred up and disappear after one time in the washer. These are the real deal, just like the kind you can buy off the streets back home.' Adoma smiled at her memories of the street sellers balancing the bundles of fabric on their heads as they searched for buyers.

Then an idea alighted. 'Maybe instead of pendants, I should buy them cloths with their own adinkra insignia! I always lose my jewelry, and it's probably the same for my friends… Yep, that is a good idea.'

Adoma left Sankofa with four different swaths of fabric, one for each of her best friends and one for herself. She bought enough so that each person could make a few items out of their own fabric, maybe a skirt, jacket, or purse. She left with two large shopping bags and headed toward the subway.

While riding the train, Adoma reflected on the adinkra cloth in her mother's closet years ago, then snapped out of that memory when she noticed Mark's missed call. She returned the call with a smile. "Hey honey, sorry I missed your call. I was totally absorbed in looking at some fabric at the store. What are you doing?"

"Just waiting on you, Adoma. Are we still on for an early dinner? You know that I have to be up early tomorrow morning for my next assignment."

"Oh my, Mark, I completely forgot that you pushed up the time of our dinner because of your flight. I would love to go home and shower first, but I will head toward your place right now. Sorry babe, see you soon."

"See you soon and no worries, but, Adoma…"

"Yes, Mark?"

"We need to talk."

While eating, Mark took Adoma's hand, "Adoma, I have to share something that I just found out."

"Yes, Mark?" Adoma gulped.

"Well, I just found out that my trip will be a bit longer than anticipated – a whole month this time."

Adoma froze. "Wait, you won't be back until the 3rd?" Adoma said, disappointed that he would miss a crucial date. "Oh, Mark! Do you realize that you will be missing my birthday by a couple of days?"

"Yeah, Adoma, you know I did, and I tried. I tried to get my trip shortened, but the regular journalist covering mid-east affairs is out with a sick parent. I couldn't get out of or shorten this extended assignment. I'm so sorry that I will be gone for so long, and I'm extremely sorry that I will miss your birthday. I will make it up to you. I promise." He then kissed Adoma's forehead, little consolation for missing an important occasion.

'How disappointing,' she thought. Adoma didn't know how this next month without Mark would turn out, especially with Duke waiting in the wings. Having Mark physically near, even if intermittently, anchored her, keeping her from completely floating toward Duke, and now Mark was going to leave her for a whole month.

Adoma thought about taking some time off from work

so that she could join him for at least the last couple weeks while he was out, but she knew that wouldn't work. Work at Joy Records became quite busy, and Sasha Pierce had a new album developing that needed all the songwriters writing on it full-time. With the record label insisting that Sasha Pierce deliver another hit, pressure on the songstress meant pressure on Adoma.

Adoma took a big gulp and stared at Mark, who, oblivious to the knowledge that this month without him could change everything between them, finished his meal. But that night, her last night in his arms for a while would not be the night to dwell on it. After dinner, they got into their routine of cleaning up together, holding each other, connecting their hearts and more. Their love still felt so good.

"Casey! Oh my gosh, it's been forever since we've spoken! How are you?" Adoma exclaimed, excited to talk to her friend after so long. "I know most of the fault is mine this time. I had to get resettled again."

"No worries, but girl once again, so much to catch you up. How are you?" Casey responded.

"I'm all right, chica, but Mark left for a while. He has already been away for about a week, and I already miss him a lot… I wonder about his travel schedule; it's brutal on our relationship."

"Why do you wonder? Do you think he's doing something?"

"Mark?" Adoma asked. She was surprised at how incredulous the words 'Mark' and 'cheating' sounded together. "No, not at all; he's perfect – it's just that he's always gone. And, I'm new here, and I don't know many people. I just know my cousin, and I forgave her, but things haven't been the same between us since the set-up, you know."

"Ah, yes I know. That was a bit messed up what she did. But, I think it's pretty cool that Duke is back in your life. I've always liked him."

"Yes, that I know," Adoma said with a sarcastic tone.

"Ha ha, not like that! That Mardi Gras was so long ago!"

"True. But, you know what?"

"What?"

"I think you would love Mark. He's great too; really special."

"Yeah, but if he is never around, what kind of relationship can you seriously have?"

"Well, we work around it and just try to factor in the absences. 'Absence makes the heart grow fonder,' as they say. Maybe this is strengthening our relationship, Casey. Not everyone is like you," Adoma teased.

"Hey! Stop that. I have changed you know?"

"Oh yeah? And what has sparked this new you?"

"Well, for one, work. My coworkers heard about one of the incidents that I had at one of the restaurant bars I go to when I need to blow off steam. I mean, really? Big deal that I need to go and sometimes drink because the job is so stressful. I know some people use exercise to relieve stress. I'm just a little bit different you know? I use a different form of exercise. I'm in man's world, and you know what? They do it. I don't know why it's such a big deal for me to meet some cuties at a bar and dot dot dot…" Casey laughed.

"Casey, now you know, there is always a double-standard. But what does this have to do with work?"

"Well, someone from work found out what I did and spread a malicious rumor – and to add insult to injury told my supervisor. They were all acting so crazy different toward me. Then Human Resources called me in and reminded me of the fact that when I began employment, I also signed an agreement, which had a morality clause. The HR director also ominously added that I am 'being watched very carefully.'"

"Ha, seriously? Why would you sign a morality clause?"

"I dunno. I guess I never thought I would get caught in my shenanigans! Plus, there is always so much paperwork when you start a new job; you hardly read anything. I also think I had to. But it's all good. The call into HR and being *this* close to losing my job was a real wake-up call, so I've calmed down. Plus, I think I'm falling for someone."

"What?! You settling down?! I seriously never thought that I would see the day." Adoma chuckled, slightly surprised to hear

Casey's revelation.

"Yup, I have changed my ways, my dear."

"How long have you been dating?"

"It's actually been a while, I just didn't want to jinx anything, so I kept it hush, hush," Casey said with pride in her voice.

"Well… You know my next question is, 'Who is he?'"

"His name is James. Remember, James, my high school boyfriend? Well, we reconnected. He's recently divorced with twins, a boy and girl. He has a great job as a school superintendent. He loves kids. And he is doing well, very well. He is really good at investing his money, too."

"Ahh, now I remember. The same James I teased was a trust fund baby?"

"Funny, Adoma. Well, I plan to move in with him when my lease is up."

"What? Then you're in a serious relationship! Casey that is so great! This is huge. Congratulations, love."

"Thank you, my friend. Well, Adoma, as you may have guessed, it comes with challenges. The twins' mother is a bit unpredictable. James told me all about her while we grew closer as he finalized his divorce. She really put him through the ringer. So, tell me, how am I going to deal with a crazy baby's mother and help raise two pubescent twins? I'm not the best example, as you may recall."

"But, you were low key in high school and got good grades. You would know how to advise them to be good students. Anyway, we all change, and you did, too. You can warn them about the mistakes you made. You know, like tell them 'stay off the pole,' don't do it just because you're curious – better still, don't ever," Adoma laughed.

"Adoma, you know there were many students who did that for money back in college. One of my old roommates did, and now she is a child therapist," Casey retorted. "Not all of us had monied families to fall back on," Casey said pointedly.

"Casey, your family has seen more money at once than my family ever will."

"Yes, but it wasn't good money, and that is in the past. You know how it turned out and what it did to my parents."

"True. Sorry, I shouldn't have brought it up."

"That's okay."

"I don't remember you keeping in touch with James through college. Does James know about the fun you had?" Adoma asked, eager to change topics, but landing on a poor choice.

"Does Mark know that you were with me half the time?"

"Touché'"

"Let's change subjects," suggested Casey. "Have you spoken to Mya or Genna lately?"

"Well, I haven't talked to Mya in a while; she's gone off the grid again. But the last time we spoke, it sounded like she is doing much better. I am proud of her; she's coming back. She may even visit New York to get away. We shall see.

"I spoke to Genna the other day, too, but we discussed everything but the ethics cloud that hangs over Fred's head, so I didn't press it. She will open up about it if she wants to."

"Yeah, I want the inside story," Casey responded.

"Me, too. It's hard to know what's true and what's rumor, you know, and the media tends to blow things out of proportion for ratings. You just never know what is real and what isn't on the internet and television. I hope it's not what they are saying, though."

"Yeah, I hope not either."

"Well, I need to get ready to get out of the house. And speaking of Duke, I see him later this evening. He is back in town and taking me out to dinner."

"Oh?" Casey seemed genuinely surprised. "Sounds like trouble."

"Hardly."

"Adoma, that man has stuck to you like white on rice since you reconnected. Are you blind? You can never tell when a man is madly in love with you, can you? Can't you see that he is trying to win you back?"

"Stop it, Casey; we're just friends. He knows I have a boyfriend."

"Then why are you having dinner with him tonight?"

"Well, because I want to and I feel kind of lonely without Mark today."

"Oh my gosh! Today is your birthday, isn't it? Why didn't you remind me?" Casey exclaimed.

"Oh, it's not a big deal. This year everyone is so wrapped up in what's going on in their own lives - I understand you ladies forgetting. It's okay."

"No, it's not. We love you so much; you are the one who keeps all of our friendships together. I am so sorry to have forgotten your birthday, friend. That never happens. I hope you have a good one with Duke. I know that after you guys had crossed the line, things were never the same between you two, mostly because you fell so fast for him. But remember that he was your friend in the beginning, and he was an excellent friend to you, Adoma. So be careful, don't push him out of your life completely again. He is a good man. It was just a bad situation."

"Casey, thank you for the birthday wishes and the sage advice on my friendship with Duke. I will keep it in mind. I don't want to keep you longer. Have a good night dear, and I can't wait to see James again."

"Ha, I can't wait for everyone to meet him, too. I told him all about you gals."

Adoma chuckled. "Oh, I bet you did."

Precisely at the top of the hour, Duke picked up Adoma in a town car. 'Wow. Impressive,' she thought as he came to the steps and handed her flowers.

"Thank you Duke; you remembered my favorite, sunflowers." She hugged him.

"Of course, I did." He smiled, beaming with pride. "Are you ready?"

"Yes, in a bit. Just give me a second to respond to a couple of texts. Mya and Genna just texted me 'Happy Birthday.' They remembered. Either that or Casey called them right after we spoke and reminded them." She smiled, wondering when Mark would reach out.

"Sure Adoma, just take your time. We still have about forty-five minutes."

"Ok, almost done. My mom just posted a birthday message on Facebook, too. Okay, I just hit send. I'm ready."

The restaurant served a lovely red-velvet cupcake with one candle in it as the birthday dessert, sweet and simple. It relieved Adoma that the waiters did not sing happy birthday to her.

"Duke, thank you again for such a lovely evening. Dinner was delicious, and I had a great time. You are truly a special friend to me. I want you to know that I appreciate you." Adoma sensed Duke had something on his mind and reached her hand over to him.

"Thank you, Adoma," he said, appearing uncharacteristically nervous. "I also want you to know something."

"Yes?"

"I know I said it earlier, but I want you to know that I am sorry for what happened in the past." He took both of her hands, held them, and gazed into her eyes. "Adoma, I sincerely apologize for hurting you before. I'm sorry. Please forgive me. I thank you. And, I love you."

Adoma returned his gaze, and at that moment, when she heard that special sequence of words, Duke seemed to embody the spirit of all the men who had hurt her before. And simultaneously, all their faces flashed through her mind. And in her mind, they all offered her the same distinctive words: 'I'm sorry. Please forgive me. I thank you. And, I love you.' And finally she could release them and the hurt they caused her.

Adoma then looked at Duke, and at that moment she could forgive – and had indeed finally forgiven him – truly, wholly, and completely.

Chapter 27
Bye, Bye Baby Doll

Mya tussled in the bed until Christian elbowed her awake. "You okay, dear?" he asked.

"Yeah, Christian, just another bad dream. Don't worry about it. I'm okay."

"Which was it this time? About Roger? About money?" Mya's former attorney asked.

"No, it was a nightmare from when I was a child, but I think I'm okay now."

"But honey, you're still sweating..." Christian pulled in closer to Mya on his bed. He caressed her hair. "Mya, you don't have to worry anymore. I just want to prove to you that love doesn't have to hurt the way you have been hurt before, and that love doesn't have to disappear the way it disappeared before. I wanted to do that for you and show you so much of my heart much earlier, but I couldn't, not when I legally represented you. So, I kept my feelings to myself as they bubbled inside of me almost painfully, and I wondered if you could tell by the look in my eyes when we spoke, or by the way I placed my hand over yours in comfort... I wondered a lot back then because that was all I could do.

"Of course you didn't notice any of this. You were in one of the most tumultuous events in your life; you wouldn't see small nuances like that," Christian continued muttering to himself, feeling ridiculous for voicing his thoughts. "But now that everything is behind us and you are my woman, I can show you how I feel, hold you tight and never let you go."

"Mmh, yeh," Mya assured him, too drowned in thought to notice his soliloquy. "I think I'm okay; it was just about what happened. The medical report at the trial brought it all back to me." Mya paused and looked into Christian's eyes. She had fallen in love again, and this time it felt right. Christian had been there and witnessed everything from the beginning. He saved her from losing her mind during those times when, as she confessed, she couldn't take much more of life with Roger – his mind games, and his attempts at every opportunity to make her feel unattractive, unintelligent, and unworthy. Christian was her relief.

"You never told me the story, babe." Christian hugged Mya. "Tell me now, and maybe the nightmares will go away."

"Well," Mya started. Her shaky but sweet voice cracked a bit as she began. "I was very young and sooo scared that day," Mya gulped and continued. "Most around me knew when the day arrived; the event was made to be a big deal." Her eyes began to swell with tears. "The day before, my cousin asked me if I was ready. But, I didn't know how to be prepared. And who is ever ready for that? No girl ever is, and not me, not as a small child." Mya shuddered.

"It's okay Mya, keep going." Christian held her quivering hand tightly as Mya rested her head on his shoulder and sobbed lightly.

"I was hoping to tuck this part of my life away and never have to relive it." Mya, with tears falling to the pillowcase, continued describing in great detail the ceremonious nature of the event, the decorations, the beautiful fabric worn by the women, and the music. "Christian," Mya sat up and spoke in a voice raised in indignation. "Can you believe they had smiles, as if nothing, nothing at all tragic was going to occur? Ugh!" She held her stomach in disgust. "I could never forget those smiles!" Mya explained that the smiles varied in characteristics; some had a tinge of sadness while others seemed cruelly gleeful, as if they held a secret joy, a satisfaction to bring another into their circle of pain and lifetime of scars.

"Then, Christian, when the clock turned noon, it was my time. My aunt grabbed my left hand, and I just remember trying to turn around and reach for my doll that fell from my right hand, but her pull was too strong, and my baby doll just lay there on the floor. I couldn't take it with me as I entered the room. I don't know that I can talk about the rest."

Mya closed her eyes and reluctantly continued, recalling what she wished not to share. Inside the room she was laid on a small bed surrounded by straw. Dried blood from the ceremony before her speckled the floor. Her aunt placed a flowery fragranced cloth over her mouth and nose and said, "Breathe," and then it started. Her aunt and her mother held her down while 'the doctor' began to carve. As her body contorted in pain, she wondered as a child why this had to happen to her or why it had to happen at all.

"Mya, I'm so sorry," Christian consoled her at the end of her story.

"It's okay. That's what happened." Mya ended with very little emotion as she wiped away her remaining tears. She composed herself, then continued. "It was just one of those things that happened in my former world, something very common. It's no longer worth my tears; it's not a big deal," Mya brushed it off.

'And perhaps I'm selfish to dwell on it,' Mya thought to herself. 'Millions of girls worldwide are subject to this practice,' Mya told herself to help ease her mental pain.

But the ritual that scarred her, physically and emotionally, took her childhood innocence - and worse, her ability to have children with a man she loved.

At this moment, a new man she loved lay beside her in comfort. But now, love-wary Mya analyzed Christian's every word to avoid another error. She loathed ending up like before or like Genna, married to someone involved in a publicly humiliating scandal.

As Mya left the bed they temporarily shared, she thanked Christian for listening. "I truly do appreciate everything." Christian helped her reestablish her business and finances. He was extremely helpful and very present – in fact, omnipresent. He lurked everywhere, and where Mya went, so did Christian. Christian said that he wanted Mya to see her friends more often, but he never gave her the space to do so.

So, Mya let another week slip by without responding to Adoma. Mya wanted to but lacked the privacy to return her call.

But this morning, she didn't care about 'ignoring' Christian and she finally answered Adoma's week-old text with a phone call.

"Hi, my lovely!" Mya exclaimed.

"Mya?" Adoma asked incredulously, "What happened to you? I have been calling and texting you like crazy, and you haven't answered me for a while. What in the world is going on?"

"I am so sorry, love. I've been so busy. I would look at your text or missed call, intend to reply, and then completely forget. Truth be told, I've been a bit distracted too. You know, the divorce was extremely tough, the most humiliating ordeal that I have ever experienced. It felt dreadful to be exposed like that and in front of strangers in such a way… It was like a sore that you don't want anyone to see but a bully finds out about it and rips the bandage off, exposing the puss-filled wound to the light where everyone can see it, and then it burns. That's how I felt during the whole proceedings. You couldn't make this stuff up. Our lives sounded like a soap opera." Mya sighed.

"During the trial, they discussed our sex life and even my vagina. 'Dreadful' is the least serious word that I can use to describe those moments. And for what? What was it all for really? Just so the lazy bastard could continue living off me? How did he even have it in him to watch me get ready to go to work early each morning while he lay asleep doing nothing? Did that not make him feel less like a man? It certainly would for any man that I know. I wish I had never met that psycho… Yes, I had trouble conceiving, but did that make me any less of a wife to him? Did he have to treat me that way, and say the things he said, and let all of those strangers know those details about me? To think I saw my future with a monster like that is unbelievable!

"Be careful who you end up with, Adoma, and watch out for the signs. Watch out for the body language, watch out for off-the-wall comments, watch out for the jokes – you know when they say something and then say 'Oh I was just joking'? Well, every joke has a bit of truth in it, so watch out for that. If you get any of these signs while you are dating, before it is too late, *run don't walk* to the nearest exit. Make an exit strategy and flee. It's not worth it to be married to or end up with someone you wish to physically harm because you can't even stomach the sight of their face. Let anyone who can't love you, won't love you, doesn't know how to love you, go."

"I hear you Mya, loud and clear. Don't worry."

"And now I'm dating my former attorney, Christian, as you know."

"No, I don't think that you mentioned it, but congrats," Adoma said hiding her surprise. "You don't think that it's too soon?"

"Probably, but it just happened. Right after the trial, he and I started seeing each other and became attached at the hips. And he offered up his place for me to crash while the property issues get finalized." She giggled in a way a woman in love does.

"Hmm. Sounds like he likes you a lot. Well, you are very lovable Mya, so I can see why he fell for you, and he probably had a case of SDDS after that dramatic divorce of yours."

"SDDS?" Mya inquired.

"Yeah, you know Saving the Damsel in Distress Syndrome that takes over a man when he helps a distressed woman and then he feels like the hero and all; and then the woman falls in love and in turn, so does he?"

"Oh, I didn't know it had a name."

"Oh, it doesn't, silly, I just totally made that up," Adoma snickered.

"Adoma, you are so goofy."

"I know," Adoma laughed.

"So, what is new with you?" Mya asked in excitement.

"Well, New York is still going okay. Work is fine. Sasha is as demanding as ever since we are working on her new album, which in actuality makes for a non-productive work atmosphere at the label, but hey. Being creative on demand is like counterproductive you know? It's much easier to be creative when you feel free. When you feel the pressure to produce, it's almost stifling. I don't know why they don't get that. Pressure and delivering a masterpiece rarely go together." Adoma exhaled in frustration. "But luckily, I can derive some material from my love life. And my has that been drama of theatrical proportions."

"Really? Do tell. Now that you finally have a love life I want to hear it all. Spill it, Adoma."

"Oh, I am. We haven't spoken for a while, and you are in for a shocker. Wait for it." Adoma paused for dramatic effect." I think I'm in love with two men."

"What, Adoma?" Mya, in shock, asked further. "Mark and who else?"

Adoma pretended not to hear the question and kept speaking. "I'm perfectly happy with Mark, Mya. I want for nothing in our relationship. I still don't need anything with Mark, other than just more time, but he's perfect. He's a perfect man. He's a perfect boyfriend."

"Then, what's the problem Adoma?"

"The problem is that Duke is back in my life."

"Duke? From before? Your off and on again friend turned lover you met during our New Orleans trip? I remember him. He seemed cool, but he hurt you didn't he? Oh, yes he did! I remember that! Really, Adoma, you let him back into your life?"

"He did cause me a lot of pain, but I forgave him, and we've moved forward. He's back in my life, and I've been seeing him when he's in town. He's been there for me – even my last birthday and other times when Mark's been gone – which is often. And I do love Duke in a sense. I also love Mark. I love them both," Adoma said passionately and continued. "One is my past, and the other is supposed to be my future. But at this point, my past is now my present and what I thought was my future," Adoma paused in exasperation "And the man who I know is better for me – seems to be fading slightly from view."

"Really, Adoma?"

"Yes, Mya, it's hard to acknowledge, but the more time I spend with Duke..." Adoma paused before ending the sentence in disbelief, "...the less I see myself with Mark. Did I just say that, Mya? Ugh. What is wrong with me? Mark is a great guy – more than great, fantastic, wonderful, and any other superlative I can think of!"

"Adoma, if Mark treats you well and loves you the way you need to be loved, you have to let this thing with Duke go. He hurt you so much. He betrayed you and your feelings. How can you even look at him and not think about all that he put you through?"

"I forgave him, Mya. He has changed, and I believe him."

"What's changed, Adoma? Is it worth losing someone you love and truly loves you for someone who didn't see your value before and let you down?"

"Hmm. Mya, you always know what to say, and now I feel terrible. Maybe you're right. I don't need to risk losing Mark by spending so much time with Duke. I will have to have a conversation with Duke."

"Yes you do, love, yes you do," Mya confirmed.

"Well, dear, thank you for the advice. I will let you know how it goes. Are you still coming up to New York to visit as you promised? "

"I will try. Maybe Christian will let me escape one of these days," Mya laughed, nervously.

"Well, I hope you make it out here soon. I have a great coffee shop to take you to in Harlem. Oh, and you will love this place called Sankofa and all of the cool stuff they have there. Speaking of Sankofa, expect a package from me next week. I am sending all of you ladies some packages from the shop."

"Really? I love gifts. Yay! Thank you in advance."

"Well, lovely lady, speak with you soon."

"Absolutely... Now that the worst is over, and that monster has gone away forever, I will be in touch so much more. I miss you all a lot, and I'm sad that I've lost touch with everyone, but I will try to get Genna and Casey together soon for dinner – most likely at our usual spot – and we will bond in your honor. Oh, and we have to a lot to celebrate – my freedom and Casey's crazy spur of the moment romance."

"Ha!" Adoma replied "She told you about him too? I can't believe Casey is in what seems to be a stable relationship with a stand-up guy. Good for her. Maybe now she will finally calm down instead of looking for love in all the wrong places."

"Yes, our Casey is growing up." Mya and Adoma laughed before they hung-up.

Chapter 28
Countdown

A month later, "I's married now!" flashed on Adoma's, Mya's, and Genna's phones. Casey texted each of them the funny quote from a well-known movie she and Adoma loved. Casey had outdone herself, upping all of her prior impulsive acts, and did the most spontaneous one yet – she had eloped to Vegas.

No one, not even Casey, knew the weekend would end with marriage. Casey left as a single woman for a romantic getaway in her second favorite city and came back a bride.

The small wedding consisted of only the two of them. Casey told no one, not Genna, Mya, or even Adoma in the moments before the ceremony, out of fear that one or all of them would try to convince her to slow down. However, in Casey's mind, there was no need to wait. Knowing that eventually in life she would marry, and since Casey had already dated James and known him for about twenty years, she thought 'why not now?'. Getting married to James was the only impulsive decision she could be proud of.

Casey and James, who were close in high school, and later in life as she coaxed him through his marital problems, had grown even closer in recent months. As they both reminisced on phone calls, becoming nostalgic about their high school romance, they had fallen in love again. They traveled down memory lane and ignited old emotions they had for each other many years ago.

James's recent divorce came conveniently; it coincided with Casey's weariness for fleeting romances and her huge wake-up call at work, where she nearly lost her job due to a lapse in judgment.

With the work episode and tinge of loneliness lingering, Casey concluded the time had come for domesticity – just one man and maybe true love. Casey hoped responsibility would abate her urges to seek comforts elsewhere.

Luckily for Casey, she deftly sensed that James seemed eager to remarry. He, accustomed to structure and routine, didn't function well without a wife. Also, since he had won sole custody of his twins, he needed help around the home. The perfectly timed coincidence pleased her.

Casey wished she could have seen the faces of Adoma, Genna, and Mya when they all received the text with the pictures of her Vegas wedding attached. The photos came out beautifully and surprisingly professional, opposing Casey's previous misconception of Vegas weddings. If she hadn't told anyone she married in Las Vegas, it would have been impossible to tell by the photographs.

In the photo, Casey wore a lovely, but casual sleeveless crème dress that stopped at her knees, showing off her beautifully tanned and toned legs gleaming with cocoa butter.

James wore a nice suit, one of the many he owned and wore to work. Casey did her hair and decided to switch her style from her sharp bob to a wavy weave. The back of her hair swept up and cascaded down in waves past her shoulders. Already an attractive woman, she looked better than she had looked in a long time, not simply because of the hairstyle, the dress, or the make-up, but because she looked radiant, at peace, and in love.

In the photo, James sported a bright grin, and Casey looked just as normal and radiant as any bride. James, blissfully ignorant of Casey's explorative years, appeared ready for the future with a new partner by his side. And even if James weren't oblivious to Casey's wild days, it didn't, or shouldn't, matter. They made a lovely couple.

Adoma responded to Casey's text with 'Congratulations, beautiful bride!!!'. The surprise wedding, ironically, came as no surprise. Well, it shocked Adoma when Casey finally decided to settle down; but since she had, it did not surprise Adoma that Casey eloped with James. Quick decision-making fit the personality of the Casey that Adoma had grown to know. By the looks of the pictures, Casey appeared ecstatically happy, like a new woman.

Adoma was excited that Casey's marriage could be another phase of her life, a whole new chapter. 'Casey, a bride, a wife, and step-mother? That would be interesting to watch… and could be perfect for her. Besides, Casey, with her personality, wit, and charm, could make any man happy. And, thank goodness she will be slowing down and no longer putting herself or her job in jeopardy with her impulsive behaviors,' Adoma thought.

Previously, Casey would never have let her personal life cross into her professional one. She drew a bold distinction between the two and enjoyed the respect that she used to receive at work. At work she had rank, but that didn't seem to matter now that the bar rumor had spread through her office. Her coworkers, even the administrative staff, now viewed her differently.

Also, Adoma had developed concern about Casey's recent actions when it appeared that the very same behaviors she exhibited in college and in their twenties had followed them into their thirties. Casey jeopardized everything for fun, and it came across as reckless, irresponsible, and plain stupid. She risked her employment and even health with her dicey activities. Heaven forbid Casey be stuck with something forever over a single night of diversion.

So, when Adoma viewed the wedding picture, she smiled with satisfaction. James seemed perhaps too dull for Casey, but at least he was a good, decent man with a decent job, decent resume, and a belief in commitment. This type of stability – going home to and growing old with someone you loved – could work for Casey… maybe. 'I guess time will tell.' Adoma hoped. 'And if not, we will certainly hear all of the stories.' Adoma smirked as she stroked one of the adinkra cloth's she had bought from Sankofa.

The colors of this particular fabric radiated a beautiful indigo and jade. She carefully folded the cloth, packaged it, and presented it nicely in the gift box. This fabric, the most colorful, would be the one for Mya. She began to fold the other two as well. When Adoma finished, she placed the carefully selected gifts inside the Sankofa gift boxes.

Before sealing each box, she wrote notes to each friend, along with a general letter to them on stationary bearing her name…

Dear Besties,

Since you are reading this letter, by now you have seen the fabric inside of the gift box. You received your fabric carefully picked out by me. I am sending each of you a unique swath of cloth, and you will notice the black emblems, an adinkra symbol. Each fabric is specific to each of you ladies. It contains the adinkra emblem on it that best suits your personalities – in my humble opinion – or what you mean to me or our friendship.

The cloth is beautiful, so please feel free to use it how you wish. Make a dress, a skirt, or even some cute pillowcases out of the fabric. But, please only use half of it and save the other half to bring with you to the reunion. Don't forget it! I will explain the significance of each symbol to you then. Instructions regarding the fabric's care are also inside the box.

As the reunion soon approaches, and to give you time to plan, I am asking that you save the date now. Yes, put it in your calendar now with frequent reminders, and start making space in your life to attend. I will initiate the planning this weekend.

About six months out, I will send the information for the trip accommodations, etc.

I trust that you all are just as excited about the reunion as I am and that you will attend. This reunion will be a success with all of us present, physically and emotionally.

My love to you all.

Lylas,

~Adoma~

'Done,' Adoma thought to herself, relieved that the first part of planning the reunion – the invitations – were finished. Still, she stressed at the thought of pulling off a successful event from a continent away. Luckily, she had some sense of where to go, from speaking with former coworkers who had visited the island destination, and from the coffee table book Mark had gifted her.

Adoma picked out a couple of to-dos and the restaurant where they would celebrate their ten years of friendship. Now, she needed to finalize the plans, and pull them all together, all on her own. She put a reminder in her calendar for about six months out to 'make hotel and restaurant reservations.'

Putting reunion preparations aside, Adoma also needed to tend to the confusion she had made of her life. 'The rest of the planning can wait,' Adoma said to herself after she mailed the packages. She needed to prepare herself mentally, get dressed to see Duke that evening, and tell him that they needed to stop seeing each other so often. Adoma fretted doing so but deemed it was a necessary course of action. She had asked Duke to meet her for coffee that evening. After first agreeing, he had canceled the coffee date and instead asked if they could meet for an early dinner.

Adoma planned the conversation over and over again in her mind. 'I will say this, and he will say that. He might spar with me a little bit, maybe be mad at me for wasting his time, but then he would understand and let me go.' She imagined Duke getting a little bit angry, as he probably had never been dumped before; but then their friendship would prevail, and he would willingly surrender to what was best for their friendship – and for Adoma as his friend.

Adoma also had the unlikely fantasy that Duke would cry and say he wished he had never let her go in the first place. Then Adoma would hold him in her arms, comforting him, but also agreeing with him that 'yes, he did make a mistake' by choosing the wrong woman. Adoma chuckled knowing that was the most unlikely scenario to play out.

So before they met, she thought she had everything covered. That she would end the date accomplishing what she had intended, saying everything that was on her mind, and that Duke, understanding and receiving it all, would bow to her wishes, and finally let her go.

And then Adoma's imagination started leading her to picture her world without Duke in it, and it seemed like a weird world for her to exist. For almost the last ten years, Duke was always there, always a constant in her life – except for that period during his marriage; but even then, she carried him with her.

Adoma felt saddened that the impending conversation may completely sever her ties to Duke. He would be gone, and there wouldn't even be an emotion on which to cling. There wouldn't be love or hate, just apathy, which was nothing, and Adoma didn't know if she was ready for that world. In some ways, Duke anchored her. In her world of constant changes, would she just float away without him? On the other hand, would Mark's love fill the void and be enough to keep her grounded and focused on what she wanted in life?

Adoma had the courage to excel in the past because Duke helped build her confidence and told her she could. He always had faith in everything she wanted to pursue, and encouraged it. And she accomplished her goals with him rooting for her.

Being around Duke made Adoma feel good in a different way than being with Mark felt. Adoma imagined the opulent lifestyle they would have together due to his high-powered position. The best way to describe it was that being with Duke made Adoma feel wealthy by association. Duke also desired Adoma. 'Am I just an object to him? No, that can't be true,' and she let that thought go. 'No, he does love me, and I love him too, but I love him differently now.' And when Adoma thought about her life and how happy Mark made her – and how stressed she had become with Duke back – it became clear. 'Yes, I am going through with it. I will end things with Duke. I have too much to lose. I love Mark, and shouldn't take him for granted.'

Adoma arrived before Duke and ordered, relaxing a bit. She had time to once more revisit what she would say and how Duke would respond so that she had all of her bases covered. 'With all of this mental preparation, nothing should take me by surprise,' she surmised.

Duke arrived 20 minutes later looking exceptionally handsome. His khaki pants fit a bit snug around his legs and his navy blue blazer worn over a crisp white shirt made him look incredibly appealing. Adoma dressed equally conservative for the meal, dressed in a light-blue button-up shirt that fit cozily at her breasts, Capri khakis, and loafer-style shoes. She placed her hair in a springy ponytail to give the illusion of carefreeness and had put on natural looking make-up, but plenty of concealer over the dark circles under her eyes – the result of a sleepless night in anticipation of this conversation.

They greeted, and he sat down. "Can I have a fry?" Duke asked as he grabbed it, moving it toward his mouth. Adoma opened her mouth to say what she planned to say to Duke, then prepared herself by first taking a sip of her lemon-water and muttered barely audibly, "Duke, you know…"

"Wait Adoma, before you say anything. I am so excited. I want to share some news with you," Duke interrupted Adoma's planned monolog while continuing to eat her fries.

"But, I have something important to say."

"But, this is important too. "

"Okay, Duke, you first," Adoma acquiesced.

Duke placed his hand over hers and smiled like a little boy who couldn't wait to be the first to run and tell the neighborhood news. "I asked for a transfer to New York. And…" he paused for dramatic effect, "…they agreed to move me here. We can be together all of the time now, Adoma!"

"Duke, that is wonderful news! I know you like the States much better than Europe. I'm happy for you."

"And what about being glad for *us*?" he asked.

"Duke, how can there be an us when I am in a relationship?"

"Adoma, I just can't accept that you think that Mark is better for you than I am." Duke leaned back in his chair and crossed his right shin over his left thigh. He moved his hands together staring at Adoma incredulously.

"Duke," Adoma paused "Now it's my turn to speak." Adoma inhaled deeply. "I love you, but our ti…"

"Adoma, I love you too, and that is why I want you to know that I want to spend the rest of my life with you." He leaned forward and embraced both of her hands, pulling them just a couple of inches shy from his broad chest. "I want to marry you

Adoma. Will you marry me?"

And with those proudly said words, spoken through his shiny pearly teeth, he looked at her most sincerely.

Adoma's mouth dropped, and she spilled her water on the table.

Chapter 29
Save the Date

Genna was surprised to receive the beautiful package and unwrapped it carefully. She smiled when she noticed the nicely done – down to the silk ribbon – professional invitation. Genna recognized the Ashanti stool stamped on the box, as she had seen one in Adoma's former loft and had asked about its significance.

'Adoma actually plans to pull off this reunion after almost ten years. Amazing,' Genna thought, then carefully peeled the lid off the box. Inside revealed a beautiful fabric. Genna pulled the cloth out of the parcel and unfolded it to fully display the pattern and colors. 'Absolutely stunning,' she thought to herself.

The cloth, much longer than her arms could stretch, had a deep royal purple and yellowish gold background, the backdrop to beautiful onyx-colored symbols designed into a swirling pattern. Genna's symbol looked like an open flower with four petals, but she'd wait for Adoma to explain it. Genna laid the fabric on her bed before she noticed a letter on the inside of the package. She reached for it, then smirked when the stationary caught her attention. Genna walked over to her vanity table and began to read the general letter first, and then the one personalized for her.

Hello, Dear Genna,

I know it has been a while since we've spoken. And though it has, you are still in my thoughts and also my prayers as I think of you and Fred during this tumultuous time. We haven't always remained in communication, but we didn't need to for me to know that I have a friend in you, and if I ever needed anything, anything at all, you would be there for me just as I would be there for you.

We've been friends since childhood and then there were the law firm days. Not only have you been a good friend, you have proven to be a confidante. We have shared a lot, including the good times like our memorable trip to New Orleans and the promise that we made to each other shortly after.

Yes, the idea to meet ten years later in the Seychelles was a crazy one made while we were having fun, but we pledged to it. Why? Because we knew back then what we are forgetting now, that our friendships could make it and they have. Now look, ten years is almost here.

I haven't forgotten our vow. Many things in my life have been unstable too. I have moved from country to country, been in multiple failed relationships, changed careers, and moved on a whim; but one thing (other than my family) has been constant in my life, and that has been my friendships with you, Casey, and Mya.

On some of the loneliest occasions overseas, a conversation from one of you or even an email could change my outlook on the day. The reunion promise we made to each other was made with the same type of hope. In that promise we assumed so many things about our friendships, and though we are all so different, we are the same.

We all have our careers, our relationships, in some cases families. Yes, we are all busy professionals too, but this upcoming reunion means the world to me, and I know we will regret it if we do not pull it off and honor our commitment to our friendship.

My heart extends to you at this time, but I know it will all be over soon. You also always have me to lean on should you wish to talk. And even if we do not speak as you deal with the pressures you and Fred are now facing, know that I am thinking of you and sending you all the positive energy and love that I can. I love you and look forward to speaking with you soon.

Big Hugs, Lylas,
Adoma

'Aww, how considerate and thoughtful of Adoma.' Genna smiled. 'She still uses our childhood phrase, Lylas. Cute. She knows how to hold us together,' Genna thought to herself, then reached down into the package and pulled out a photo Adoma had added to the gift box. The picture showed all of them on Bourbon Street the day before they made the promise to reunite.

The cute photo pictured Adoma looking young and positively happy with her signature smile and dimples. Mya looked regal and gorgeous as usual, with her arm draped around Adoma's shoulder as they stood cheek-to-cheek. Casey played around and posed in a crazy B-girl stance, and Genna joined along in Casey's playfulness with a Posh girl type of pose with her tongue sticking out to add a bit more humor to the moment. This picture brought back so many memories. Life seemed easy then; back then they were just really all getting into the swing of their careers and life, and everyone seemed so optimistic.

Then Genna cracked a smile as she remembered the crazy drunk guy who took the picture. 'So funny! New Orleans was so wild that even taking the picture was like herding cats. Imagine getting four girls to sit still for that long and to find a sober person on that street to take a picture.' But they found someone, a guy who was walking alone looking sad, like he had lost the rest of his crew. But Casey approached him and struck up a conversation; then he was happy to take a picture of the girls, but only after insisting that he moon them. So he did. 'Yuck,' Genna thought, recalling his hairy derriere. But the bystander got his thrill, took their picture, and yes, received the treasured Mardi Gras beads.

Genna laughed at the memory to abate the nostalgia it also brought of innocent times gone too fast. She looked again at the photo wistfully, tearfully. The New Orleans trip almost ten years ago created memories, fun laugh-out-loud memories. They always laughed when they came together; the ladies would certainly have a good time at the upcoming reunion.

When they had promised to reunite, at first Genna had concerns. At that time and a few years afterward, she never really felt like she fit into the group completely. She and Mya rarely spoke, and Casey and her had often butted heads. Genna accepted that part of the fault lie with her, as she had an issue with letting down her guard or fully trusting other women. Truth be told, she would rather spend time with her man than another woman any day, and on occasion she had ditched Adoma to spend time with Fred. However, even when Adoma knew this, she always let her off the hook and maintained their contact as if nothing happened.

Soon Genna began to feel more comfortable with everyone, and after a few years the idea of the reunion seemed like a good one – a plan, a concept, easy to commit to and achieve. But, life differed for all of them back then; they were younger, in their twenties, more carefree, and their lives had less issues. Now real life and the unexpected occurred.

Genna would love to take a vacation to an exotic island off the coast of Africa, but the timing could not have been worse. Even strong-willed Genna began to bow to the strain and pressure brought by rumors of an investigation. She hoped that this time next year, it would all be over, but had no idea if it would be so.

Through the fundraisers and political events, Genna maintained contacts and was able to garner a few favors, resulting in a source who claimed to know what was going on. Although Genna's source would not divulge details, Genna found out that an ethics committee continued to look into the allegations of ethics violations and specifically focused on abuse of power and the possibility of the acceptance of improper gifts in Fred's congressional office. The worst part was that, due to the nature of the allegations, authorities may have the option to freeze their bank accounts until the probe concluded and the findings were released.

Genna prayed none of this would happen, or equally important, hit the *real* press, in addition to the political blogs that currently circulated the speculation; because if so, the embarrassment would damage the image she cultivated. Already, as she visited the country club or other places around town, she would feel self-conscious. 'Maybe they did or maybe they didn't know anything,' Genna thought, suspicious that the women, the ones she looked up to, were whispering behind her back or when she entered into the room. So, as a result, Genna stayed to herself and stopped socializing as much.

Genna looked back over at the beautiful package and the

save the date invitation. 'Adoma definitely put a lot of thought into this, wow. Sending fabrics and loving notes this far out.' The thought-provoking note, amidst Genna's turmoil, almost made her teary-eyed.

'Adoma has a point, we do have something special, being of four different backgrounds, most of us immigrants, and to have had a continued friendship together for this length of time. It's remarkable.' Genna looked at the photo again and giggled, relaxing a bit more into the idea of going to the fast approaching reunion.

Truth be told, Genna couldn't wait to get away from home and unwind on an island, because being home now irritated her. Going to the Seychelles for the reunion sounded good, but a local beach would do just fine, and the islands were so far away, they would take almost a day to reach. The timing in Genna's life seemed too problematic.

At present, her relationship seemed the most complicated – more than it had ever been. Fred had changed drastically since being associated with the rumors. Politically ensconced, even hand-picked into his present position, Fred obviously had more to lose, and now faced professional uncertainty, whether or not the allegations proved correct.

'What will we do if the congressman is forced to leave office and Fred has to look for a new job? Surely he will struggle to find work,' Genna worried about Fred. 'His career would blow in the wind and what if that taint gets on me? I would have to leave my cushy position as well.' Genna frowned, knowing the speed with which rumors spread and became real – even if not. And with the absence of information, people tended to fill in the void in their own way, which is usually stranger than the truth. The gossip that Genna heard ranged from kickbacks for a construction project to abuse of power claims involving threats and harassment.

'Hmm, if there was a kickback, where was the money?' Aside from their homes, cars, and Genna's clothing, they were not living a super-plush, luxury lifestyle. They could afford a big house and nice trip every now or then, but it wasn't like their bank accounts bubbled over with money.

Those accounts reflected that Fred earned a modest salary and Genna still paid off her student loans. However, most of their lifestyle spawned from Genna, the breadwinner. Her money led to her ideas of how she wanted it to be and Fred didn't care as much about the material things.

Genna imagined that no matter the outcome, she'd still remain the primary wage earner and didn't worry as much about her employment security as she worried for Fred's. If, unfortunately, the allegations appeared accurate and a formal investigation proceeded – and especially if it seemed Genna may have had knowledge or involvement in wrongdoing – her firm might ask her to leave for appearance's sake. But, Genna, the professional star of the family would be welcomed with open arms to any smaller boutique firm. Like flipping a switch, Genna could be back to working and earning money. Genna just hoped that scenario never arose.

Chapter 30
Sharing in Happiness

Adoma gazed at her left hand as she rode in the dusty yellow cab on her way to catch a flight. The platinum ring adorning her fourth finger commanded attention, even her own, and she looked at it often and intently, as if awaiting messages from it like a crystal ball. The sun's rays hitting the cushion-cut stone through the barely tinted taxi windows reflected its facets. The gem beautifully responded to the light with flickering rainbow-colored reflections.

Adoma cherished her ring, though she never wanted or cared for diamonds. After learning about the horrors of the diamond trade, Adoma would have much preferred her birthstone for an engagement ring. But her fiancé guessed that she'd be conscientious even in her jewelry preference and made sure to propose with a conflict-free diamond that came with an attached certificate. So, the glowing gemstone happened to be the only diamond she could love. She fixated her eyes on her hand during most of the cab ride, not only owing to the diamond's appearance, but for the romantic night it reminded her of – the unforgettable moment she became engaged to the love of her life.

And now ecstatically happy, Adoma headed to the airport to meet and vacation with Mark as he concluded his latest assignment.

Adoma nodded to herself, knowing that she had made the right decision when she said 'yes'. All of this, she and Mark, resulted from her opening her heart to real love. She had also made the right decision when she said 'no' to Duke and let go of what no longer served her. Though it took some time.

Duke's true love and commitment had been so elusive before that when he announced to Adoma that he wanted to marry her, she felt as though she had been vindicated. But as Adoma thought more about Duke's 'proposal' she began to have second thoughts. It hurt her to do so, but she had to decline. Before Duke proposed, Adoma had already planned to sever relations, but she faltered, and in a moment of temporary confusion, she almost did the unexpected – and said 'yes.'

Adoma went over that moment repeatedly. A lengthy friendship with Duke meant that Adoma knew him well enough to predict his behavior. Adoma concluded that if Duke had intended to propose that day, he would have done so in a more grandeur manner and not during a meal in a casual restaurant on an early Saturday evening, without a ring. Duke excelled at everything, so he certainly would have wanted his proposal to be an event that Adoma could brag about, a thoroughly successful one, where Adoma would cry and do all the stereotypical things women do when surprised with an engagement ring. Instead, Duke asked Adoma to marry her over a bowl of fries.

During the meal, when Duke proposed at the same time Adoma tried to end things, Adoma realized that the proposal became Duke's way of controlling the situation and, in turn, controlling Adoma.

After this immediate understanding, Adoma metaphorically woke up, wiped her eyes, and perceived Duke as Duke – without the romanticism of their friendship and without the added benefit she gave him for knowing him so long. On that day, she could finally see Duke for exactly who he was. Duke was a good man, an accomplished, well-educated and polished man, who always wanted to win and dominate all of his relationships – professional or personal; he always played for control, even if undetected by his pawn.

After Duke's proposal, Adoma did the hardest thing she had to do in years. She gazed at Duke through tear-filled eyes, and as she stifled a cry, simply said to him, "Duke," then blinked hard and released a tear. "I am so, so tired." Then Adoma placed her right hand on his right cheek, and walked away.

"Hi, Mya!"

"Hi, Adoma! How are you? And where are you? I hear a lot of noise in the background."

"I am well. I'm at the airport. I thought I would give you a call during my layover. I'm on my way to see Mark in California. How are you?"

"Oh how nice, Adoma. I am doing well also. Glad to hear all is well with you."

"Yeah, things have been going great. It has been a really good two months since I uncomplicated my life and ended everything with Duke. As we discussed before, some loves are better left in the past, un-resurrected." Adoma exhaled at the thought.

"I'm proud of you love. Never spite the true love you find by straying back to someone who hurt you, especially when you have the right one in front of you, and when the right choice shouldn't even be a question. And look, it paid off shortly after."

"Yes, and so far so good for my first month of engagement. My lease ends at the end of the month, so I'm going to move into his place. There's no point in continuing to pay exorbitant rent when I'm always at his place and we're getting married anyway. In fact, we're even wondering why wait. We know that we want to be with each other forever."

"Yes, I understand. Sometimes it feels as though you can't wait, but just be sure it's right. Do you see yourself with Mark forever, no matter how he turns out?"

"Well, I don't see him changing that much or for the worse, which is good. No matter what happens, I can't imagine not being with him. So, yes, no matter how he turns out, I am by his side."

"Well, you may want to come clean to Mark about spending the last stretch of time with Duke."

"Hmm, I don't know what good that would do." Adoma frowned.

"Adoma, you don't want to start forever with someone and have secrets."

"It's not a secret. It's just not relevant. So why bring it up? If he were to ask though, that would be different, and I would tell him. But really, I just want to put it all behind me, especially after realizing so much."

Adoma gauged that this whole time Duke viewed winning her back as a challenge, as a conquest. And that once he would win, he would no longer pursue her. He may even no longer want her at all and move on to pursuing another woman for sport. Adoma assessed that Duke derived power and self-worth from external sources. 'A man like that could never be fully satisfied with what he had,' she guessed. When Adoma thought about their love or what she reasoned now to be their co-dependency, it became very clear. And Adoma theorized that what she thought was love actually wasn't love, or at least not the type to sustain her forever, the type for a lifetime that she had hoped for. It wasn't the kind of love that you grow with or that helps you grow; to the contrary, it was the kind that Adoma, who strove continuously to evolve, would outgrow.

Yes, Adoma had forgiven Duke and the hurt that he caused her in the past. She had absolved his betrayal and the way he misled her, and they continued to see each other. But intuitively, Adoma sensed that something wasn't as right as it should have been. Inside, Adoma had changed. They both had changed in fact, but matured differently over the years, and Adoma valued freedom while Duke valued power.

Adoma imagined the type of person she would devolve into if she had ended up with Duke. She couldn't see herself in ten or fifteen years growing into the woman she wanted to be as Duke's wife. On the contrary, she imagined herself swallowed up into his world – living a life centered around him, his ego, and his status, but not around their hearts or around their love. Adoma wanted no more of that type of love – she wanted a higher love. She had finally resolved there would be no more "Wasted Time" citing her favorite Meshell Ndegeocello song.

"Adoma," Mya said, "I'm glad you realized it all before someone got hurt. But also try to release Duke now. I can tell you're still disappointed, but you can't carry that baggage with you into your relationship with Mark. I've learned and grown through my own experience – enough now to be able to see my emotional pain differently. I can appreciate that it gave me clarity to know what I do or do not want in the future and what is acceptable or unacceptable in a partner; but I also had to let it go. I want you to also know that you have to let go of the pain too. You may say you are okay, but it could be held deep inside," Mya explained.

"The divorce with Roger was the worst thing, really…" Mya continued, "…and as I said earlier – humiliating. But it's time to move on, and I am. There are new experiences to have and new beginnings to start, and this time, I know will be better than before. I have forgiven Roger and I have forgiven myself for loving him. I had to do this so that I would no longer be stuck in the past. Do the same for yourself… just forgive and let it go. Let Duke go, release him completely and wholly from every part of you, so that you can now be fully present with Mark, the one who truly loves you. I am no longer stuck, and I don't want you to be either. Be in the now, the present, not attached to the past or worried about tomorrow. You will have true peace of mind if you do."

Adoma paused for a moment to think of Mya's poignant words. "Mya, you're right. All your therapy sure has paid off!" They laughed.

Mya continued, "Sometimes we try to keep wilted relationships from dying by holding on to them as long as possible. We hold on because we remember what they used to be and don't want to throw them away or cut them off, even when they have become shriveled, toxic, and without life."

"So true. That was how it was with Duke and me before – way back. We kept in touch for a long time, seeing each other occasionally. He'd even go out of his way to visit, but in truth, the relationship had become stagnant. And though it was comfortable between us, our relationship did not evolve, it did not grow, it was not healthy. And when he returned in my life I knew all of this, but let myself forget it. I had what was right for me, a new partner in front of my eyes, but he was the unknown and I was more afraid of that, the unknown… Geez Mya, now I sound like you!"

"Ha!" Mya giggled.

"But I still don't think I should tell Mark about Duke."

"Okay Adoma, do what you want, but I still believe that you should confess every…"

"So," Adoma interrupted unwilling to go down that path for the third time in their conversation. "How was dinner with Casey and Genna?"

"Genna didn't show up," Mya explained. "Some excuse about having to work late, so it was just Casey and me."

"That's a bummer. But why am I not surprised about Genna bailing?"

"Yes, we were hoping to see how she was doing, because she hardly keeps in touch any more. But what can you say? She's an adult. We can't make her come out and connect with us."

"And Casey?"

"Yes, Casey. She, on the other hand, is doing wonderful. We both talked about how happy we were when we heard you were engaged last month. And, really Adoma, I don't think you would even recognize Casey now. She is really getting into marriage and motherhood. It's hilarious, almost like she is playing a role in a movie, because it is so unlike her, yet she is really umm… assimilating into it. She even showed up to dinner in a floral dress." Mya laughed.

"A dress with flowers on it?" Adoma giggled; she couldn't believe it either. Casey never wore dresses or floral prints.

"Yes ma'am, but it wasn't A-line, I know that's what you're going to ask next, ha ha. She's probably saving that one for next time," Mya chuckled.

"Yeah, probably. I bet she doesn't want to shock you all at once," Adoma snarked. "Hmmm."

"I know. She filled me in at dinner and she sounded so good. James seems like a solid type of guy, very grounded, intelligent, and family-oriented. How did she let him get away before?"

"Well, he was her high school sweetheart, and after high school, Casey had her eyes on different types of men. She really enjoyed the fast-paced social scene of college, you know the fraternity guys and the college athletes… and then later, the professional ones after we graduated. You know there are so many temptations in a big city like home. Temptations are hard for Casey to resist and the guys did flock to her in college, after college, and I'm sure they still do. But it's not as bad as before I'm sure. Back then shiny objects easily distracted Casey. She has more focus now, and I know she told you about what happened at her job, right? I think that's what really scared her."

"She told me just a little. She mentioned that things seemed tense and that she got called into the HR director's office and that the director claimed Casey's outside activities, if they were to become public, would shed a negative light on the company and risk its reputation. Was there more to it?" Mya excitedly inquired.

"Oh, so she didn't tell you the specifics? Hmm. Well, I think I can say, 'Old Casey' wouldn't mind, but don't bring it up to her. Wait for her to tell you herself. Okay?"

"I promise, but please go ahead. The suspense is killing me."

"Well, she went to a restaurant bar after work and caught the eye of one of the managers, and he gave her a 'restaurant tour' where he showed her his office in the back. And things got ... out of control. One of the busboys in the restaurant, who also moonlights as the janitor at her company, saw her go back there and told his cousin, the receptionist, at Casey's job. That's when the rumor spread like wildfire around the office. And you know with office gossip, they added a few details that simply didn't happen. I think Casey said the HR director had said she violated the employee handbook, specifically the section pertaining to off-duty misconduct unbecoming of an officer in her company, or something formal like that. She almost lost her job for it."

"Are you serious?!"

"Yes, I am. How embarrassing for her. I am embarrassed to tell you the story. But, as we said earlier, good thing she has changed."

"Wow, Adoma, those details are quite, umm, shocking. Hmm, Casey didn't tell me all of that – just that she said that work had improved a lot. She also mentioned that the embarrassment seemed to be behind her after she spoke with the HR department. She really took the warning seriously. And, I think she thinks she's redeeming herself by working additional hours and volunteering for some of the projects others don't want.

You know she still felt unfairly scrutinized and in many ways ostracized for actions that, according to her, her male colleagues would get away with. However, she decided to put that behind her and continue proving herself as an asset to the company. And the good news is that a few of the proposals she submitted even received high-level attention. And the best part is that two of them – if awarded – appear to be on the verge of winning the company millions of dollars in billables."

"Good for Casey!" Adoma responded. "I hope that since she's worked so hard for her accomplishments that all of the doubts about her off-duty conduct are in the back of her supervisor's mind. But we have gotten a bit off topic. I called to find out how things are going with *you* Mya."

"Oh me? Things are going well with Christian and me, extremely well actually. I thought the living arrangement would be temporary, but we're enjoying each other's company a lot. I never knew a relationship could be this good, Adoma. And I'm so happy to have found out. I think I'm falling deep in love again, but this time, I want to take it slower. I think Christian has already fallen for me, as he'd told me earlier that he felt like he loved me the first time we met, but as my attorney instead of showing me, he had to suppress his feelings in order to represent me to the best of his ability."

"That makes sense. I'm sure there are also rules against divorce attorneys dating their clients."

"Umm. Yeah, I think there are. But it was the trial that brought us together, and now we can laugh at the time in court when I stood up to Roger and tried to stuff twenty-dollar bills into his mouth, but instead sprinkled them all over his face. Ha ha. Christian told me that he secretly cheered me on and wished he could have been next to me giving it to Roger, too."

"Mya, that is hilarious… and I'm glad you're happy right now," Adoma added. "We all deserve it, Mya, but you, with all you have suffered, you have paid your dues. It's your time. Many people say they want love, but don't fight for it to be in their lives the way that you do. You never gave up on it and you take the risks because for you, love is worth it. You have been brave and courageous to risk loving again when you have lost it the way you have. Mya, this is a particular type of courage that deserves its own credit. I've noticed sometimes people can be brave or take risks in some areas of their life, but do not take risks on something as important as love. You've taught me that true healthy love's always worth the risk. You don't know until you trust. And yes there will be bumps in the road, but you still love because you know that out of all of the things that are important in life, the greatest is love. With a strong foundation of love everything else is so beautiful and all other things can change for the positive. Mya, your endurance, and strength have taught me a lot. And, I'm so happy that we are both happy right now. We're both in love, and it's great. And look, even Casey is happy!"

"I know. Isn't that wonderful? The best thing in the world is when your friends can share in your happiness as they experience their own!"

"Yes, that is the best thing in the world," Adoma said as she heard the gate agent call announcing the boarding.

Chapter 31
The Garden

When Adoma saw Mark approaching her she accelerated and jumped into his arms, straddling his hips like a delighted child. He, equally as excited, spun her around and gave her a loving kiss. "Hello, my love."

"Hi, babe."

"I'm so excited to see you and even more so to see that you are so happy to see me. I haven't had a welcome like that in a while!"

"I know," Adoma said smiling. "It's been a long time you know, and on the plane ride here I thought about you so much and how much I appreciate you and your presence in my life."

"Ha, my dear. I've heard that one before. Show me!" Mark said facetiously.

"I show you all of the time," Adoma responded, enjoying their flirtatious banter.

"I'm so glad you could join me here. So this trip is for you to get out of the city and relax, but I also have a surprise for you."

"What is it?" Adoma asked with a bit of anxiety, unable to hide her mixed feelings about surprises.

"Well, if I told you, then it wouldn't be a surprise, right? You'll find out soon enough."

"Okay, Mark, but I don't know about you and secrets. I bet I will get it out of you before you can surprise me."

"True, I'm not good at keeping secrets, but I seriously doubt you can get me to spill the beans on this one."

"Many have regretted underestimating me," Adoma laughed. She and Mark walked hand-in-hand to the hotel reception. Before they reached the check-in desk, Adoma observed her surroundings. Her environment reminded her of the descriptions of the most opulent mythical gardens. She didn't know which one, only that the plants, the shrubs, the flowers, the streams trickling everywhere – all of the flora together worked like a symphony, in an explosion of beauty.

The architecture of the hotel – just as elaborately designed and meticulous in detail as the garden – reminded her of the homes in Morocco. The hotel had a lush, open courtyard, like those of Marrakesh. A gilded table, decorated with fresh fruit baskets and a tea jug on top, stood in the center of the reception area. Behind the table, water trickled gently from the waterfall fixture set behind the desk clerk for a relaxing backdrop.

"Welcome. Have you enjoyed our lovely hibiscus tea?" asked the desk clerk.

"Thank you, we did," Mark politely responded before Adoma could correct the lovely young lady and inform her the tea was mint, not hibiscus.

"Here is your room key. Enjoy your stay," the reception clerk continued with the formalities. Adoma and Mark went to their room to relax before planning to have sun setters later at the hotel outdoor lounge.

After the long flight and cocktails, Adoma could no longer keep sleep at bay, so she prepared to retire for the evening. She did her routine yoga exercise and ended in Shavasana, quietly giving thanks and gratitude for all the good in her life, for all of the love she received from Mark and from everyone who loved her – her family and her friends and even strangers who showed her kindness. Mark first gave her space, then kissed Adoma before lying down next to her and holding her hand until they fell asleep.

Adoma woke the next morning and noticed that Mark had changed her into pajamas. 'How sweet,' she thought, 'but where did he go?'

"Mark?" Adoma cried out. Receiving no response, Adoma stood up. She found no note; he had just disappeared. Adoma went to change and to look for him, and discovered that all of her clothes were gone. 'What happened to my luggage? Were we robbed?! Where is Mark?!' Adoma thought, unnerved.

Adoma called the front desk, and after apologizing profusely, they promised to investigate. The clerk further confirmed she had not seen Mark either.

"In the meantime, the hotel will send up a complimentary dress from the boutique," said the front desk clerk. But this did not console Adoma, who began to panic.

'Where are my clothes, and where is Mark, and why the heck is he not answering his phone?!' In about five minutes the room's doorbell rang and a porter handed her a dress to wear.

'Now shoes... okay, great, my sandals from yesterday are still in the closet. Now, let me go downstairs and try to find out what's going on. Maybe Mark just got hungry and left me to eat breakfast,' Adoma said mentally, embarking toward the elevator bank. When Adoma reached the lobby, and as the elevator doors opened, there stood Mark waiting for her. He wore a crème linen suit, matching the color of Adoma's flattering dress, and a big smile.

"Where were you? I've been worried sick. I couldn't find you, and my luggage is missing. I had to wear this dress. I'm about to file a report right now! I thought we were somewhere safe!" Adoma hadn't noticed the flowers in Mark's hand.

"The dress looks lovely. Here are some flowers. I hope they help you feel better. You can file the report later. Let me escort you to breakfast first."

"Thank you. But..." Adoma responded. Mark took her hand before she could finish her sentence about the missing luggage. He led her down the hall, past the breakfast area, and into the courtyard, which looked different than the day before. This morning it was decorated with white lilies all around.

Adoma turned her head and saw Mark's parents sitting next to her own. She looked further... and Genna, Casey, and Mya beamed at her. Adoma covered her mouth and gasped as she realized what was happening.

The familiar melody began to play before Adoma could display her immense surprise, and then Adoma, on cue, proceeded down the aisle, holding Mark's hand toward the awaiting priest.

"...I too vow to be the keeper of your heart, promising never to hurt you, keep secrets, or diminish your happiness in any way," Adoma repeated Mark's vow.

"...then, I now pronounce you husband and wife!" exclaimed the priest.

Immediately after the pronouncement, Mark and Adoma passionately embraced. After many hugs and kisses, Adoma looked into his eyes and to the small audience and then separated from Mark, hastening to hug her parents.

"Oh, my darling, congratulations!" Adoma's mother lovingly touched her face with her right hand, then pulled her toward her ample bosom, kissing her on the cheek. She rocked Adoma back and forth fervently. Adoma didn't want to leave her embrace, even though the pressure hurt.

"Thank you, Mom. I am so happy, yet surprised to see you all here. How you all pulled this off under my nose, I can't believe." When her mother's embraced loosened, Adoma smoothed out the front of her crème dress. "Even the fact that I am wearing this wedding dress right now is funny. Amazing. I thought we were robbed," Adoma laughed. Her parents both looked at each other, and smiled with a sense of pride in having played a part of the surprise. No doubt Adoma's mother helped Mark pick out the dress, the style entirely befitting her.

Adoma's father took her right hand into his own and covered it with his left. "Today is a blessed day and now you are married and no longer living in sin. God is faithful. God is good. Your mother and I prayed that you would meet the right man and get married. We prayed for you everyday – for your safety, too, of course, but also a marriage. Praise God."

"Thank you, Dad," Adoma replied. Eager to avoid awkwardness, she spoke again, "I will be right back. I want to say hi to my friends."

"Yes, of course," Adoma's mother replied. "We spoke to them earlier. Yes, say hello to your friends. We will be here."

"Mom and Dad, go and get to know Mark's family over there. You've only spoken to them once before."

Adoma looked over. Mark was still talking with his parents, and before she could shuffle over to her friends, she caught his eye, and he motioned her over.

"Hi, Mom and Dad!" Adoma said as she shrugged her shoulders and turned her palms up in a lighthearted facetious fashion.

"Give us a hug dear!" Mark's mother pulled Adoma into her and Mark's father's embrace, and with Mark on the outside, they had a nice group hug. "Welcome to the family, dear."

"Thank you so much." Adoma's eyes began to swell with tears.

"Aww, tears of joy," Mark's mother said, smiling.

"Yes. I had no idea I would be going to my own wedding today! Oh my gosh Mark, you have outdone yourself. You *did* surprise me!"

"Yes, that's my boy," Mark's dad said in a deep voice.

"Yes, that's our son," his mother's eyes glimmered lovingly over to Mark, echoing the sentiments.

"Babe, go over and greet your friends. I see Casey looking over here, and you know they must be ready to congratulate you," Mark said.

"Thank you, babe, I'll be right back." Adoma kissed him on his cheek and spun around in the direction of her friends.

Adoma, brimming with exhilaration, almost ran a sprint to her friends, who in hushed tones were trying to guess the reason for the rushed wedding.

"Do you think she's pregnant?" Genna asked as she dabbed her red lips with the cocktail napkin.

"Noo," Casey retorted. "She would have told us, or at least Mya."

"Yup, she would have told me when we spoke over the phone yesterday. She did mention that they were ready to marry, though," Mya said, fixing the straps of her top that were sliding down from her shoulders.

"We'll find out soon, though. Shh, she's coming." Casey pushed a flute of champagne across the cocktail table. "Mya, hand her this glass. If she avoids drinking it, then we will know for sure," Casey suggested.

As Adoma walked within ten feet of her friends, they all reached their arms out in front of them and squealed, "Yay!"

To further convey excitement, Adoma even threw in 'jazz hands' moving her fingers up and down like she were playing an imaginary piano. Once they made contact, they clasped arms into a huge group hug and hopped up and down in unison appearing as a single entity.

"Oh my gosh ladies, I am so happy to see you all!! We are finally together again! I can't believe Mark pulled this off! And Mya, I didn't know you could be so sneaky! We just spoke yesterday. How is it that you were able to keep quiet about this? We talked for an hour!" Adoma rejoiced.

"Oh, that was easy. What was harder than keeping quiet on the phone was all of us arriving last night and hoping you wouldn't see us accidentally in the lobby or around the hotel. Mark told us you were knocked out, though."

"Yes, I was extremely tired last night and fell asleep completely dressed only to wake up in pajamas minus my luggage. Hmm, now I'm suspicious. How conveniently timed. Did that man drug me?!"

They all laughed.

"Here, why don't you relax a bit more? Here's a glass of champagne." Mya handed Adoma the flute and Adoma received it, holding the stem with her left hand while gesturing with her right hand as she spoke about the whirlwind day.

The ladies tried to act naturally, but could not avoid staring at Adoma, anticipating her next move. They collectively wondered if she would eventually sip the champagne.

Adoma ignored the drink in her hand and continued to speak. "Hey! The music is getting louder, and what is it that I hear?" Adoma talked over the music. All of the guests, relaxed by the food and drink, began to loosen and sway too. "Drop It," the latest Sasha Pierce hit that Adoma had written blared through the speakers. Because the song had played ubiquitously on the radio, everyone began to dance to the recognizable beat.

Adoma put down her champagne glass to join the fun. "I'm so happy to see y'all here. I love you!" Adoma shouted over the music and continued to dance as Mark approached her to steal her away. Mark and Adoma swirled to the dance floor and rocked their shoulders and hips, constraining themselves, though they both wished they could sneak away. Soon, their foreheads touched and they just moved slightly, noticing only each other. When the song ended, Adoma rushed back to everyone.

"Woah, I am flushed," and she fanned herself.

"Here, have your champagne," Casey tried again. "You still know how to move. I guess you still have your rhythm, even now after you're all big time and stuff."

"Oh stop it, Casey," Adoma smiled and sighed, again ignoring the sparkly.

"You know, I could never lose my rhythm; it's in my blood!" Adoma swiveled her hips side to side and began to lower and 'drop it' before she caught herself halfway down, raised up, and looked around to see if her father noticed.

"Adoma, you know Mark's mom and dad might faint if they see you 'drop it like it's hot' right now in your wedding dress – in broad daylight at this luxurious hotel." Genna reached out her arm to pull Adoma toward her.

"They would wonder who they just let into their family!" Casey added.

"Leave my baby Adoma alone," Mya cooed. "It's her wedding day, and she's allowed to have all of the fun she wants!"

"Yeah, Mya is right! Isn't this fun ladies?!" Adoma exclaimed, finally sipping her champagne. "You all are always here when I need you, through whatever we're going through, and despite the fact that we're so different, from different backgrounds, from different parts of the world. We're still and forever friends!" Adoma, pausing, looked closely at the ladies and noticed something that touched her heart. Mya, Genna, and Casey each wore the adinkra cloth that Adoma sent them as part of the invitation for the reunion.

Genna made her adinkra cloth into a cute purse; Casey used hers as the collar and border for her dress; Mya's fabric turned into a stylish skirt.

"You all made it to my surprisingly short notice wedding and are wearing the adinkra too! I couldn't ask for better friends! I love you all!" Adoma hugged them and continued "...And we get to do it all over again soon in the Seychelles!"

"Yay!!!" they all said, and group hugged again. Everyone planned to attend or at least told Adoma they would. Even Genna eventually confirmed.

As the other three ladies laughed and hugged, almost clinging to each other from the effect of the champagne, Genna sat back and observed with a dry smile.

Chapter 32
Fake It 'til You Make It

The drama swirling around Genna made attending the reunion seem uncertain. A week after she returned from Adoma's wedding, Genna drove to the other side of town to bleach and add new extensions to her hair. From the time she and Fred had moved to their exclusive community, she had avoided getting her hair done nearby, in an effort to keep her hair business and her personal business to herself. But now, the neighborhood ladies quietly shunned Genna because of the scandal, so she had even more reason to avoid the local salon.

She preferred to get her hair done in the old neighborhood anyway. That's where they knew how to blow out and straighten her tight curls just the way she liked. Getting her hair done gave her respite from the usual, often judgmental, environment where Genna, a shrewd observer, could see the women tilting their heads to whisper something at the gym or the spa.

Even at work some of her colleagues looked at her differently. Gone now were the looks of envy she once received from her coworkers. They had been replaced with something else, an unrecognizable look that until that time, Genna had never experienced. She soon realized the look to be one of pity. And, pity felt horrible; she never wanted anyone to pity her. Even when she and her family barely had anything, she held her head proudly and dressed and appeared as though she did. No one at her school had known how poor they were. So being the object of pity felt like a shot to Genna's heart, especially for something her husband had done, not her.

Just as Genna sat at the shampoo bowl, she received an alert. Her worst nightmare had come true. The scandal broke on the national news, validating that a formal investigation had begun. Genna would no longer have to wonder if the country club ladies knew anything. The news report just confirmed that everything they were whispering about was true.

Even Genna's hairstylist subtly asked about the report that was now on the television in the salon, trying to hear the dirt about the probe directly from Genna. She dodged the questions by pretending not to hear him through her earphones, strategically worn during the visit so that she could avoid conversation. No one, especially not a busy-bodied hair stylist, needed to know her business.

Genna listened to a classic album Adoma had introduced her to years before, *The Miseducation of Lauryn Hill,* and focused on the song "I Used to Love Him" to block the static coming from the outside world. While the music played, Genna drifted away into a fantasy of being anywhere but in the tense situation entwining her life. She wished it would all go away – the scandal, the investigation. And mostly, she wanted to feel like her old self again. 'When would that ever be?' she wondered. 'Will it ever be? What if the investigation ends with a conclusion that the congressional office was guilty? Would the taint spread to Fred and me? How would our exclusive community and people around town react? Will they ask us to leave?' All of these questions buzzed in her head.

Life no longer looked optimistic. Genna and Fred would not become the power couple she had always imagined they would be. They would never again be featured in their local society pages, and would probably not be invited to fundraising events. It appeared the nice cushy life she had was slipping away from her.

With all of the thoughts circulating in her brain, one question began to form: 'Why work so hard if it's all lost?' She even considered quitting so the firm wouldn't have to ask her to resign. She decided against that. If her law firm wanted her to leave to save face, they would have to work to do it. Maybe then she could get an excellent package and relax for a bit. 'Maybe we should move before they kick us out.' She quickly nixed the idea. 'No way! Why should I feel shame for anything? I did nothing wrong, and I don't even know if Fred has because he won't tell me anything. All of this self-pity has got to end, and I need to be the woman I know that I am!'

On her drive home across town, Genna had time to think more about the state of her affairs. Despite her freshly done hair, when Genna got home she put on her running shoes. She had to plan, plot, strategize, and rehabilitate what had become of her social image and pre-empt any damage to her professional standing. She didn't know how she would achieve this yet, so she ran to clear her head. And suddenly the familiar phrase 'fake it 'til you make it' came to her. 'Oh yes, I know how to do that indeed.'

Genna faked being engaged so that colleagues wouldn't ask questions about her relationship with Fred. She faked not resenting Fred for his lack of commitment. And now Genna faked that she still loved Fred. And, tomorrow she was going to fake to everyone at work and the neighborhood that everything was going just fine.

'What scandal?' Genna said facetiously to herself. 'There's no reason for me to shrink because there's absolutely nothing wrong going on in my world. Move right along everyone, nothing to see here. All is perfect. Of course they won't find anything wrong, because Fred had no part in anything at all. No more ducking and diving.' Genna said all this to herself to double down on her confidence and firmly imprint her self-motivational talk. 'Be strong and everyone else will fall in line.'

Yes, 'fake it 'til you make it' had served her well. How could Genna have forgotten the words by which she lived for so long?

Casey didn't have to fake anything. She slipped nicely into being a good wife and a step-mother to the twins. The twins thought Casey was 'cool' and they started bonding with her. Her new step-daughter borrowed some of her clothes and at times flattered Casey by asking her for fashion advice.

The twins took after James in their height and in their sweet personalities. However, the budding good looks they inherited from their mother made Casey wince, because in their faces, Casey was reminded that she was not their biological mother. That knowledge started to erode some of the security she felt within the family. However, the twins' easy acceptance of Casey as a maternal figure made Casey fall in love with them. She had never imagined being a step-mother, but now couldn't imagine life without her 'ready-made' family – a complete unit already there to love. She just had to show up and nurture it and they would love her back for as long as she kept loving them.

Based on their strong friendship, Casey and James built a solid, stable marriage. Above all things, stability ranked number one in what Casey wanted most since her family had lost a small fortune, and she, in turn, lost her family. Having James be such a good provider allayed her concerns.

Casey had become unrecognizable, and not just in physical appearance, as Mya duly observed, but in her behavior. Casey would pick out James's suits, and make breakfast for him and the twins. After Casey got the twins and James their breakfast, she'd then get herself ready for work. First by slipping into masculine clothing, completely contradicting the domestic goddess role she played each morning. Keeping her work clothes simple, Casey usually wore slacks or trousers with a button-up or polo style shirt. There was no reason to focus attention on her figure or her looks in her mostly male work environment. Casey wanted to stay under the radar and keep her male colleagues' attention trained on her analytical abilities and her stellar job performance, not rumors.

Chapter 33
The Facts

Adoma returned to work a newlywed and beamed all day from ear to ear. She smiled about her personal new beginnings and also that her new song hit number one on the Billboard charts. Adoma heard it all around the city and in some of the oddest locations as it garnered substantial radio play. Now she could momentarily relax at the job and use the downtime to plan the reunion.

Adoma researched The Republic of the Seychelles, a small island nation, in her spare time and became fascinated with the country off the east coast of Africa in the Indian Ocean. She gained an idea about the populace, the topography, and about the many pristine beaches the chain of islands showcased.

Just as Adoma began to return to where she left off in her trip planning, she heard a ping come from her computer. 'Sasha can wait for a minute. I just delivered her a huge hit,' she thought and went back to trip preparations. 'Well, at least I have one thing down – where to celebrate on our last night. Great.' She then sighed at the enormity of her tasks. 'Now I just have to plan the flight, the events, how long, and where we will stay,' Adoma added sarcastically. 'Hmm… This is interesting – no visas or malaria medicine required? I'm surprised that malaria is one major thing we don't have to worry about. How could that be? We are traveling to an island in Africa, but the tourist information on the internet says that there is no need to take malaria drugs, as the island does not have cases of it? Hmmm.' Adoma found this information to be incredulous, but additional research supported the fact to be true.

The type of mosquito that carried the malaria virus existed all around the world, except for five countries. Antarctica, three other countries, and the Seychelles lacked the malaria-carrying mosquito. 'How incredibly fortunate we don't have to take those horrible pills – the one that gives you the funny dreams or the one that you have to take everyday. They are both gross, ugh. If one of those pills can give me acid-like vivid dreams, just imagine what it could be doing to the brains of people who take it all of the time? Oh well, not my problem for now, but certainly something to think about on my next trip to see my relatives back home. So no malaria medicine will be required, and we also don't have to worry about getting visas. Thank goodness! I can check those off the list. Lovely.'

After returning Sasha's email about the latest deadline for the revised version of another new song, Adoma continued to research. The fact that the Seychelles did not have malaria was peculiar – though an extreme blessing for its inhabitants.

Adoma recalled the stories that her parents told her growing up about malaria taking the lives of a couple of their childhood friends. In fact, she learned that malaria ranked in the top five causes of child mortality worldwide. This reality deeply saddened her, and Adoma could not let it go. 'Drugs exist to prevent and cure malaria, yet it not only sickens but kills so many children around the world?'

Adoma read one statistic that cited a medical journal saying that one child a minute dies from malaria each day. The numbers shocked and disgusted her. 'Why do so many children unnecessarily die each day of an illness, yet it rarely garners attention, or discussion, or even given a thought?' Adoma sadly muttered to herself.

Even after Adoma left the office and had gone home to Mark, the facts haunted her.

"Babe, have you ever covered malaria?" she broached the topic right before bed.

"No, honey why?" he asked, surprised by Adoma's odd selection for pillow talk.

"Well, did you know that it's a preventable and curable disease that kills a child a minute?"

"What, a child a minute? Are you sure about that? I thought that the statistics had improved; that it's a child every two minutes?" Mark, shocked by the numbers himself, began to rattle figures.

"Yes, I know babe, I did the math already," Adoma interrupted before he could finish. "A child a minute or every two minutes doesn't matter. How many more children have to die before it's brought to the attention of the world? Not only children, but healthy adults die from it too." The emotions that had built up in Adoma throughout the day began to bubble to the surface, and Adoma spoke more quickly than usual. "And since the Western world barely gives malaria a thought, western travelers to malaria-prone countries have died in the U.S. or in Europe – amongst some of the best medical technology – because the doctors didn't know to test for or how to treat it. Every death is tragic, but even more so because none of them have to happen." Adoma's eyes welled up again.

"Yes, honey. You're right. The deaths are all sad and preventable. I can tell you that most people in countries without malaria probably don't even think about the virus until they're planning an exotic vacation and want to protect themselves from getting it."

"How can we be okay with that?"

"I know baby, but there are so many other things to worry about in this world. The media bombards us with terrorism, natural disasters, and crimes. Issues like malaria, which have been around for a long time, just will not get the same coverage as these other stories."

"But, Mark, malaria kills more people than all of those other issues combined. Whether a child a minute or a child every two minutes, no one should die just because they got bitten by a mosquito."

The last part of Adoma's sentence stunned Mark, but he pushed it aside. Adoma was right. "Baby, let's get some sleep. I'm exhausted." He moved her night scarf away from her face and kissed Adoma on the forehead. "Goodnight."

Then Mark turned off the metallic colored lamp on their nightstand.

Chapter 34
'Keep Moving, Nothing to See'

Genna occupied herself with damage control. She didn't take any significant actions; she just made sure to project herself in a way that appeared that everything in her life continued to be under control and as perfect as it could be. Genna wanted to portray so much confidence that those who observed her would wonder if *they* were crazy for thinking that the reports could be true.

'No, the stories are wrong,' Genna imagined telling anyone who dared to ask. 'Image is everything,' Genna thought. 'Perception is the reality.'

Genna needed to shut down the sneaky glances and the whispering, and take control. She needed to show up with her head held high and not emotionally cower, as she did when the rumors started. Then, she had shrunk out of embarrassment; now she would not. 'Why should I? I did nothing wrong!' Genna thought defiantly, striving to regain her power.

Other than the looks and whispers, no one dared say anything to Genna in the office. So far, the reports had not affected her work. She labored just as diligently as before, and even more because she needed a distraction from home.

Perhaps owing to the fact that Genna and Fred did not share the same last name, no major clients of the law firm raised an issue. This encouraged Genna to stay focused on the partner track, despite the controversy swirling around her. To abet this goal, Genna acted pre-emptively, laying a foundation around her that she had no knowledge whatsoever of any potential wrongdoing. Genna created an imaginative protective barrier between her, Fred, and his problems, so that colleagues would disassociate the three. Genna would slip a comment here and there in attempts to influence her coworkers to believe that she and her husband had a relationship with little communication about anything – especially work.

Recently, this had come to fruition. Fred went about his daily business rarely speaking, acting as if nothing bothered him. They didn't discuss much at all let alone the news story. Instead, they discussed the most mundane of topics. "Fred, should I buy the orange juice with the pulp this time?" Genna would ask, when instead she wanted to interrogate him and find out what the hell was going on. All of his silence, all of the unspoken words began to wear on her.

'Maybe Fred's in shock, taken aback by the allegations that seem to have sprung out of nowhere,' Genna thought to herself, trying to rationalize her husband's behavior. Before this moment, Fred's office had received accolades; the representative himself applauded Fred for running a transparent office. Track records are forgotten in the midst of scandal and sensationalism.

Genna continued to pry as much information as possible from her source, all the while attempting to appear above the fray. However, even before the scandal broke in the mainstream media, Genna had been having difficulty gleaning information from her contact. 'How far along are they in the investigation? Do the allegations have substance? Would there be a charge and what exactly could it be?' Genna wondered about all of these possibilities. 'All of this drama and stress for something that may not even result in anything seems so ridiculous,' she had thought at the time.

Genna looked down at her phone as an email titled '6-month countdown!' flashed on the screen. 'Adoma, bless her heart; she keeps sending countdown emails and updates like everyone cares as much as she does about the reunion.' Genna read them but rarely responded to the emails.

In reality, Genna could use a distraction in her life – a girls' trip to a tropical island sounded nice, but not entirely enticing. It was feasible, but still too far away for Genna to take seriously at this point, especially with all that was going on in her world. She hadn't spoken to Adoma directly about the spider web of instability that entrapped her. However, with Genna's current burdens, she felt no obligation to go. 'They would all have to understand if I change my mind and can no longer make it.'

Genna forgot about the reunion for a moment and went back to planning her crisis management. She thought about starting a whisper campaign, a countering rumor about herself to balance the prevailing one. But Genna had no idea what that rumor would be, and did not want to besmirch her character if it backfired. So, until necessary, she would continue with her denial, acting as if nothing was wrong, everything was fine, and that this all couldn't possibly be true. Truth be told, the possibility of losing her husband, her job, her life – everything she held dear – scared her deeply to the core.

Chapter 35
Don't Go

Mark surprised Adoma with news of another long-term assignment in an East African country. To avoid disclosing his true need for travel, he lied.

Mark kept the real reason – that he just needed a break – to himself for the two days he had contemplated leaving. Indeed, he had an approaching deadline for on an important story, for which he could not write a single word. However, it did not require travel to research the material for what he hoped to be a thought-provoking, important piece.

Truthfully, Mark had a debilitating case of writer's block, one so severe it frightened him. If Mark could not write, then he could not make money, and that concept caused him additional stress. Mark glanced at Adoma as she prepared herself for the day. He felt guilty about keeping a secret but reasoned away his pangs of conscience. 'I didn't lie to Adoma; I just didn't tell her the whole truth, which is that I need to get away.' He said to himself.

Adoma dressed, thinking it peculiar for Mark to be so elusive about an assignment when usually he had been very forthcoming about previous ones. However, Adoma accepted his uncharacteristic silence the past few days, resisting the urge to press him about his emotional seclusion and let him work out his issues in peace.

Mark had been nothing short of an understanding, loving husband, so Adoma had no reason to give Mark a hard time. 'If he needs a break,' Adoma thought, 'if he feels that he needs to leave for whatever reason he isn't sharing with me, I will give him that space. He would do the same for me. I don't need to know details, and I trust he'll return with a renewed sense of liveliness, back to the Mark I'm used to.' Adoma hoped that would happen and entrusted Mark like no man before in her life; she would not let go of that trust no matter of how uncertain she felt.

Adoma had felt a shift in Mark's behavior in the past week. They usually spoke about everything – or rather Mark usually listened to Adoma speak about everything. 'Perhaps Mark never felt like he had an ear to hear him when he needed one,' Adoma wondered. She hadn't given that a thought until Mark had already packed to leave. However, Adoma still made a last minute effort to correct her observation.

"Mark is everything okay? Do you need to talk about anything?"

Mark kissed her on the forehead and said, "I think it will all be okay; I will call you when I land."

Adoma had waited too long to engage, and with a tight hug, Mark walked out the door with only his brown leather duffel bag over his shoulder.

Adoma shuddered from the emotionless good-bye. She questioned, 'Could Mark be too good to be true? Could he be like Duke, with a girlfriend in every city, and be on his way to see another woman?' All of those scenarios swirled through her mind.

She wiped a tear from her cheek. She never really let Mark know how much she respected and loved him. She didn't know why she hadn't, but now she never wanted him to feel like she took him for granted, as he truly blessed her life.

Adoma pulled out a pen and began to write out and make sense of her thoughts in the best way she knew how – a new song.

Am I scared to love you because I know we won't make it?
Or because I know we will?
Am I scared that I will end up without you?

Or forever with you? I don't know.
But for now, stay near me
Because I can't dream of a life with you so far away
To have to close my eyes and only see your face in my mind is not right.
I want your skin next to mine, every night, all night
So you tell me you have to go, for how long you don't know.
But you can't leave again, without me again
Don't go. Don't go. Don't go.

It's not sometimes
But all the time that work calls you to leave.
And when you do, I feel something isn't right,
I feel not as safe at night.
Don't leave again without me again.
Don't Go. Don't Go. Don't Go.

Some things just belong together like you and I
Like clouds in the sky,
Like sad movies and misty eyes.
So don't leave again without me again.
Don't Go. Don't Go. Don't Go

Adoma's hot tears fell onto the paper, almost erasing the last words she wrote. But, maybe her tears could bring someone else small comfort knowing they are not alone in missing someone who is emotionally or physically distant.

'Sasha should like this,' Adoma thought. "Don't Go" will make a lovely ballad.'

Mark regretted such a sterile good-bye, but it preserved his focus. His seriously long writer's block was affecting his livelihood, although thankfully, he hadn't yet missed a deadline. But his creative block had affected his serenity.

Fortunately, Mark knew what to do. The ocean, his first love, would be the perfect cure. Whenever he needed refreshing, he headed to the shore to allow the sea to speak to him like it did in his childhood. 'Get out of the city. Be on a boat. Do some work with my hands. In that order,' Mark recited as he nodded to sleep on the plane.

Maybe later Mark would ask Adoma to join him, but for now, he needed to, wanted to, be alone and not shower, and not shave – to just sail. Then, eventually, when the mood struck him, he would write the story he had been commissioned to write. Just not at the moment.

Mark had not been able to type a single word on the piece, nor did he want to open his laptop. The thought of touching the equipment made his body cringe. This contrasted the days his laptop served as another appendage, always at his side. But now, even the sight of the silver rectangle brought more attention to his current inadequacy as a writer. Instead of beckoning him to open it, the computer taunted him, reminding him that he had not been productive in a very long time.

Back in the city with Adoma, Mark wanted to keep this to himself, sleep all day, and stay inside. He didn't want Adoma to see him this way, so he just left. Mark didn't want it to affect her; instead, he wished to protect her. He sensed an old familiar feeling coming, and his will to shake it diminished with each day. Mark knew its imminence. If he didn't control the lurking melancholy beginning to take hold of him, it would grow, evolving into an uncontrollable beast.

And that is why he had to leave.

Chapter 36
Casey, Where Are You?

When Adoma picked up the phone to dial Casey, like her previous calls, it went to voicemail. In dismay, Adoma huffed with discontent.

'I will call you back,' Casey texted her.

When Adoma had not received the return call, she waited a few more days and buzzed again, multiple times, to no avail. Casey had stayed on Adoma's mind for two months, although they hadn't spoken in that time. But Adoma persisted, ignoring Casey's lack of response.

'Strange,' Adoma thought and wondered for a moment if Casey was avoiding her, but let those doubts slip away. There was no reason for Casey to avoid her, 'unless new and improved Casey, a changed woman, is attempting to sever all ties to her colorful past.' Adoma did know Casey's secrets. However, she had no intention of telling anyone, and certainly not Casey's husband, James.

Adoma remembered James from their large high school, but because she spent so much time on the 'other side of the tracks' with her high school boyfriend and eclectic friends, she didn't know him well. Adoma just remembered that James was one of the most popular students, and through Casey, heard that he had done well after high school. And, over the years, in addition to his job, he had become very well off in his own right by making wise investments. He also dutifully tithed his money to his local church, in which he was very involved.

Adoma never imagined Casey attracting a religious man or vice versa, but perhaps they both remained attracted and attached to each other via their old memories of love in years passed. Or, maybe James appreciated the way Casey showed up for him during his marital issues.

The way Casey described James's previous marriage, he had divorced an erratic woman who had left him for a richer man, and although she had returned after two months away, they could no longer salvage their relationship. James's marriage disintegrated quickly after that, and when it did, Casey had been there for James as a confidante. In being that, Casey listened intently to the details of their daily fights, and the general angst his previous wife, an attention seeker, put him through. Then later, James shared his heartbreak with Casey after he decided to file for divorce.

In Adoma's opinion, James over-shared with Casey in a manner that did its own damage. He should have shared his concerns with his wife, not Casey. 'Those long conversations he had with Casey could have been long conversations with his spouse. But that's none of my business,' Adoma said to herself.

Adoma dismissed feeling ignored by Casey and thought instead about how well Casey seemed to adjust to marriage and a new life. Adoma had presumed that the monotony of marriage could not keep Casey's attention for very long, but perhaps the tradeoffs – stability and commitment – outweighed the feelings of boredom and restlessness Adoma imagined Casey to be feeling right about now.

'As long as Casey is still coming to the reunion, I guess that's all that matters.' Adoma knew she could count on Casey to be there. Casey remained committed to the reunion, like she had been committed to their friendship, unlike Genna, who seemed to be waffling in her agreement to attend.

Sometimes Adoma wondered if Genna saw her as a true friend; or if she, Mya, and Casey, being the few friends Genna had, were just friends by default. Since Adoma tended to see the best in people, she focused on Genna's good qualities, such as her spirit of generosity and closeness with her family, and dismissed her doubts about their connection.

There were times, however, that Adoma felt drained by their friendship, especially when Adoma could perceive Genna's sense of superiority over her – and everyone else. Adoma picked this up from off-handed comments Genna made, or the way that she expected a gaze to be trained on her when a handsome man looked at the group. This was evidence of what Adoma had assumed all along – that Genna thought she was the most beautiful one of the four. This led to an occasional strain between Genna and Casey, as Casey too was accustomed to male attention. That tension between Genna and Casey sometimes played out in a cold war, with Adoma and Mya becoming unwitting proxies in their disagreements.

Adoma tried for the last time that day to reach Casey. 'Voicemail again. Wow,' Adoma sighed. Although Adoma hadn't spoken to Casey in what seemed like forever, she knew that the silence would not last. Friendships like theirs were the best kind of friendships. And just like with Mya at times, Casey and Adoma could go months without speaking and then catch-up as if they had never missed a beat. Even so, with all that Adoma had going on in her life, she wanted to share it with Casey and missed talking with her. Adoma hoped to speak with her well in time for the reunion, but at this rate and length of silence, Adoma was unsure that would happen.

If they didn't speak for the next few months, there would be a lot of time to catch up in the Seychelles. Adoma anticipated hearing all about Casey's complete 180-degree turn. 'And, Casey a step-mother too?' Adoma could hardly believe it. And then she would remember that Casey, though unpredictable, had always sought structure and had mentioned becoming a mother before.

For the sake of Casey's new marriage, Adoma hoped that the 'old' Casey had completely disappeared, now that she had morphed into a suburban housewife. But at a group dinner once, Casey had made a strange comment that Adoma hoped did not foreshadow anything: "I don't know about that," Casey had said, doubting whether she could remain monogamous forever.

'But, everyone changes, so it is certainly possible for Casey to have completely changed as well.' Adoma marveled at that thought, and wondered as well, 'Or is the 'free-love' wild child Casey still hidden deep inside?'

Adoma and everyone else would find out soon enough on the

vacation in the Seychelles. And, if Casey could keep to her vows during a girls' trip to a far-away island with gorgeous beaches and people, then Casey had indeed changed.

Chapter 37
Mind Your Manners

Casey never intended to ignore Adoma for months, but marriage to James thrust her into an unfamiliar world. A world she remembered observing in high school but had since pushed its memories to the depths of her mind, where she suppressed them and other difficult periods of her life.

Casey's teenage anxieties bubbled to the surface as she and James stepped out of his black BMW and onto the cobbled driveway of his parents' home. It had been many months into their elopement before his mother and father finally summoned them for Sunday dinner.

As they approached the front door, Casey tilted her head back to digest the full size of the home's stone facade and the beautiful attention given to it by the builders. She walked through the threshold with the mild escort of James's mahogany hand directing her from the nook of her back.

"It is *beautiful* inside," Casey commented.

Casey had never been in a home like this, as she had come from more modest beginnings. Her family, just for a split second, had seen riches, and then it disappeared. Having financial prosperity and then economic calamity, propelled Casey to form a bipolar relationship with money. She would sometimes spend extravagantly on clothing or meals, and then hold on to her money tightly or complain about spending an additional dollar on something.

Financial stability evolved into a significant value for Casey later in life and occupied an ample amount of her attention. Casey, who earned an excellent salary, still regularly discussed money – needing, wanting, having, and losing it. Fortunately, her recent union lessened much of her anxiety around finances. Being that James's income provided a nice cushion for her, he made her very happy and was certainly the reason Casey had not mentioned money in a while.

"Thank you," James said with pride in response to Casey's compliment. He stopped walking for a moment and looked deeply into Casey's eyes. "Don't worry Casey; it will be okay. I'm sure my mother won't bring up the Vegas wedding at all."

"Well, they surely couldn't be pleased about the impromptu wedding of their only son – or with my lack of communication as a new daughter-in-law. I hadn't spoken to your mother during the engagement and barely muttered a sentence to her or your father after the wedding – and vice versa. I'm practically a stranger to them."

"That's behind us now. Tonight is the night to get to know my mother and the rest of my family. And you don't have to worry about my father; he stays in the background, quiet as a mouse."

Casey and James stepped onto the marble of the majestic foyer, and the younger of James's sisters greeted them. Warm hugs and formalities followed. As they waited for James's older sister, Casey took a moment to admire the family photos comfortably placed in the cozy den.

Over a dozen photos decorated the fireplace mantle, with a picture of James next to all of his tennis and football trophies in the center of them all. 'James still looks the same,' Casey thought to herself as she recalled him in high school. James, an active student, attended all of the school social events in addition to his extra-curricular activities. He managed the high school trifecta – social popularity, sports achievement, and honor roll. No one knew how he did it, but the other students and their parents esteemed him for it. As did Casey, from afar, until a chance pairing led to their brief puppy love.

Further to the right of the mantle, pictures of the entire family smiling happily in exotic locales evoked a twinge of envy, as Casey remembered how dissimilar she and James had grown up. James was raised in this beautiful home in which they would dine. In contrast, Casey lived in a much smaller home with working-class parents, her mother a high school counselor and her father a laboratory technician for a big pharmaceutical company. They lived comfortably in a modest home in a decent neighborhood. Casey's family's life was simple. And although she rarely needed for anything, the simplicity of her upbringing had bothered her, especially after Casey transferred to a more affluent high school.

A later monetary windfall enriched Casey's family, but not enough to warrant entree into the world of ski trips and elite organizations with fairytale names whose members were the wealthy and respected women of society, such as James's mother. Casey's mother never joined those groups, perhaps out of lack of interest or perhaps out of lack of invitation. Casey never knew the real reason, but she wished her mother had so that she could have been a part of the groups and invited to the social events too. Often in high school, she felt left out when other students would attend an event or a party for members' children, and Casey knew that she could not go. James's mother hosted many of those events.

Casey heard the sounds of high heels clicking on the hard wood of the stairs and braced herself for the imposing matriarch's appearance.

"Son!" She exclaimed, squeezing James tightly. "Darling!" she hugged Casey, not at all appearing displeased they had eloped to Vegas. James's father greeted James first and then gave Casey a cordial hug.

"Let's go to the dining room," James's mother said as she ushered them forward. The housekeeper scurried out of the room as the family sat down. Casey observed James's mother's presence as the 'Mrs.' of the house. Her spirit thoroughly permeated the home, setting the tone of each room, even in her absence. The activity in the house hummed to her rhythm, and the decor appeared as she did, beautiful, feminine, and resilient.

"You look lovely dear," James's mother complimented Casey's dress, pleased that Casey and James dressed up for family dinner as she had asked, explaining that 'dinners should not be casual affairs.' His mother always insisted that guests and relatives wear their best for formality, and also so that she could take advantage of the evening to show off her newest garb. This night,

James's mother dressed in an expensive golden cocktail dress barely containing her plump, cosmetically-enhanced bosom. James's mother, still gorgeous, 'grasped too tightly to her beauty and remaining youth in an unflattering way' Casey thought to herself, as she studied her mother-in-law's face for signs of enhancements.

But, other than her distracting cleavage, James's mother exuded class, and also exacted perfection in her mannerisms and speech. Though she stayed well-maintained, with beautifully coiffed hair and dazzling manicured hands, she wielded a powerful, controlled inner femininity as well.

However, her personality toward some people, Casey would argue, did not seem so elegant and graceful at all. James's mother's fixation on and constant references to manners and etiquette both exhausted and terrified Casey, who already felt like an intruder in their world of cotillions and debutante balls.

"Jay," as James's sister called him, "Could you please pass the water?"

"Sure. Rather, sis, just hand me your glass, and I'll pour it," he responded and reached toward her. James's eldest sister smiled as she accepted the newly filled glass with her well-jeweled left hand.

'I wonder if James's sisters realize the gilded perfection in which they grew up?' Casey thought to herself. They seemed perfect in Casey's eyes, beautiful and self-assured, but not in a conceited fashion, just self-assured about their lives, about where they belonged in their surroundings, assured about everything – the clothing they wore, the way they looked – everything.

They acted carefree as if nothing bothered them and nothing ever could. Casey envied them, especially the freedom they unknowingly possessed within their structured lives. She envied them for not needing to fret over many things that concerned women. James's sisters probably couldn't see it, but even as teenagers, their suburban upper-middle class future had already been mapped out for them. They need not plan a thing. They would go to the best universities and graduate schools. There, they would pledge a sorority and inadvertently get their 'MRS' degrees by meeting and marrying a well-brought up male member of their worlds. James's sisters would work in the most notable professions, most likely becoming lawyers or doctors, and their husbands would work in similar jobs. Of course, they would also have the perfect children – one of each, a boy and a girl. Of course.

"Casey," James's other sister began to ask, "I think my sorority sister went to school with you. Did you know a Kayla..."

"Oh, my school was huge," Casey interrupted, eager to avoid any discussion of college and possible connections for James's sister to investigate. Not that it would necessarily matter, or perhaps it would, but James had no knowledge of her scandalous early adulthood. He remembered a different Casey, the high school Casey with the wonderful parents that all the kids loved being around. And Casey kept it that way, never sharing further details with James out of concern he may see her differently.

"So Casey, what's it like being a step-mother to pre-teens?" James's younger sister asked.

"Oh, it's great. The twins are lovely. I love being a mother," Casey responded. She did everything expected of a mother and more to ensure the twins loved the heck out of her, though even Casey had to pinch herself about becoming a step-mother. She also made sure that she and James exemplified a loving couple, just as Casey's own mom and dad did – before her father's accident.

'If I'm now a wife and step-mother then I will be the best dang wife and step-mother there ever was!' Casey's competitive spirit encouraged. Although Casey, who worked in a military-like environment, felt accustomed to performing duties and following instructions to a 't,' she didn't have to play a role because she loved James and his children so much.

"How are your parents doing Casey?" James's mother asked. "I think James mentioned they are still together; just like my husband and..."

"No, they separated at the beginning of my freshman year in college – three months after the accident," Casey interrupted her. Casey kept her eyes focused on her plate, and specifically on her fork and knife as she cut her food. Casey ate carefully, attempting to avoid an etiquette faux pas. However, holding attention to her manners was made more complicated by the glare of James's mother's constant observation.

"Oh, yes your father's tragic work accident. I remember reading all about that in the papers back then. How devastating. The accident damaged his lungs, right? Even all of that money he won from the pharmaceutical company in the settlement could never compensate for what happened."

"Mother!" James interjected, and placed his hand on Casey's arm to comfort her.

"Of course it couldn't," Casey responded to her statement. "The accident took the father I knew as a child, and the money destroyed our family life." Before the tragic incident, Casey's mother and father loved each other dearly and gave Casey and her two brothers a warm and loving home. Not only were Casey's parents very happily married and very much in love with each other then, but they also loved Casey and her siblings dearly, providing Casey and her brothers all the attention growing children deserve. They actively involved themselves in parental activities, rarely missing school events or PTA meetings. They both did everything they knew to show Casey and her siblings they were deeply loved.

Regardless of this shower of affection in childhood, one many would covet, Casey confessed that she felt as though she lacked as a teen. These feelings intensified in high school when Casey became acutely aware of the distinction between the rich and everyone else.

In the beginning, she couldn't shop like some of the other high school girls or drive convertible VWs like them either. In comparison to some of the students with brand new cars and designer labels, Casey felt poor – although she was not. Casey had perfectly fine clothes and a modest first car like most sixteen-year-olds, but that wasn't enough. She kept these feelings to herself so that her hard-working parents wouldn't feel as though they hadn't provided enough.

But, treasures come in many forms, and later Casey wished she had realized the richness of her family life because it changed one winter day. That change provided Casey everything she ever wanted materially but took so much more.

Casey tried to refocus her attention on the meal, but distracted by memories, she absent-mindedly reached to her right for the bread plate. Instead of biting into her bun she bit into James's older sister's newly buttered roll.

James's mother noticed the etiquette error and the look of disdain emanating from her eyes caused Casey to excuse herself abruptly from the table. James followed.

"James, can we leave?" Casey spun on her heels and asked curtly.

"Why?" he asked in genuine curiosity, brushing down his tie.

"I'm just uncomfortable right now around your family."

"Oh, you mean my mother, specifically? Don't worry Casey. She will come around. I think she may still be upset we eloped."

"Yes, that, and more upset because you eloped with me."

James noticed Casey's tears and rubbed her arms to console her.

"I can tell that your mother never liked me, and still doesn't – even though she barely knows me," Casey continued, "and apparently I was so insignificant to your sisters they don't seem to remember me at all."

"Casey, that's not fair. High school was ages ago."

"Can we just leave? Please?"

"Ok," James acquiesced, in light of Casey's vulnerability. "I will tell them that you aren't feeling well."

Casey sat in the car waiting for James to say his goodbyes. The dinner left plenty to digest and left Casey feeling uncomfortable about her place in the family – particularly whether or not she would indeed be accepted. 'The important thing is not whether James's family loves me, but rather that James does,' she said to herself as she waited. Casey dismissed his mother's behavior toward her, yet wanted to win her over at the same time. Just like she had felt before, Casey couldn't help feeling inadequate with a deep longing to belong. She wanted to be seen as the wife James's mother could love.

To do so, Casey needed to continue her pursuit of being a role-model wife, step-mother, and daughter-in-law. So, she wished that all vestiges of the 'old' Casey would die, to be laid to rest and forgotten. She wanted no connection to the old Casey. She needed to distance herself from that woman.

Casey had a lot on her plate, adjusting to James's mother, adjusting to the twins, adjusting to monogamy and routine, and to a newer version of herself. She told herself she never intended to ignore Adoma's calls, but a part of her did. She wanted to reinvent herself completely, and Adoma with all her reunion talk and friends-forever business reminded her of the old Casey she was trying to forget as she crafted her new life.

But she couldn't put off speaking to Adoma for much longer; the reunion approached in just a few months.

Chapter 38
Rejuvenation

The spring in Mark's step and the glimmer in his eyes both returned when he came home from his self-imposed exile. The ocean waves washed and lifted away Mark's melancholy and oncoming depression; and positive, outgoing, and affectionate Mark had returned.

Physically, Mark's appearance changed as well. The extensive length of time he spent on the boat, mostly in the sun, darkened his olive complexion a few shades. Mark returned beautifully bronzed with a bit of a mustache, a slight beard, and the hair on his head grown out into a small afro. As he walked through the door into their home, the sun shone brightly behind him, and partial rays peeked through Mark's fluffy shock of hair, giving his head a halo. Mark, seeing Adoma in the kitchen, smiled broadly upon entering and approached her with a longing sense of urgency. He gripped Adoma in a tight embrace.

Adoma welcomed him back and lovingly grazed her fingers over the top of his head. "I love your hair," she said, admiring the additional inch to his height.

"Oh, how I have missed you," he murmured in an extra baritone pitch. He then leaned down and pulled Adoma even closer to him.

"How much have you missed me babe?" she teased slightly.

"Oh, so very much."

"I've missed you 'oh so very much' more," she cooed while gazing lovingly into his eyes and still only rubbing the surface of his hair. They both smiled and stared at each other. Then silence.

Mark nuzzled his nose into the nook right above Adoma's collarbone where her neck and shoulders met. She instinctively tilted her head in the opposing direction and lovingly caressed his forehead and right temple. Then, he put his hand over hers, squeezed it, and led the way upstairs.

The next morning Adoma and Mark woke up in each other's arms with a newlywed aura hovering around them. Neither dared move, but the obvious needed discussion.

While away, Mark had been in touch in the beginning, but the phone conversations were brief; and later, for a while, he became unavailable. Still, Adoma stayed in trust, knowing that all would be okay.

"Mark, how did your piece go? Did you get enough information? Were you able to complete it?" Adoma asked all of her questions at once while looking toward the ceiling, anticipating a canned response.

"Adoma… the truth is," he turned to face her, "I left to get away… I'm sorry to have left you. It had everything to do with me and nothing to do with you. I'm embarrassed to say that I felt stuck with the piece, and then with life, and then like I was going to a dark place – so I left. It probably would have been best to talk about it before I left you, but I didn't have the energy to deal with it and also worry about how me disappearing could affect things. So I used the article as an excuse to get away… I went to the sea – to feel the openness, to feel its majesty, to feel insignificant against it. The ocean puts the problems we all make grand into perspective. I needed that space, and I am much better now for it… So thank you for allowing that." Mark hugged Adoma to convince her that everything remained okay between the two of them.

Adoma inhaled and waited a moment before speaking. "Mark, I know that a lot of time I talk about what is going on in my life, with my work, and with my friends – especially lately as I plan the reunion… But, if I ever made you feel like you couldn't speak with me about anything difficult you are going through, I am sorry. I am sorry, Mark… I love you for all of your pieces, not just the fun, loving ones. I know you are sensitive –

just like me – and that this sensitivity brings us extreme highs, and if we are not careful, the same level of lows. We are similar, Mark. I get it. But don't beat yourself up for not being positive all of the time. It's okay; that's life; we are human. But you never have to feel as if you have to be 'Mr. Sunshine' with me 100% of the time. I love you for all of you."

"I love you too, Adoma." Mark embraced her once more. "Being away helped, but, I wasn't *completely* self-absorbed while I was gone; though for most of the time, that was true. And, yes, I did buy it for my mental vacation, but now it's ours."

"Mark, what are you talking about? What is ours?"

"I bought a small – a very small yacht; a cabin-cruiser really. I got the boat for a great price from a man whose family was leaving the country for security reasons. I sailed it from Mombasa. It was incredible. I felt so amazing, working the sails and being out in the ocean like that - just like as a kid with my father."

"Aww. That's so nice. It sounds like the sea really calls you."

"Yeah, I think it does."

"So where did you leave it, babe?"

"Well, that's the surprise for you." He paused, then smiled and looked at her. "I docked it in the Seychelles." His grin became as wide as a Cheshire cat's.

"What!?" Adoma covered her mouth. "How long did you sail to get it there? Mark, what about pirates and stuff? Are you crazy?"

"I know babe; it was nuts to do that, but I needed that rush, that adrenaline, too. And it gave me material to write. Plus, the coast guard there escorted me a bit and gave me navigational tips. It was all right. I know it was a bit dangerous, but I feel good because of it. I feel alive. Also, more and more yachts pass through; even some luxury liners and cruise ships. Some of the yachts, you should have seen them. Oh my goodness."

"Mark, I can't believe you, but yet this also excites me at the same time," Adoma giggled.

"Yeah, I didn't want to tell you I was doing it, knowing you would worry about me, and especially since once at sea, phone reception was not guaranteed."

"How long did it take to sail?" Adoma asked.

"It didn't take too long – about a week. And now you and your friends have a boat to get around the islands of the Seychelles."

"This is the oddest surprise a girl could get Mark. Thank you!"

"You're welcome. I banked on this getting me out of the doghouse." He smiled as he nuzzled her cheek.

"You're so funny," she replied, and they hugged and closed their eyes again.

A couple of hours later, during breakfast, the reunion slipped back to the forefront of Adoma's mind.

"Mark, how many can the boat sleep?" Adoma asked as she played with her thick hair twisted into four sections.

"It has a place for sleeping, but no, it really isn't big enough for all of your friends to sleep comfortably. It's a nice size boat; some might call it a yacht, but it's really considered a cabin cruiser like I said earlier. So don't plan on sleeping on it. You can have fun on it and get some rest on it, but it's not for the entire trip," Mark responded and playfully yanked one of Adoma's twists, which quickly sprang back to its chin-length position.

"Okay, then that means we still need to get a place. I think we should rent a house or a condo. I believe that will be the better option for us, right?" Adoma did the math in her head and quickly concluded that indeed that would be the better choice.

"I think you're right; renting a place will be much better and more cost effective than a hotel. Also, it will be relatively inexpensive for you to hire house help, someone to help clean and cook. The place where I docked the boat also has boat staff. You can hire a captain there to help you get around."

"Sounds like a good plan," Adoma agreed with Mark, though she never really liked the idea of domestic help. For some reason it always made her feel uncomfortable to have someone waiting on her and calling her madam. Adoma thought it seemed pretentious, though she knew that for some, having help in other countries significantly eased the day-to-day living.

And since the costs were so low compared to the U.S., she had to admit, renting a house and hiring temporary help seemed the better way to go. 'And why not splurge? This is the ten-year reunion. I should get a chef, too. These ladies are going to have a ball!' Now Adoma's to do list for the day became slightly longer. She needed to find a place and trustworthy house staff.

"I should be able to ask my contacts there about domestic help for you, and also about the best places to rent," Mark said as if sensing her concern. "Don't worry babe. I can take care of this part. You keep planning the best week ever with you and your crazy best friends."

"Thank you, babe." Before she could tiptoe to give him a kiss on the cheek, Mark had already reached down to kiss her forehead and poured her orange juice. Before he finished, Adoma added, "Will you let me know when you get the details sorted out?"

"Sure, do you have a time limit or something? We may need to wait until a month before your arrival date to finalize, but I could start checking and getting everything started. Are you okay with leaving it all up to me or do you want me to check with you about the place before I commit?"

"Well, considering that I have so much to do and that you know my taste and the country better than I do, I trust you to get something that will be suitable for all of us – even picky Genna. Just let me know as soon as you start everything so that I can send the ladies another update as soon as possible and get another round of confirmations. They all say that they are going, but they haven't bought their plane tickets yet."

"Well it's a bit far out to buy plane tickets, don't you think?" Mark asked.

"Not in my opinion. But maybe you're right. I haven't even bought mine. I just think I need the reassurance. Maybe I'm afraid that my friends are starting to flake," Adoma responded in a discouraged manner and added, "Genna never responds to the emails, and I haven't even spoken to Casey since our wedding."

"Hmm…" Mark paused a second to think, then asked, "Have you tried calling Casey instead of texting?"

"Of course I have. The phone just rings and then goes to

voicemail." Adoma sighed.

"Well, we know what Genna has got going on, but what could be keeping Casey from speaking with you?"

"I have no idea babe. I wish I knew the answer myself."

"Hmm, how is Mya, and has she spoken with either of them?"

"Mya is well, but she hasn't talked to Casey or Genna recently either. I asked her the last time we spoke. Everyone is busy with their lives and with work."

"You should consider calling Casey at work then."

"At work?"

"Yes, what if something's wrong? Call her at her job. Desperate times require desperate measures. In the end, she will appreciate the effort. Trust me," Mark said convincingly.

"Okay, I will think about it. You have a good point," Adoma conceded.

Chapter 39
Are You Insane?

Genna looked at her color-coordinated shirts on the rack, trying to decide which of her silk blouses she would wear that day. 'Neither,' she concluded. 'Today, I feel like wearing a dress.' She retrieved one of her designer dresses from her closet and laid it on the bed. Genna walked over to her vanity table to pick out her jewelry. She had started to put on her earrings when Fred sauntered in holding two cups of coffee.

Genna groaned internally. Amidst the drama, she detested Fred, scrutinizing everything he did, from his walk to the things he said. And Genna could not stop playing their relationship over and over in her mind again for clues to her current situation.

Her thoughts often drifted to the early days when Fred delayed marrying her for so long. His not wanting to take the formal step had insulted Genna, yet he seemed completely comfortable living with her in the home she purchased. Yes, Fred helped with the mortgage and the bills, but Genna made the sizable down payment and held the home's deed. The day he asked to share the title, Genna almost choked with laughter, but contained herself, promising him to get to it later.

Genna filed those thoughts away and proceeded to get dressed.

"Hi darling," she half-heartedly said as she put on her diamond studs.

"Hello, dear. Good morning." Fred walked up behind her and handed Genna her cup of coffee. He looked over to the bed. "Nice dress. What's planned for the day?"

"Oh, the usual, mostly meetings with clients, and then I meet with one of the senior partners," Genna replied as she continued putting on her jewelry, dismissively engaging him. She turned around, crossed her legs, took another sip from her mug, and then leered at him. "And you? How is work going for you this week?" She continued to peer above the rim of her mug through the steam, wondering which lie he might tell this time.

She never remembered Fred lying so much before. Genna had always been the most dishonest one. Not by telling direct lies, but through omission and hiding her true self. She cared so much about Fred's approval that even as her husband he never saw her stripped down. Recently, she had stopped caring so much about that, but not to the point where Fred had ever seen her without make-up.

Later in the marriage, Genna even tattooed her eyebrows so that she wouldn't have to go to bed with her thin eyebrows shaded in and risk rubbing make-up on their expensive, stark-white pillowcases. But the foundation she slept in still stained the sheets, so she switched to darker bedding, foregoing her preference to feel like she slept in a hotel.

"Things are great, doll. You know, busy and all. The congressman is putting together an exploratory committee for re-election," he continued in an unusually animated tone.

'Unbelievable,' Genna thought and could no longer play along. This morning it had all gotten to her – and now he was insulting her intelligence. Thoughts whirled through her head. The news reports whirled through her head. Then the time years ago when she resented him almost as much as she did now whirled through her head.

That was years ago when she thought she was pregnant, and she had never brought it up again. She still could not believe Fred entertained the notion of giving up their child. But she began to wonder why she had not gotten pregnant again after that. Without Fred's knowledge she had stopped taking the pill, yet every month her period would return like clockwork. Her doctor mentioned that it could take a while for the hormones to leave her system. 'But it shouldn't take this long,' Genna thought.

"Fred, are you insane?" Genna snapped back to the present. "Do you think that I am that stupid? You have not once discussed with me as an adult and as your partner the details about what's going on with your job and the investigation! Do you think that I don't realize that you could be involved? Or, that everyone is treating us differently now? Or that we have not been invited to the same events we used to attend? Why have you been so quiet?" Genna walked over to him in her silk panty hose and undergarments. Genna placed her hand on Fred's angular chin and pivoted his face directly to hers. "Tell me why, Fred," she lowered her voice, knowing better than to yell in his face.

"Tell you what?" Fred's voice slightly rose as he removed Genna's hand from his chin as delicately as possible without bubbling irritation.

"I would like you to tell me a lot of things, Fred, because we certainly have not spoken about anything significant in a long time. But just a couple of things would suffice for now – now that you ask. I would like to know, Fred, most importantly, number one. Tell me why we aren't a team anymore?" Genna suddenly raised her voice again. "Number two, Fred, number effin two," Genna raised two fingers, but in a sideways fashion making her hand appear more like a gang sign. "Why don't you discuss the ethics scandal with me, Fred?" And then she sat on the bed to ask what recently caused her consternation. Genna lowered her voice and asked, "And last but not least, why the hell haven't I gotten pregnant again?"

Fred paused momentarily, appearing to gather his thoughts. Then, he returned to the argument, "You don't get to yell at me, Genna! I have a few questions of my own!" Too angry to stay, Fred stomped and stormed out of their bedroom. Less than a minute later, Genna heard the jingle of keys, and then a few seconds after, the slamming of the door.

Genna didn't know what he meant but stunned by her outbursts and equally as stunned by Fred's response, became suddenly overwhelmed. A tear welled up in her right eye and rolled down her cheek, leaving behind a blackish trail of mascara along the side of her face, dripping down to her beige sheets. She breathed in deeply, then leaned back all the way on her bed, laying there in only jewelry and undergarments. Genna looked up at the ceiling, and she wept.

Genna stopped suddenly, remembering that she needed to get herself ready, both physically and emotionally, for her meetings. She contemplated calling in sick to work, but couldn't bring herself to do it. The closest she could get to doing so was to call the legal secretary and advise her that she would be late for her first meeting and ask if she could reschedule it for the afternoon. Genna acknowledged the unprofessionalism in this request, but couldn't go to work in her present emotional condition.

She needed to regroup and refocus on her day ahead, instead of the bizarre argument she and Fred just had. She thought about taking a quick run to clear her mind but didn't have the time. Genna tried to call Fred, but he didn't answer the phone. "Seriously!" she gasped out loud while throwing the phone onto the bed. His lack of responsiveness angered her more.

"I don't have time for this!" Genna said aloud. She fixed her make-up, put on her dress, collected her phone, and stormed out in the same manner as Fred had just a few moments before.

Genna sat in her car and revved the engine. "Darn it!" she muttered through clenched teeth. She had forgotten her wallet. Genna hastily left the car and in her rush tripped on her high heels. "Aargh!" she wailed in pain, holding her left foot. Her yelp caught the attention of a runner across the street. He looked in her direction and ran toward her, rushing to her aid.

"Are you okay ma'am?" he asked confidently in between deep breaths of air.

"I don't know," Genna replied softly, pursing her lips tightly to suppress the pain.

The man bent over and touched her ankle. "You're quite the lucky lady. You took a nasty fall, but it appears to be just a sprain," he said while examining her foot. "I hope you don't mind, but we are going to have to take off those fancy shoes of yours and ice the sprain before it gets too swollen," he continued with the slight twang in his voice. "Ma'am, may I help you get back inside?"

Genna nodded 'yes' to the handsome stranger while wincing in pain from the accident.

"Okay then. On the count of three, I am going to lift you from the ground and into the house. Is that okay?" Genna nodded in response. "Could you hand me your house keys first?" he requested authoritatively.

"Here you go. Thank you," Genna responded softly.

"One … two … and three!" Genna groaned as he lifted her body and carried her through her doors and onto her living room sofa. "Can I get you ice?" he asked.

"Yes, the sandwich bags are in the top drawer opposite the dishwasher."

He walked over to her with ice and gently placed it on her swollen ankle. "Okay, I think you should be all set until your husband comes home."

"Thank you so much Mr…?"

"I'm Rob," he said as he stretched out his hand to shake hers. "Do you think you will be okay?"

"Thank you, Rob. Yes, my husband will be home soon. I will call him to be sure. Thank you again." Genna closed her eyes to fall asleep as Rob moved toward the door. "Oh, Rob, I forgot. My phone is in the car; could you please get it for me before you leave?" she asked dangling her keys to him.

Rob returned with Genna's phone. "And one more thing, please, if you don't mind. I'm dying of pain. Could you please grab the pain medicine from that closet in the hallway on your left-hand side?"

"Sure." He walked down the hall. "You have a beautifully decorated home," he complimented as he gave her the pain medicine.

"Thank you again. I'm lucky you were there, or I would still be outside crying in pain. I owe you so much."

"Oh ma'am, it's not a problem at all. As a gentleman, I am much obliged to help." He smiled broadly. "Here's my card. Let me know that you mended alright, Mrs….?"

"Genna. Please, call me Genna," she quickly said as she tried to smile back.

"Okay, Genna. Keep me posted. I feel bad leaving you like this all alone. Are you sure you will be alright?"

Genna hoped Fred would return quickly, but she had her doubts after the way he charged out.

"Yes, my husband will be back soon…"

Chapter 40
Worthy

Casey wondered, 'Where does my friendship with Adoma fit into my life right now?' Casey's personal life began to connect perfectly, except one big piece – her old friendships. Casey still cared for Adoma, and by extension Mya – and even Genna – but they just didn't fit in her life anymore. She accepted that friends outgrow or grow away from each other. If not for the reunion their friendships would have died of natural causes or gone to friendship heaven or 'Iwonderwhathappenedto' land anyway.

As a matter of self-preservation, Casey started to distance herself from her friendship with Adoma. In Casey's mind, she needed to choose whether her new family or her old friends were more important; the two universes seemed to conflict. Casey and Adoma's bond began to slip into a coma and Casey hastened to pull the plug for the sake of her new marriage.

Casey didn't want James to hear her speaking with Adoma, and then eventually want to see Adoma, and accidentally learn things about Casey from Adoma. However, Adoma also 'didn't deserve the silent treatment' simply because she had been Casey's accomplice.

Casey succumbed to her feelings of guilt, and instead of going about her regular business, picked up her phone to call her best friend.

On the other side of the country, Adoma sat at the foot of her bed watching the news and missing her friend. 'Okay Casey, you can't keep ignoring me,' Adoma thought as she scrolled down her contacts list, tempted to call Casey again. Ignoring the temptation, Adoma looked at her to-do list instead.

Casey and Mya had RSVP'd for the reunion and Mark had already secured the home and domestic help. Everything began to coalesce, and she moved forward with plans. 'Casey would have to call soon,' Adoma decided, still wondering if her intuition that Casey wished to untether from her past – and anything connected to it – were accurate.

'Did Casey want to rid herself of witnesses? Good friends let each other change, mature, and grow as well,' Adoma thought. Though Adoma had fun with free-spirited Casey, she never wished to pigeon-hole her into a certain character simply for her entertainment. 'Whatever resistance Casey has in connecting with me, or if she thinks that I want her to remain the same, or that I would tell James anything, exists solely in Casey's mind,' Adoma discerned. 'Hmm… Unless Casey has become too paranoid and self-conscious to see that.'

Adoma's phone rang just as the news reported additional details on Fred's work scandal. "Geez," Adoma said to herself. 'This doesn't look good. I hope Fred doesn't take the fall for anyone. The representative may get out of this unscathed. How crazy is that?' Adoma thought while answering her phone. "Casey!" She exclaimed.

"Hey, chica. Yes, it's me. I've been resurrected and have come back from the dead," Casey joked.

"Yes! Seriously, you have! It's been months! Why have you been hiding?"

"I haven't been hiding," Casey responded a bit bashfully.

"Well, then… Why has no one heard from you lately?"

"It's just been an adjustment is all. You marry not only a person, but also their family. I have his children to think of, and the mother-in-law, and sometimes the ex-wife," Casey explained. "There's a lot to adjust to."

"And, well, how is everything going?"

"No sleep for the weary, as they say." Casey chuckled. "But on the bright side, I'm not restless. I thought maybe I would get bored, but the new lifestyle keeps me on my toes. I played tennis for the first time last week."

"You, in a tennis skirt Casey? That sounds so funny. How is your backhand?" Adoma asked, smiling at the image of Casey on a tennis court.

"Horrendous, but I grunt as though I am killing it out there like Serena Williams." They both laughed.

"You're still funny, Casey. You mentioned staying on your toes. What's that about, hunh?"

"Nothing really; just issues of fitting into his family. They are very different from mine. He grew up the way, you know, the way I kind of wish I had. So I feel like an imposter – and ungrateful all at the same time." Casey sighed. "His mother looks at me a bit contemptuously at times, though she tries to hide it. I know she hates to see us together, though neither she nor James would ever admit it. But I feel the looks, and it makes me feel inadequate, like back in the day all over again."

"Casey, you have to let that go. How many years ago was that? Geez. No one, not even an intimidating mother-in-law should make you feel that way. You are more than enough and perfect as you are. Even if you've turned into a Stepford wife," Adoma joked, unable to resist.

"Funny, funny Adoma, I know. But I've been thinking a lot lately, and now I fear that she or James will find out about all the crazy things that I have done in the past. I wish, because I love James so much, that I hadn't been so wild, even though I can't say that I regret my experiences. I had a great time, and even my mistakes have made me who I am. And, I think I have turned out perfectly fine, thank you very much… I just know how James's family might view it. I know it's crazy, but I am getting paranoid. Because if they do – if they were to find out – I don't think James would love me the same anymore, and that would mess up the equilibrium I have in my life… this new life I have made for myself."

"Casey, if he found out and it bothered him, he would need to let it go. People change, everyone evolves, and most people for the better. You are no different. And by the way, I don't think that James would love you any less. That seems immature."

"But how do I know? He fell in love with me the way that he thought that I was. He fell in love with his high school sweetheart, a domesticated fairytale version of me. A part of me that I love, but the other side of me is still there; it's suppressed desires, but I can still feel the impulses bubbling below the surface. My behavior has changed, but I still want to go to a bar and get to know someone new. I just don't. I've learned instead to save my energy for James."

"Casey, have you considered speaking with anyone?"

"Adoma, I am not a sex-addict, please. I don't think that's a real thing. I didn't say that I would *do* anything like that. I'm just saying that it's back there."

"Yes, back there like the Hulk is just back there?"

"Adoma!" Casey exclaimed. "This is a serious conversation; come on!"

"I'm just sayin', Casey."

"Arrgh, let's just change topics. So how is our dear Mya?"

"She is doing wonderfully. She is happy with Christian. Also, she is thinking of adopting. She contemplated getting a surrogate, but ruled against it, as she thought about all of the children in need."

"Oh yeah, she has a point. And is Genna still MIA?"

"Yes, a little bit. I hear from her by text every once in a while, but in general, we haven't spoken. And the news just now reported more to the story. Mya says it doesn't sound good."

"Oh really? And how does she know that?"

"I don't know, but I guess it may be pillow talk. You know, Christian being an attorney may have heard and then maybe told her something."

"Well, I am not surprised to hear that, but I hope that everything turns out okay for them."

"Yes, I do too."

"Well, the good thing is… In a couple of months we will all be very ready for a vacation," Casey added, knowing that this would make Adoma feel happy.

"I know. I'm ready too. I have everything almost set for us as well. We have the house, a boat, and we have the help. And I have a bit of a surprise for you ladies as well."

"Cool, I love surprises, and I can't wait."

Adoma walked to her closet and retrieved what she had

remaining of her adinkra fabric. Adoma had already turned the other half of it into a lovely top. "Don't forget your fabric," Adoma reminded Casey.

"I know, I know. You've told us like a million times. I don't think anyone is going to forget it."

"Good." Adoma sighed in relief, tracing her finger over her family's adinkra symbol adorning her neck.

Adoma hung up the phone glad to know that Casey had not completely pulled away, though not entirely convinced that Casey wouldn't dump them all for a fresh start shortly after the reunion. 'Does running from your past work?' Adoma pondered. Adoma remembered some things in her life that made her cheeks darken in embarrassment. But she learned from them, and probably wouldn't have realized what a gem Mark was if she hadn't 'kissed a few toads' before. Adoma knew that these mistakes didn't define her. Had she let them, she would not have felt worthy enough for Mark's love. And she knew better than to think that. She was worthy enough for *anyone's* love. Adoma hoped that Casey would soon realize the same thing.

Chapter 41
Ready, Set, Go!

The media reported that documents were subpoenaed from Fred's office. Ironically, Genna couldn't care less. Though she and Fred coexisted mostly in silence, except for perfunctory intercourse, lately, Genna had not a care in the world. She finally enjoyed her days. She and Rob, who assisted with her injury, began to run together frequently. In those moments, they spoke and shared, and Genna received the emotional connection she needed. Soon, Genna started to feel like Genna again.

"Ready, set, go!" Rob started the stopwatch and stared intensely at its numbers as Genna sprinted. "Time!" He yelled after about two minutes.

Genna appreciated the feel of her hair blowing in the wind and likewise having a running partner. Rob was smart, someone with whom she could discuss intelligent issues and matters.

Yet, he either didn't know about or didn't dare mention the political scandal playing on the cable news stations, and that was fine by Genna. She enjoyed his company and the escape it provided from her home life, an unintentionally, self-created, gilded cage. Luckily, now she had a distraction, something shiny and new.

Better still for Genna, her campaign to detach from Fred's troubles began to work. No longer did she receive icy stares at the country club or the looks of pity in the office place. The newer associates looked up to her again. She had fun using her acting skills and convincing everyone that *this* Fred, the one allegedly involved in illegal activity, wasn't the man she married.

She didn't know anything or even what happened to the man she married.

It was partially true; she didn't know what happened to Fred. In more than ten years of marriage, though he had always seemed selfish, never before had he been so secretive. Previously, as a power couple on the rise, they had shared everything and planned everything together. His current secrecy around the house tired her, and she now tired of him.

"How did I do?" Genna gasped in exhaustion. Genna's pace slowed as she returned to her original starting point, and she collapsed inward, placing her hands on her knees to provide support while she breathed heavily.

"You did about five seconds better than last Saturday."

"Good, then that means that I am improving." She let out a huff that blew her hair out of her face.

"Yes, you are." Rob smiled after first stealing a glance to notice the way Genna's sweat glimmered along her skin. "Is your ankle still feeling okay? You recovered so quickly from the sprain. And now look at you. You are sprinting faster. I'm not sure why you're pushing so hard, but you are."

"No reason, I just want to increase my time." Genna bent down to tighten her laces. Rob stole another quick glance. Genna continued, "And you're right, I did recover quickly from that sprain. Thankfully, by the next day, I was up and running." Genna laughed. "Figuratively of course! But I do hate to be still."

She looked down at the previously injured foot. "It took about two days before I even attempted to run again," she gasped. "I certainly hated those two days." She rocked back and forth on her foot and continued speaking. Fred rarely entered her mind when she spent time with Rob. This finally allowed her the opportunity to entertain the idea of life without Fred.

'What would happen if Fred got in trouble?' She asked herself. Though Fred insisted that there was no wrongdoing on his part or even on that of the congressional office, it became apparent that was untrue. Fred blamed the whole controversy on partisan politics, a conspiracy resulting from party affiliation.

Fred may have had a point when he asserted that the upcoming election cycle fueled the claims. Regardless, now

Fred's future employment seemed uncertain. Previously, the representative had always won the seat hands down. This time it would be a close election or even a possible loss. Even with a win, public opinion would not likely be forgiving to indiscretion or the appearance of impropriety to a politician who ran on an anti-corruption platform.

It was all a mess. Genna was not quite sure what Fred would do. Former employees of the political world could assimilate quickly into the corporate one, in particular by attaining plum consultancy or lobbying positions in the private sector or even professorships in academia. But with the taint of the scandal, it didn't seem that such a transition, should it have to occur, would happen as seamlessly for Fred. This appeared to be a cause for concern, but not at the present. Genna finally enjoyed not worrying about a thing.

Genna, returning to the run at hand, said, "I'm glad to have called you and that you were willing to be my running partner, to make sure that I didn't re-injure myself," she said flirtatiously.

"I'm glad you called too," Rob responded. "Are you ready to hit the trail?"

"Yup, I'm ready," Genna said while stretching her calves. When she finished, she waited for Rob to complete his stretch.

"Let's go!" he said and patted her on the behind – in a sportsman-like manner. Genna felt the jolt of electricity, but dismissed it, as she had been ignoring the feelings she felt between them – the constant tug of energy and tension as they spoke and interacted; the slight reading in between the lines of what they said to each other; and the want of innocent words to mean more. Going against her legal training to take words at face value, she enjoyed playing in the space of uncertainty – pretending she didn't know where things were headed.

They both ran forward toward the trail, Genna slightly ahead, Rob purposefully just at her heels, a step behind.

Chapter 42
Back to Basics

Mya smiled at the cuteness appearing on her computer screen. While looking at their photos she grinned, optimistic that one of these children could soon be her future son or daughter.

With effort, she also dismissed the sadness and disappointment that hid in the back of her mind, the longing to have a biological child of her own. 'What matters is the love,' she told herself and continued looking through the website, trying to glean as much information as she could from the orphanage.

Christian peered over Mya's shoulder as she clicked on the different pictures and information. He took it upon himself to help the process as much as possible. Mya gladly accepted his help, as it would allow her to save thousands of dollars on the expensive, complicated process.

From helping Mya rebuild her finances to assisting in her business, Christian was involved with everything, though Mya had the intelligence and the business acumen to do it all on her own. But, he insisted. How he found the time to help with a demanding law practice impressed Mya. She allowed and soon welcomed his involvement, and almost depended on it. More and more, Christian made himself indispensable, and Mya didn't mind. His involvement was maybe too much, but it far outshined what she had before. Now, as Mya began to consider her life's aspects – her business, her living arrangements, and now her future child, she factored in Christian.

As Mya scrolled through the website, she paused at a young girl smiling widely with big onyx eyes. Her broad smile made her appear incredibly radiant as she stood in the center of a group of young girls, all holding on to each other as they posed for the camera. The young girl's hair was cut short like a young boy's style, and the dark yellow and brown school uniform only added to her cuteness. In the remaining pictures, Mya viewed the young girl again and again. In whichever picture included the small child, randomly or not, Mya's eyes would instantly be drawn to her. Looking at her made Mya forget her previous desire to have a child of her own. Mya already felt a connection, and she had to meet her.

"Christian, look, isn't she adorable?" Mya asked excitedly.

"Yes, she is," Christian nodded.

"Let's contact the orphanage about her."

"Sure, dear. I'll get right on it, but don't you think you should do more research before getting too excited?" Christian said, trying to sound supportive.

"Hopefully they will let us schedule a visit soon." Mya ignored his hesitant response and the jealousy that seeped through his smirk.

"Soon? But this would be an international trip. Are you sure that you want to leave so quickly and go so far to adopt? There are plenty of children without homes and loving parents here."

"I know babe, but I have already made up my mind that I want to adopt from back home. I feel more of a connection with the orphanages there, and in my opinion, their need is greater there," Mya responded intrepidly.

"Okay, so it looks like next month we are traveling to East Africa. I look forward to it. I have never been."

"Yes love, I can meet you there from the Seychelles. Our trip needs to be *after* the reunion."

"Oh, yeah, the girls' trip to the pristine beaches of the Seychelles. Remind me why I can't go again?"

"Sorry, my dear. The answer to your question is in the first part of your sentence. No cylindrical extremities allowed." Mya giggled. She'd picked up a bit of Adoma's sense of humor. She rubbed Christian's arm in comfort, but it appeared to be his ego that needed stroking. "It's a promise to reunite that we made almost ten years ago. We can't change up the trip now. I really can't believe we stuck to the plan, and it's really going to happen. I'm proud of us."

Christian appeared to pout; Mya noticed and responded. "I wish I could bring you with me babe, but it's just us ladies. We don't always have to be attached at the hips, you know?"

Just as Mya spoke, she received a new message in her inbox. "Speaking of the devil... Adoma just sent out another reminder email. I hope it's the last. I think we all know the drill by now."

"Darlings," Mya started to read Adoma's email aloud but changed her mind as she observed Christian huffing in the background. She continued reading, silently.

I hope by now that all of you are just as excited as I am to be headed out to a luxurious vacation in the Seychelles next month. Though none of you has confirmed your flight information with me, I am not going to worry about it and trust that you all will buy your tickets soon and show up as planned and promised. As mentioned, I will be arriving to the islands early, so as long as you all are there on time (see below), it's fine.

What: Welcome Night
When: Next Month the 20th
Time: 6pm
Where: Port Victoria
Contact the Harbor Master if necessary, but the boat 'Emerald' will be easy to find.

As you know, this is an awesome place with crystalline waters. It is a luxury hide-away for many celebrities and jet setters. There is no telling whom we may run into. So pack well.

A few important reminders:

1. Make sure to check your passports! If they are expiring or have too few pages left in them, you may risk an issue.

2. Pack bathing suits.

Also remember, there is no need to worry about the hotel thanks to Mark. For an incredible price, we have secured a lovely little villa and – we're gonna be on a boat! I will continue to plan our activities, but the first one is noted above. Be on time. And if there is anything special you ladies would like to do, please let me know. But mostly just plan to relax and bond.

3. Remember your adinkra cloths!

Oh, and in case I have to remind someone, remember it's just us gals, the original posse from back in New Orleans. Back to basics baby!

I can't wait!

Lylas,

Adoma

Part III

Chapter 43
The Tenth Year

With her head against the window, Adoma stared at the multi-colored, turquoise and emerald water. The plane approached the runway, and even before landing, her destination exceeded her expectations, appearing more beautiful than depicted in photographs.

Adoma disembarked onto the tarmac of the small airport. She breathed in the warm, humid air and adjusted her hat, grateful that she had decided to braid her hair before the trip. Typically, Adoma avoided humidity for appearance's sake; this time, she welcomed the warm damp air, which revived her skin and nasal passages after the dry air of the plane.

"Gorgeous," Adoma whispered, surveying her environment, as the seagulls danced in and out of the water as if playing games with the waves. Their sweet songs welcomed Adoma to their home.

Adoma steadied her ebony gaze to the distance, focusing on the remaining archipelago of islands surrounding the main island where she stood. The magnificence, the enchantment of the Seychelles, more than she could have ever imagined, awed her. Her eyes continued to revel in the verdant flora and the sparkling water.

Disinclined to follow the direction of the crew, Adoma trailed off, away from the airport, toward the ocean, her stride broken only when redirected to her correct destination, the arrivals gate. Upon exit, she scanned the colorful crowd of drivers holding signs for their intended passengers. Not seeing her name, she abated disappointment with the small consolation of a latte before hailing a cab.

On Adoma's final sip, she noticed, parked off to the side, a handsome taxi driver on his phone reclined in his seat, calm and relaxed. He rubbed his sienna fingers through his jet-black curls, unconcerned with entrapping tourists to pay inflated fairs.

"Combine d'obtenir a Rue Long?" Adoma approached him asking in the little French she could muster.

"I speak English," he replied with a huge smile and thick accent. After he stated his price, a third of the going rate, Adoma hastily mounted his cab before he dared change his mind.

"...And there you will see our clock tower, a replica of Big Ben in London." The taxi driver pointed to the tall clock tower as they drove through the city center through a historic area that reminded Adoma of the French Quarter in New Orleans. They passed Creole restaurants, museums, and galleries. "...And there you will find Victoria Market," he continued.

"The market is colorful and beautiful, just like this area," Adoma remarked, observing the cobbled streets and the French colonial-style architecture.

"Yes, it is, madahm," the driver answered with a pride befitting more than his responsibility. He continued, "I'm also a tour guide. Please allow me to drive you around a bit more. There will be no additional charge.

"Did you know Victoria is one of the smallest capitals in the world?" the driver asked proudly, trying to impart onto Adoma his knowledge of the island chain. And while they drove he recited the country's history after the arrival of its first inhabitants, then the details about the merchant trade and the local folklore before French control of the island.

Adoma took copious mental notes to remember the details so she could share them with Genna, Casey, and Mya when they arrived. She knew that she had better make the trouble of getting to the Seychelles, nearly a thousand miles away from the nearest land mass, worth every effort.

"I'm so impressed with your knowledge and charm," Adoma said, looking over to the taxi driver. "What's your name?"

"Jean," he flashed a broad smile and replied with glistening eyes. Jean reached into his shirt pocket for a business card and handed it to Adoma, who readily accepted it. "Maybe later, I could be of service and show you and your guests more of the islands? Oui?" He suggested.

"I think that is an excellent idea, Jean. In fact, why don't you drive for us the entire trip? I will call you soon," Adoma said as Jean dropped her off, "but for now, I will stroll the neighborhood alone a moment before dinner."

Adoma inhaled the flowery fragrances blanketing the air and mentally noted the places to eat, drink, and shop as she walked. While doing so, she began to imagine all four of them sitting together at the restaurant tables catching up on their lives these past few months.

Chapter 44
Third Time's the Charm

After severe procrastination, Genna succumbed to pressure and at the last minute had bought her plane ticket to attend the reunion. 'Just what I get for waiting so long to purchase,' Genna bemoaned her discombobulated itinerary, which included a long layover in an unfamiliar West African country. 'And the timing could not be worse. The only good thing about leaving right now is that I avoid being at home while the investigation heats up. And, maybe now, I will stop feeling so sick,' Genna thought as she drove to the airport.

When Genna reached her layover destination, the dripping humidity of the air gripped her. "No jetways?" Genna mumbled, walking the tarmac toward the main terminal, as she wiped sweat from her forehead. 'I can only imagine what the airport must look like inside. Forget the airport. More importantly, what will I do for ten hours?' She weighed her options, eager to escape the dusty airport after having learned that a mechanical issue had doubled her layover wait. 'I don't think I want to sit around here without a business lounge pass. And, for close to the same amount to buy one, I could probably get a room at the airport hotel. I have enough time to rest. Yup, the hotel sounds good, and it would probably be worth the trouble.' Still unsure, Genna walked toward the information desk. Then, a bubbling in her stomach aided her decision; she opted for a hotel.

Genna surveyed the stark décor. After being pleased with her comfortable and clean surroundings, she quickly fell into a deep sleep; a slumber so deep even the persistent mosquito in her room could not wake her.

While laughing with Casey and Mya, Adoma stopped to investigate the unexpected sound.

"Oh, it must be the house phone," Adoma called out, correctly identifying the ringing that interrupted their lively conversation. Over the last few hours, they regaled in the recent events of their lives while awaiting Genna.

"Okay, ladies," Adoma announced. "That was Genna. She just landed and apologized about missing last night due to her layover. She should be here in a moment, in enough time to join us on the boat for our first outing – Praslin Island."

"Great. What happened? I thought maybe she decided to ditch us again when I saw that I was the first to arrive," Casey commented sarcastically.

"Stop, Casey," Adoma lightly reproached. "What had happened was, she already had a layover, but then there was a mechanical delay that made it even longer. But it doesn't matter now; she will be here soon, so I will call Jean to pick her up from the airport."

"Oh, yeah. I am excited! Now that Genna is here we can open our secret papers, the ones we've waited ten years to see again!" Mya delighted.

"You mean the ones that have been trapped in Adoma's doggy bag for a decade, holding all of our hopes and secrets? Funny, I don't even remember what I wrote on my sheet," Casey added.

"Hold your horses ladies. We will do that later," Adoma explained. "I have something special planned for that. But, for our first couple of days on the island, let's not think about that. We'll just enjoy the beaches, some good wine, and connect. We haven't all four been together or spoken to each other in a while. Plus, when's the next time we'll be in the Seychelles? Let's take advantage of it, and tomorrow we will do even more touring of this place I now call heaven. The captain will take us to a granite island, home to cool birds like blue pigeons and black parrots. " Adoma paused, smiling, grateful that this day had finally come to fruition. She turned to Casey and Mya. "I've missed you all so much."

"Genna!" they all exclaimed less than an hour later, rushing over to embrace the last friend to arrive.

"Hey, ladies! Well, I made it, though it feels like I went through hell and high water. What a brutal flight! You guys just don't know what I have been through in the past 24 hours. I had the longest flight and layover. I'm exhausted, but, I'm finally here."

"You don't look exhausted. How do you manage to stay so flawless?" asked Mya, smoothing Genna's sleeve.

"I woke up like this, but, thank you for the compliment. I'm surprised I still have some energy right now and haven't passed out on the couch yet. Due to the stress of my life, I've been sick to my stomach – literally. But at least I managed to make the last leg of the flight without throwing up in the airplane bathroom."

"Aww babe. Sorry about that," Adoma consoled. "We're about to leave in about an hour for the harbor to sail out to another island. The captain is waiting for us, as I told him 10 o'clock. Do you need to stay here while we go sightseeing? If so, it's okay. You can stay and catch up on your rest while we're out, and that way you'll be refreshed in time for dinner. How does that sound?"

Genna, unable to keep her eyes wide open, yawned. "Yes, I think I do. My body's tired of traveling, and I just want to be on the ground for a moment. You guys go without me this time and have fun. I'll be ready by this evening for dinner and then I can catch everyone up on everything. Is tomorrow the lazy day on the beach? I hope so. I am so ready to relax by some clear blue water. I could stay out on the beach all day! But for now, I just need sleep. I'm sorry for bailing on the first day, but I need a shower, and a nap, and..." Genna grimaced, "...maybe some Pepto."

"Oh?" Adoma asked. "Hopefully you didn't drink the water from the tap during your layover. But yes, we will have plenty of swim and relaxation time. We can even dive off the boat right into the middle of the ocean."

"The boat?" Genna inquired.

"Have you not read my emails?"

"Well, yes, but sometimes I had to scan. Adoma, there were so many in the beginning, and they were long sometimes, too."

"Yeah. I could tell you all were getting tired of them when y'all stopped responding. So that's why I just gave up and sent a final email one month out. But in the last email I mentioned a boat, I think."

"Oh yeah, the surprise boat. She will tell you more at dinner probably. She already filled us in." Casey clamored to add, "Mark decided...."

"Hey hey hey," Adoma interjected. "No more guy talk now that we're all here. Today is just about us. And, we have plenty of time later to reminisce together, starting with dinner tonight." Adoma smiled, proud of her restaurant find. "Oh my gosh, Genna!" Adoma exclaimed." I almost forgot to catch you up on the latest good news we discussed yesterday! Mya's going to be a mom!"

"Oh, really?" Genna smiled.

"Yes, she is going to adopt!"

"Congratulations, Mya!" Genna managed to squeak out an excited tone in her exhausted state. She averted her eyes, which would've betrayed her, exposing the tinge of jealousy she felt for having not been the first to announce the welcome of a child.

"Thank you; though Adoma is ahead of herself," Mya responded. "I'm still in the early stages of figuring this all out, but I plan to visit the orphanage after the trip. Christian and I'll meet up there. There's a young girl who is holding my heart; she is so beautiful. I'm in love. Love at first sight."

"Wait? Are you going to the orphanage with *Christian*? That's a big step. Where's that heading?" Casey asked.

"Well, I don't know, but I am in no rush to be engaged again so soon. It would be my third engagement, so I'd just as soon wait."

"Well, third time is the charm, they say," Casey encouraged.

"True, la tercera es la vencida. Yes, third time is the cha- " Genna unsuccessfully stifled a yawn.

"Genna, get some rest." Adoma moved toward her. "Here, I'll walk you to your room." Adoma assisted with Genna's luggage as they walked deeper into the hallway. "But before you forget, please get out your adinkra fabric and leave it in the basket over there." Adoma pointed to the wicker basket almost filled to the brim with the other cloths. "They'll be taken care of early tomorrow."

Chapter 45
After Dinner

Adoma returned with seashells she had collected on the beach, and Casey and Mya, bronzed from the afternoon activities in the sun, tumbled in after her. With Genna sufficiently rested, they prepared for dinner and awaited Jean.

While Jean drove, he engaged his captive audience in more history and island facts. "Also, if it might interest you madahms, I could show you the nightlife treasures of the island as well – after you have dined, of course, and only if it pleases you," Jean offered as he steadied a gaze at Casey through the rearview mirror.

Casey and the other passengers looked at each other to assess mutual interest. Jean continued speaking, sweetening his proposal. "Oui, my cousin owns a lounge, a very popular one in fact. All the tourists enjoy it, and I can escort you madahms there after dinner - if it pleases you."

"Hmm, that sounds good," Adoma replied on behalf of everyone." We'll see how we feel when you pick us up from dinner. Then we can decide."

"Yes, madahm. I am at your disposal."

"Yes, we can decide later, if it pleases us. I think I can guess that it will, Jean," Casey flirted.

Most of the dinner conversation consisted of Genna's long account of her arduous travels and Adoma, Mya, and Casey recalling the day's activity of sailing from Mahe Island to tour Praslin.

The waiter, leaving their check and extra glasses of water, interrupted a deeper conversation that had begun brewing. "So Adoma, if you never really liked Roger and could tell that something was amiss with him from the beginning, then why did you let me marry him without saying anything?" Mya incredulously asked as she folded her napkin on the table.

"Well, Mya, I didn't think that you would listen to me because you were so into him and you guys were together all of the time. I barely even saw you alone anymore after you met him. I was also afraid that since I was single at the time, you might have thought that I was envious or something."

"Adoma, I would have never thought that. You thought all those things and never told me? Wow, I figured we were closer than that. Well, why are you saying something now?"

"I am saying something now because I want you to be careful, you know. I just mean, don't fall too hard for Christian like you did with Roger. Just take a moment," Adoma said. In response, Mya sighed, sipping her water, contemplating.

"Adoma, why don't you call the driver to get us, since we've finished," Genna said, eager to change topics.

"Yeah, let me call Jean," Adoma said, paying the bill.

"Jean. Cute name. It sounds nice rolling off the tip of my tongue. Where'd you find that cutie?" Casey asked. "And I hope that I'm not the only who wants to take him up on his offer to take us to the lounge. Does it not *please* anyone else to go?" Casey smiled as she turned to Adoma. "Do you think that Jean could still take us out to the lounge he mentioned?"

"He probably could, but I'm too tired to go to a club right now," Adoma replied, a bit annoyed.

"Me too," Genna and Mya both added, almost in unison.

"Does this mean that I have to go to the club by myself?" Casey asked. "Because I can and I will, you know."

"No, it means that you are coming home with the rest of us," Adoma said firmly. "Haven't you heard the phrase 'leave with who you came with'?"

"But, I want to have fun. We're on vacation, you know."

"Yes, I know. For the last ten years, I planned this special vacation you're on. The point is that we all should be spending our time together. But, we're all grown-ups, and if you just can't see yourself going home and you just *have* to go out, please Casey just go on – go right ahead. But be good."

"Be good? You don't have to tell me to be good like I'm a child. I just want to have fun and the lounge sounds like fun. But now that you have guilted me into staying with you gals and doing nothing but going to bed – never mind."

"Casey," Mya interrupted, as she separated the bickering friends, putting her arms around both Casey and Adoma. "I promise on behalf of the group that we will all go out and party before the trip ends."

"Yeah. Now we're talking. Can we bring Jean too?" Casey joked. Her smile diminished as she noticed Genna's rolling eyes and Adoma's shaking head.

"Gosh ladies. I feel like you're judging me," Casey bemoaned.

"I'm not judging you. How you live is up to you. Everyone has free will and chooses to live life differently, deciding to experience it in their own way. You just choose at all times to experience life physically, through the lower half of your body," Adoma sneered, giggling at her snarky quip.

"But you're married now," Mya quickly added.

"You see, *that* is the judgment I am talking about; I'm kind of over it," replied Casey. "And, just because I'm married now doesn't mean that while on vacation I shouldn't want to go to clubs and dance and look at attractive men like our driver… guide…whatever the eff his job is!"

"Casey, Adoma was just kidding," Genna said, trying to temper the situation.

"Seriously, ladies," Casey continued. "I'm just acting – well used to act – in the way most men have been doing for generations. But besides that, why would it be so shocking to want to go out and enjoy the nightlife while I'm on vacation? I've been mothering, advising, caring – 'being good' – for a while now. Now, I just want to hear a little bit of island music and shake my hips, but that seems like a crime. When did we all get so boring? Especially *you,* Adoma. I don't know when you became so square, but I will not join you in your new life of boredom. 'Mark this and Mark that.' That is all you talk about now," Casey parroted, accusingly.

"Oh, I didn't realize that I spoke so much about him." Adoma responded bashfully.

"Well, it's true, you used to have your own life. It sounded exciting frankly. Now all you talk about is Mark."

"Well, I have kissed a lot of toads; so many that now I just feel so blessed. He is all that I think about – because, Casey, I'm still madly in love. We're still newlyweds for goodness sake. Isn't that perfectly reasonable? You may not talk about James, but I talk about Mark, and frankly I don't care."

"Umpf," Casey grunted, expressing disagreement.

"I think it's normal. Adoma should enjoy the early days while the glow of romance still lasts because it doesn't last forever," Genna added, thinking of her and Fred's recent emotional distance.

"Come on, Genna! Stop being a bummer! Why would you say that? Some things *do* last forever; true love can," added Adoma.

"Agreed," Mya finally chimed in. "I believe that. Look at me. I'm not giving up."

"Yes, Mya, I know. Never give up," Adoma demanded.

"Third time's the charm!" They all encouraged her together.

Chapter 46
Daybreak

In the wee hours the next morning Casey, Mya, and Genna found paper jewelry boxes with their names in calligraphy awaiting them on the kitchen counter.

"I promise you I never looked at the papers – even after all these years," Adoma said, pleased her friends were enchanted with the decorated squares. "I did have to take them out of the shoe box though because I thought it would be nicer to have the hopes and secrets in these cute jewelry boxes when we get to read them on the beach today."

"That's fine. But, tell us again why you insisted that we be up so early in the morning to do so?" Casey asked, rubbing her eyes.

"To give us enough time to get to the beach before sunrise. You all know that I love daybreak. I think it will be symbolic to let go of what's been in those boxes at the rising of the new sun. There is just something so profound about daybreak and seeing the first rays of the sun peek out over the earth. It reminds me of smooth transitions, and you know in some ways it reminds me of trust, too. Think about it. We don't ever notice it, but we trust the universe because we can always count on some things. After winter must come spring; after daylight comes sunset; and after the darkness, there is always the sunrise. Always."

Adoma tested the salt water and retracted her toe just as quickly as she had dipped it in the water.

"Come on Adoma, step in all the way. It isn't that bad. Stop exaggerating," Casey, who had already waded up to her calves into the water, urged.

"Noo, it feels cold!" Adoma shivered, whining to Casey, Genna, and Mya. "I think I've changed my mind. I don't want to walk any farther."

"This was your idea; come on and stop whining," Genna joined Casey in the peer pressure.

Ignoring the tension in her body, Adoma shyly eased her way through the crystalline waves to join the others. When the four of them had formed a straight line, they continued in unison about ten inches forward into the sparkling waters of the Indian Ocean.

The water teased their knees, and Adoma abruptly halted. She turned around to look at the curvaceous boulders jutting out of the flora of the island's coast. Then she continued and, without retreat, moved forward into the ocean toward the horizon until, eventually, the pressure of the waves stilled her and her friends.

In their right hands, they each held the small jewelry boxes laid out for them in the morning. One-by-one they took a turn reading aloud the hopes and dreams that they had planned for this time in their lives a decade ago. Adoma smiled that her hope 'to live a joyful life' had come true.

They snickered at the vagueness of Adoma's wish. "Adoma, you're always optimistic anyway; your dream was bound to come true no matter what."

"Ha, ha, Genna. Yup, I kept it open-ended so I could get what I had wanted. See – it worked!"

They all laughed, but after the laughter, a silence came over them.

"Ladies, now it's time to read our secrets," Adoma announced.

With reverence, they all looked at their secrets silently. All but Mya grimaced at what they had written ten years ago.

"Are we going to read them out loud?" Mya inquired.

"Umm..." Adoma spoke up, cheeks darkening. Seeing her secret as a matured woman embarrassed her. "How about instead of doing that, we just let go of the *burden* of our secrets

– without sharing," she quickly replied. "So on my count of three, we can just release them, okay? Is that alright with everyone?" Adoma asked with the hope that they'd agree.

"Yes!" They exclaimed.

"Okay. 1-2-3!!!" And upon the last syllable, the small ornamental boxes floated into the ocean toward the horizon. The four boxes soon disappeared into the distance.

When the last cube left their sights, Adoma clasped Genna, then Casey's hand, who in turn reached for Mya's, and in unison, they lifted their arms to the heavens in celebration. "We did it!" They embraced as the sun's rays alighted the brightening sky.

Chapter 47
What's Your Secret?

"I'm excited for tonight too, everyone," Adoma, shaking off the drowsiness of their two-hour sun soak, responded to Casey's comment. "I have something nice planned, and I think you all will like the restaurant I have in mind."

"Speaking of restaurants," Casey said, rubbing her stomach. "Being on the beach is making me hungry. I'm starving now. Let's get packed and head back home," Casey suggested.

"Good idea. Let's get some lunch before we go to the house, and then we can rest some more in the air-conditioning before washing up," Adoma added.

"Thanks." Casey lowered her voice and nudged Adoma in the rib. "Psst, Adoma. What was your secret?"

"Umm," Adoma hesitated, contemplating whether to tell Casey. "I want to keep it to myself. I'm embarrassed about it."

"Seriously, are you ashamed about something from so long ago? Didn't you tell me once there was no point in feeling shame? 'Just do better when you know better'– or something like that you said once. I can't remember what we were talking about, but you said something about evolving as people. Geez, I can't remember what we were talking about."

"I don't think I remember that conversation, but still…"

"Come on A; you can tell me. I will tell you mine," wheedled Casey.

"Casey, I think I know all of your secrets." Adoma smiled.

"Maybe not all. You know…."

"I feel sore ladies," Genna, with a crimsoning face, interrupted. She had hardly moved a limb while in her beach chair and finally opened her eyes to speak.

Mya placed her hand on Genna's forehead. "Oh my gosh, and you are burning up!"

"Oh, I am? I thought I just had too much sun. I don't feel very well at all," Genna slurred, with dull eyes and heavy breath.

"Oh my gosh, Genna, I'm worried," Adoma added with urgency after also feeling Genna's forehead. "You aren't looking too good either. I am calling Jean now to take us back home straight away."

As soon as they mounted Jean's car, Genna announced, "I'm skipping lunch," and promptly fainted.

Genna's eyes fluttered open and squinted from the blazing harsh white lights above her. Mya, Casey, and Adoma waited anxiously by her side as she gained consciousness. They smiled with relief seeing Genna awake.

"What happened?" Genna mumbled, looking around to make sense of her new surroundings.

"You passed out, sleeping beauty, when we came back from the beach." Adoma smiled and caressed Genna's curled lockets that obscured her right eye, imparting an angelic innocence. "You're in the hospital."

"Oh?" Genna replied with disbelief. "Do they know what's wrong with me? Is it from stress?" she inquired, remembering how much she had been vomiting earlier.

"They don't know what's wrong, but they ran some tests and hopefully we will know something soon," said Adoma, holding her hand cautiously while avoiding the IV tube. Just as Adoma answered, the doctor on duty entered the room.

"Good evening ladies," the doctor greeted them. "Who in this room is her relative? I need to speak with a family member and kindly ask the rest of you to leave just for a moment," the doctor requested.

"I'm her sister," Adoma lied. "Do you know what's wrong with her?" Adoma asked the doctor as Mya and Casey patted Genna's arm and departed the room. Adoma and the doctor stepped to the other side of the room to discuss Genna's status.

"We don't know the cause of her fainting spell, nor the high fever, but we are doing the best we can. Do you know of anything odd that she may have ingested during this trip or before she arrived?"

Adoma thought about all the places they'd eaten and toured. She replied, "No," then remembered that Genna had stopped in West Africa during her layover. "Wait. She had a layover in West Africa!" Adoma exclaimed to the doctor. A cold dread came over Adoma. Genna had all of the symptoms she had found in her trip research. "Could she have gotten malaria?"

"Malaria?" The doctor asked in surprise. "What? Well, we don't have that test here at this hospital. The islands don't have malaria. But we will call out to get the test."

"Thank you," Adoma said as the doctor turned to leave. She turned back to Genna and smiled, receiving a weak smile in return before Genna closed her eyes. Then suddenly, Genna's face lost all color as the beeping of the machines increased in pitch, volume, and frequency. Genna's body fluttered.

"We're losing her!" the doctor yelled. "Nurse!" A nurse rushed in and pushed Adoma out of the way. Adoma heard a shout in the duress. "We have to stabilize her!"

Hours later, the commotion in Genna's room had subsided completely. "Doctor!" Adoma yelled out to him from the waiting room as he left the ICU. She, Casey, and Mya had waited hours to see him again.

"Ma'am sorry for the delay. We finally have your sister stable, and your suspicion proved correct. She indeed has contracted malaria. Walk with me; let's talk privately."

Out of earshot, the doctor resumed his diagnosis. "The patient, pardon, I mean your sister, indeed has contracted malaria. Left untreated the disease had grown almost fatal, but luckily we caught it just in time. It's okay, don't worry." He placed his warm hand on Adoma's shoulder. "We have begun treating her with a course of anti-malarial medicines, and your sister is going to be okay. But…" he paused, lowering his eyes, as if searching for the right words to console Adoma before he added his final words, "Unfortunately, the nurse broke the news to her an hour ago that she lost the baby."

"She did?" Adoma tried to remain stoic, successful in not revealing her utter shock.

"Yes, she did, and I am very sorry."

Chapter 48
Going Home

Since the hospital, Genna had barely whispered a word but finally attempted an utterance in the final moments of their return journey home.

"Adoma, thank you for flying back early with me," Genna murmured, looking up at Adoma with bloodshot eyes and a sincerity that showed through her sunglasses.

"Of course. And, there is no need to thank me. Of course, I would accompany you to come back home early. That's what friends are for. You were very sick you know, and you may not have realized this, but we almost lost you. I'm just glad you are okay now, and it's time for you to recover your health. Just focus on getting better now. You've been through a lot." Adoma wrapped her arms around Genna, holding her closer to reinforce her words.

"And Mya and Casey? Where are they?"

"They are changing their flights to come back earlier as well. They both should be back within a couple of days. We are going to be here for you Genna, don't worry. Shhh," Adoma tried coaxing Genna back to sleep. "Shhh, Genna, we are almost to your house. Just relax."

"I lost our baby," Genna whimpered.

"Genna, I know and I am truly sorry." Adoma stroked Genna's hair as the taxi turned into Genna's neighborhood.

"I lost a baby I didn't even know that I was carrying," Genna sobbed. "How did this happen? How did I ever become the type of woman who doesn't even know she's pregnant? I never thought that that could happen to people." Genna heaved, remembering all of the times she dismissed her pregnancy symptoms as being caused by stress. "But it happened to me... and I lost...."

"Genna, it's okay, don't blame yourself. None of this is your fault."

"But it is, Adoma, and I don't know how or if I should tell Fred."

"Shhhhh, don't even worry about that now. You just need to worry about physically and emotionally healing," Adoma affirmed, unable to imagine keeping such news from Mark.

When they reached Genna's home, Fred met them at the door. "How's she doing?" Fred asked Adoma as he helped Genna, balancing her on his arm.

"She's okay Fred," Adoma explained after he had tucked in Genna. "She started speaking more today, but she needs more rest." Fred nodded and blew through his mouth, moving the hair that hung over his forehead. Adoma, ignoring his disheveled appearance, added, "I think she will be all right if you just let her sleep because she is exhausted." She continued, "I believe it's the physical and emotional exhaustion from the long flight and what happened, which is the issue at this point."

"What exactly happened?" Fred asked, raising an eyebrow in curiosity more than concern.

"Fred," Adoma replied, reading his mind. "I will leave it to Genna to tell you all of the details."

"Of course. Well, thanks for bringing her back home early – and safely, I might add. And sorry about this. I know you had planned the reunion for a while and it didn't end the way you expected."

"That's okay. We kept our promise. We reunited and there was a ten-year closure, so it's in the past now. Genna's well-being is my top priority at this point. I didn't hesitate to cancel the rest of the trip. Actually what happened shook everyone up and both Casey and Mya will be on their way back tomorrow," Adoma said, glancing at the time. "Well, I need to go. The cab is still waiting for me, so I will leave you two alone so that Genna can continue to rest. Don't let her sleep for too long or her sleep schedule will be off because of the time difference. I think you can handle it from here. I will call you all later."

"Thank you again, Adoma." Fred hugged her.

"My pleasure Fred. Take care of her," Adoma said as she walked out.

"More soup?" Fred asked, checking Genna's forehead for signs of increased temperature. She didn't rouse.

At that moment, he looked down at her and realized that, for the first time in their marriage, he had seen her bare-faced, no added color, no added anything, just Genna in her natural form appearing like an angel. And, he fell in love with her again.

Fred, fully clothed, ignoring resistance, lifted the sheets and climbed in slowly, gently as not to stir her. He caressed Genna's hair, cooing softly, "Shhh sweet Genevieve, shhh. Sweet, beautiful dreams, my love," until the wrinkles in her forehead relaxed and her chest moved rhythmically up and down, confirming once more that she had fallen deeply asleep.

Chapter 49
Revelations

Adoma paid for the taxi as her mother opened the front door, welcoming her for the weeklong stay. When Adoma reached the threshold, she embraced her mother tightly.

"Welcome back home, dear. I made your favorite dish, red-red," Adoma's mother said while inspecting Adoma's face for clues to her daughter's well-being. "I am so happy to see you, even though it's not under the best of circumstances – from what I could ascertain.

"Adoma, put down your things, eat some red-red, and relax. And after you do, tell me again why you had to cancel the last part of the trip and come home? Yes, you said Genna got sick; I know that. But, something very terrible must have befallen her. What exactly happened to Genna?" Adoma's mother asked in surprise.

"Mom, thank you, and you know I love red-red, but I don't have an appetite."

"Well, if it's something so serious that you could pass up your favorite meal and fried plantain, then I want to know what happened now. Sit down and tell me."

"Well, Genna is fine now. I just dropped her off at home. But the reason we had to come back early is that we almost lost her during the trip."

"Lost? What does that mean, you almost lost her? Do you mean she almost died? What happened?!"

"She caught malaria en route to the Seychelles and she hadn't realized it. Then, while we were all on the beach, she said that she felt very hot. It was a fever, and she fainted. We rushed her to the hospital and though we got her there in time to save her life, it was too late for the baby."

"That's so tragic. You never mentioned that Genna was pregnant. Why would she travel pregnant?"

"I never mentioned it, because I didn't know she was pregnant. Even Genna didn't know. She said that she had been too stressed to notice she'd missed her period and thought that her nausea was related to stress too," Adoma explained, thinking of the irony of Genna not being in tune with her body. Adoma stopped speculating and re-focused her attention on her mother, who had sunken into a withdrawn haze.

"Mom, did you hear me?"

"Yes, I did, Adoma."

"Then, why aren't you responding?"

"I just need a moment." Adoma's mother blinked her eyes slowly. After her third blink, her eyes refocused with a far away expression. "Adoma, I think it's time for you to know." Her distant eyes gazed through Adoma, who rubbed her mother's hand to help coax out the thoughts that seemed to burden her mind. Adoma longed to know the reason for the silence that hung between them; she needed to know the truth.

Adoma's mother first stiffened and then relaxed her body as she released her breath to speak.

"There was a coup," she muttered, seemingly unable to fight back the flood of memories that had burdened her. "There was a coup a few years before we arrived in America," she paused as if gathering the courage to continue. "Shortly after the first vehicles rolled in through the capital, we lost contact with your father, who had worked for the former government, the one being overthrown. And I was terrified."

Adoma listened, rapt in attention. For all of these years, she had never known this tumultuous part of her family history.

"For the first day, no one heard from your father. We were all scared and didn't want to speculate about where he could have gone. I had hoped he was hiding somewhere and safe. I begged everyone I could think of for information, but no one knew anything or they were too afraid to say. Everyone was scared. Fear gripped the capital."

Her mother clutched her stomach instinctively. "I was pregnant at the time." Her hand moved up and down her belly, as if a child still slept there, "so pregnant then that I could hardly walk straight. I waddled like a duck." Adoma's mother smiled through teary eyes.

"On day two, we all still waited anxiously for word on your father. Then later that day, I will always remember it – it was a beautiful Tuesday afternoon – I received a call with news." She blinked slowly and looked up as she spoke despondently, her eyes trying to hold back the spilling moisture. "A relative found out that your father had been captured." She inhaled deeply and continued. "And I just knew then that he wouldn't make it back home to me." She grimaced. "News already began to filter out about what had been happening to ex-government officials. And with the thought of never seeing your father again in the forefront of my mind, I collapsed, crying out in agony, clutching the floor." Adoma embraced her mother who had sunk into her arms.

"A sharp physical pain, matching the emotional pain that ripped my heart, flooded my entire body. At that moment, I ignored it – far greater was the pain I had for fear that I would never see your father, my first love, ever again. I sunk further and further down onto the floor as my mind tried to comprehend the collapse of my world. I cried deeply, so deeply. I kept crying, incessantly – until I felt dampness… and when I looked down, I saw the scarlet liquid that caused it. And then, I screamed out for help." Adoma's mother shook her head and wiped away her tears. "We went to the hospital. But, with many of the doctors gone to tend to their families during the crisis, I didn't get the needed care. Nothing could be done; it was too late."

Adoma's mother drifted from the memory and slowly refocused her attention to Adoma to exhale words that she had long wished to say: "Adoma, you had a sister."

Chapter 50
Endurance

Adoma greeted Mark the following day. "Hi, Love. Sorry that it's been a while since we've actually spoken. I know you don't like texting, but things have been so hectic, that's all I could manage for the last two days."

"Yes, I know honey, it's fine," Mark responded. Eager to find out more, he asked, "So is Genna okay? Has Fred been around to help take care of her? And how are you managing?" He tried getting his questions out all at once before Adoma could say she'd have to leave again.

"I've been managing okay. A lot's happened since we spoke last week." Adoma proceeded to update Mark on the details – from the emergency plane ride back to the taxi ride to Genna's home. Then Adoma changed the subject to the important revelations of her mother.

"Yeah, I think my mother only opened up because I told her what happened to Genna," Adoma said, after giving Mark the initial details of her mom's recount of the coup. "But, I am so glad she did; it explains a lot about her distance toward me..." Adoma sighed, "...why she had rarely said 'I love you' or barely embraced me. I can't believe she held that information in for so long," Adoma commented, finally understanding her mother's past behavior. "Considering that none of my aunts or uncles ever spoke about it, I assume she swore them to secrecy." Adoma switched the phone to her other ear. "And you remember the mystery of the hidden cloth, right?"

"Yes – the one you found years ago concealed in your mother's items?"

"Yes, that one," Adoma confirmed.

"So, did you solve the mystery?"

"Well, my mother just told me the rest of the story, and then I figured it out on my own, the reason she keeps it tucked away."

"Oh?"

"Yeah. After she had gathered herself from the initial flashback, she finished."

"Oh?" Mark replied again.

"Yeah. Our family had a private burial. I was way too young at the time, so I don't remember it. But, remember how I explained to you before that families wear a common adinkra cloth for the church service after a funeral? Our cloth was a different emblem back then, and, well, after the funeral, my mother could no longer bear the sight of the old family symbol, so my parents changed the pattern.

"That makes sense. What was the previous family symbol?"

"Aya, the fern – for endurance."

"Interesting, Adoma. But what happened with your father? You know, after he got swept up in the government overthrow? You mentioned that he went missing; obviously he ended up okay. But how?"

"Oh yes, I forgot that part. It has to do with what I told you my cousin had explained. My dad, part of the old regime, was captured and no one heard from him for about two days. My mother believes they let him live because of his value to the new regime in the financial sector. Maybe since he was an accountant they needed to know from him where some of the money had been held or how to decode the old books. This is all just my speculation, though. I don't know."

"Okay, that's all plausible. I can see that, too."

"Well," Adoma continued, "my dad stayed and worked for the new government. I can only assume that he did it for as long as he could and then soon, he may have realized his utility would run out; that they'd soon wonder if he would remain forever loyal. I guess that's when he came here to the U.S."

"That's an incredible story. Adoma, you can't make that stuff up. How tragic and captivating all at the same time."

"I know. I'm exhausted from just having told you about it. The crazy thing is, I think there is more. This story explains some of the family secrecy and the distant looks in my parents' eyes when I pressed them about back home. But it doesn't explain everything. My dad and mother still speak in hushed tones when they think that I can't hear them."

"Are they speaking in your native language?"

"Yes. They never speak it with me, but always to each other. Maybe it's that they hate the sound of my American accent butchering our language."

"Funny," Mark remarked. "Well, hon, I'm glad we could finally talk about everything, but I'm an hour ahead of you and it's getting late."

"Yeah, you're right, and now I need to get in touch with Genna. She hasn't been answering her phone or returning texts. Fred hasn't responded today either."

"Don't worry. She's probably still jet-lagged or just trying to recover, and Fred is likely to be busy helping her get re-acclimated," Mark spoke circumspectly to lead Adoma away from a worrisome conclusion. "But yes, you do indeed need to get in touch with them eventually; the sooner, the better," Mark commented, yawning. "I'm tired, so I am going to have to let you go and call it a night. Have a good night baby."

"Good night Mark. I miss you."

"I miss you too. I love you, Adoma."

"Love you more."

Chapter 51
House of Cards

In his rush to make breakfast, Fred tripped over Genna's handbag, casually strewn at the side of their bed. He looked down, glancing at the bright pink paper peeking out of the front pocket, which barely roused his interest. If not for the word "embryo" Fred would have pushed the paper back into the purse without notice. Instead, he felt inclined, rather obliged, to remove the document and read it.

His fingers trembled as he mumbled the words he read again and again. On the fifth pass, he finally comprehended the medical report. After digesting its impact, he sighed, "I can't believe she would do that."

"Fred," Genna said as she ate breakfast. "I'm regaining my strength, so I think I'm ready to start running again. You know, get back into my old routine. I think the fact that I stopped running three weeks before I left for the Seychelles completely threw me off balance and out of tune with my body. Had you noticed that I hadn't been running?"

"Yes, I did. How could I not notice that you suddenly stopped waking up in the wee morning hours? Instead of getting up before 5 am, you'd barely be up at 6 am."

"I always thought you were asleep. Have you been awake all of those times?" Genna asked in surprise.

"Sometimes, yes." Fred added, "Don't you think you should wait before you begin running again. You know, to gain all of your strength back instead of pushing yourself? Let's see; you almost died of malaria… and miscarried a child. Now you want to start pushing yourself again?"

Genna inadvertently displayed shock. "How did you find out about the miscarriage?"

"When were you going to tell me?" Fred countered in a measured voice.

"I didn't know how to tell you. It's hard for me to think about it. I didn't know how you would take it and that's why I didn't say anything. But since you know now, yes I miscarried. I'm not sure if it was the virus or the anti-malaria pills that did it, but the doctor said that I was around six weeks pregnant. Fred, I'm so sorry," Genna explained, relieved to reveal the truth.

"Genna," Fred said slowly, putting his hand over hers. Reflexively, Genna rested her fork. "What we have isn't real. Do you see that?"

"What do you mean, Fred?" Genna asked, incredulously. The direction of the conversation rapidly changed, contrasting the comfort and support Fred had been providing as Genna recovered. Genna couldn't comprehend his accusing tone. "Do I see *what*, Fred?"

"That we have been living a lie to each other; that our marriage is a sham, Genna. That it's not real. That it's a house of cards. That we are not faithful to each other in the way a married couple should be. We've been lying to each other, and I've been lying to you by omitting the truth regarding the investigation, and other things."

"Fred, *what* other things?" Genna asked, indignantly.

"And you have done the same," Fred continued without acknowledging Genna's question.

"Fred, what are you talking about?" Genna's voice was becoming hysterical.

"The baby was not mine Genna!"

"Of course it was! Fred, what are you talking about? What are you trying to say? What are you accusing me of?"

"Genna, I will not play this game with you," Fred continued calmly. "We have been tap dancing around things for far too long. If you want to play stupid, play stupid, but I will not join in on your game. I am just stating a fact, and the fact is the baby was not mine."

"Of course it was!"

"Genna, do not insult my intelligence. The child was not mine and I know it was not mine. Now, I don't know whose child it was or whether it was conceived by immaculate conception; but it was not *my* child, Genna!"

"Fred, I am sorry that I lost our baby, but you don't have to behave this way. Fred, I'm sorry that it happened!"

"Genna. Just. Stop!" Fred, now standing, turned away from her.

"Stop what Fred? Just say what you want to say!"

"Stop lying to me and stop lying to yourself! The child was not mine!"

"And what gives you the audacity to make such a nonsensical claim and all that it implies?" Genna spat out.

"I know the child is not mine because I cannot have children!"

"What? Fred, stop lying!"

"I'm not lying, Genna. I took care of it. Snip. Done. Easy. In and out."

Before Fred had finished the last word, Genna's face curled in pain, as she balled her hand into a fist. "What? You did *that*? Without telling me? You know that I've always wanted to be a mother – to be a mother and give my child, my children, everything that I never had growing up! And you robbed me of that without even telling me?" Genna said through clenched teeth, trying to steady her stance and hands as she spoke.

"You cheated on me, Genna," Fred answered.

"You're not the victim here Fred. We cheated on each other – just in different ways. Like you had started to say – our house of cards has crumbled. And now I finally see the writing on the wall." Genna walked calmly over to the kitchen sink and put her plate away. She departed the conversation and the kitchen.

Before reaching the bedroom door, she turned around, speaking slowly and deliberately. "Now… what I want… is for you… to… leave… my… house."

Chapter 52
When It All Comes Down

On the third day of silence, Adoma drove to Genna's home. Although it was a breathtakingly bright afternoon, the blinds to the stately home were closed. Adoma retrieved the parcel abandoned at the door and rang the bell. 'Hmm. No answer.'

Adoma, grateful that Genna and Fred didn't own a dog, tiptoed to the backyard. When she reached the kitchen window, Adoma peeked through a tiny space between the blindfolds and saw Genna sitting at the counter in a bathrobe, sulking as she drank coffee. When Genna noticed the disembodied eyeball peering through the kitchen window, she screamed.

"Genna, it's just me!" Adoma yelled before Genna could reach her phone.

Genna, through her sunken eyes, leered suspiciously at the shadowy figure. She then slowly raised and reluctantly opened the kitchen door.

"Genna! What in the world is wrong with you?" Adoma exclaimed upon seeing her emaciated friend. "You're completely dehydrated. And where is Fred? You should not be alone right now!"

"Fred is gone," Genna said, collapsing back into the kitchen chair.

"What? How could he leave you alone in this condition?" Adoma responded in astonishment. "When is he returning?"

"He isn't returning. He's gone. Gone, gone. I made him leave."

"Seriously, Genna. You aren't making any sense right now." Adoma contemplated that Genna had become momentarily delirious. Genna rambled on incoherently below her breath.

"You need water, Genna. And when was the last time you ate anything? You can't survive on just coffee." Adoma rushed a glass of water to her friend, fearing that Genna would collapse without it.

Genna still collapsed, not from dehydration, but in tears. She cried with an abandon Adoma had never seen in her friend. Throughout the entire ordeal – the hospital stay in which she almost died and the long plane ride home afterward – she stayed stoic. But, now, she wept.

When Genna's strength to remain upright failed her, she gave in to the exhaustion and collapsed her head onto the surface of the kitchen table. While sulking, she muttered, "I'm on my own now. I don't have a family anymore."

Adoma rubbed Genna's arms. "Genna, I feel guilty; like it's my fault you got malaria. What are the odds. Even so, I'm sorry."

Genna continued to sniffle. "Adoma don't beat yourself up about it. You're right. It was completely against the odds. And maybe..." Genna paused "...and maybe it just wasn't meant to be. It wasn't even Fred's."

Adoma sat her glass of water on the table as she tried to comprehend what Genna just told her.

"I would go running on the weekends with a new friend, and then one day ... well... it happened. But only once! I realized I made a mistake and also why I did it. Fred had stopped speaking with me. He stopped sharing with me, and so I stopped sharing with him. We were in the midst of a storm caused by Fred. I made the life we had and now here he was trying to break it down. And all I needed from him – the only thing I needed was communication. Not what I could get from sources or the news. I needed to know what was going on – from him – so that I could counter the attacks and to protect myself – protect us. And he just left me in the dark. He stopped speaking with me; he stopped caring.

"And then there was Rob. He was there. He saved me one day after a fall; that day when Fred just stormed out after a fight," Genna continued. "After I made the mistake with Rob, I couldn't really look at myself. I stopped returning his texts. Naturally, we stopped running together. Then, shortly after that, I saw him on my morning run, so I stopped running altogether right before I left for the Seychelles. I didn't want to bump into him again. And now this... My entire world has fallen apart and ... and ... all these emotions are going through me at once. I just want to die. I want to burn the house down and just go away. What have I built anyway? None of this is real. I betrayed Fred and he betrayed me. He robbed me of our future without even telling me. He didn't even bother to let me know."

Adoma became confused. "Let you know what, Genna?"

Genna didn't notice the question. "He was aware of what I valued the most, the one thing that's important to me. I know it looks like I put material or superficial matters above all else, but that's not true and Fred knows that. I've been taking care of my parents since I've been able to. And I've wanted a family of my own ever since Fred and I met. I put family above all else, and now – and now I've lost my family." Genna paused from sobbing to stare into space.

Adoma sat still, fearing the slightest move. She didn't want to scare Genna, who appeared erratic, with any sudden moves, especially while in a kitchen surrounded by knives. In response to the rare outburst of emotion from her usually controlled friend, Adoma's body reacted with a quickening heartbeat and tightened hands.

Suddenly, Genna glared at Adoma with possessed, burning eyes and slowly raised herself. "I'm going to bed now Adoma. Please see your way out."

"Genna, it's 11:30 am, almost the afternoon," Adoma protested.

"Please leave."

"No," Adoma resisted.

"I'm going to call the police if you don't leave my property right now!" Genna yelled with clenched fists.

"Go ahead," Adoma responded as nonchalantly as possible.

"Fine!" Genna yelled. Then she completely dismissed the phone call and instead retired to her bedroom.

After Genna's door had slammed, Adoma looked around the home. Glasses and plates of uneaten food littered the kitchen and den; dishes overflowed in the sink. And, a putrid smell,

Adoma assumed to be trash, emanated from a nearby closet. Adoma disposed of the garbage and placed the dishes in the dishwasher, struggling to figure out the complex stainless steel machine.

While the dishes ran, Adoma thought about how long she had known Genna. It had been over twenty years; and in those early years as new immigrants, they had been inseparable. Meeting Genna helped Adoma with the loneliness of being an only child.

Awash with childhood memories, Adoma remembered the imaginary friend she had before knowing Genna. 'My tea parties with Abena...' Adoma smiled in recollection of her make-believe games with her invisible friend. Adoma still wondered how she came to know Abena's name, which means born on Tuesday. They were close until the day Adoma told her mother about Abena, and her mother reacted in a way Adoma would never forget. After that moment, Abena never returned to play.

Genna finally stirred from her bed, but still wore a bathrobe. "Genna, its 1:00 in the afternoon, don't you think it's time for you to change?" Adoma asked as she organized the clean dishes.

"Don't you think it's time for you to shut up and leave?" Genna responded.

"Excuse me?"

"You're excused, Adoma."

"Genna, I don't know what I've done to aggrieve you, but I am just trying to help," Adoma said while approaching Genna as closely as Genna's body odor would allow.

"I never asked for your help, Adoma. Actually, I would have preferred to have stayed in my filth without any witnesses. And now here you come, humming along."

"Yes, uh huh. Here I come along cleaning your house for you."

"I didn't ask you to. Just leave, Adoma."

"Genna, you're falling apart."

"I know that Adoma. I have a law degree, remember? That means I'm smart enough to deduce things. Therefore, I, like you, know that my appearance, smell, and the condition of my home – when all put together – mean that I am falling apart. You don't have to state the obvious."

"If you know this, then why won't you let me help you? Just let me help you. Let me open up these blinds. Let's get you cleaned up. Let's get some fresh air. Let's breathe!"

"No, Adoma, I'm fine!"

"Genna, you don't have to be strong all the time! *We* don't have to be strong all the time! You're *human*! You are always the provider, but now you need help, Genna! Let yourself receive my help! There is no dishonor in that!"

Something in those last words triggered Genna, and her penned up contempt began to release like a pricked balloon slowly wheezing out air. In Adoma's last few words, Genna received the permission that she had never allowed herself – the permission to be vulnerable – and to just breathe.

Genna ran to Adoma, and they clung to each other in a tight, tearful embrace.

Chapter 53
The Sun

The next week, Adoma, Casey, Mya, and Genna met for lunch. Genna, aided by the love of her friends and the resumption of her morning running routine, looked nearly restored to her original health.

Still, out of trepidation, this less boisterous meal hardly had a mention of the reunion trip, until Mya cautiously spoke.

"Adoma, I brought you back something," Mya said discreetly, to avoid an emotional relapse from Genna. "It's from the seamstress. It came in after you had to leave."

Adoma claimed the package and, unable to contain her excitement, tore into the plain brown box. Her arms spread wide to view the fullness of the seamstress's creation, and Adoma approvingly inspected her work. The adinkra symbols of Adoma, Mya, Casey, and Genna were carefully woven into four patchwork quilts with each of the ladies' respective adinkra symbols interwoven in the center of the patterns.

"This is gorgeous!" Adoma exclaimed as she passed the remaining quilts to her friends.

Each woman took a quilt and followed Adoma's lead in draping it over their body. Adoma swept and layered hers over her shoulder like a shawl; Casey wrapped hers over her leggings like a short skirt; Mya made a beautiful headdress out of hers, and Genna draped hers over her suit like a graduation stole.

"We look so beautiful my friends," Adoma said, satisfied.

"We do," Genna agreed, then continued. "Well, not to damper the tone by bringing up what happened, but Adoma, I'd like to thank Mark one of these days for his article in *The Times* on malaria."

"Aww, he'd be happy to know that you read it. I will make sure to pass on the kind words to him," Adoma responded. She knew the beginning words of his article by heart....

My wife had asked me if I had ever written about malaria and I hadn't. I never planned to. The editors never asked me to. The readers never thought about it. I had no reason to. No reason until now, when it affected someone dear to my family.

Malaria kills. Malaria killed my friend's unborn child and almost killed her too. These deaths would not have been noted, but simply added to the numbers of those who did not have to die...

Seeing Genna's eyes moisten, Adoma squeezed her friend's hand in comfort and received an equivalent squeeze in return.

"Shots anyone?" They all smiled and welcomed Casey's intentional interruption to keep a light atmosphere.

"No!" they all grumbled in response.

"I think I will have a tea instead," Mya said, and everyone else followed suit.

"Well, ladies," Adoma spoke as they reviewed the bill. "This has been a great ten-year adventure. Shall we do it again, let's say in another ten years?" Adoma added in jest.

"Well, another decade may be too long to wait. Let's say in another five instead?" Mya countered.

Adoma, Casey, and Genna nodded in agreement with the more reasonable time frame.

"Who knows where we'll all be in the next five years? I'm going back to school to get a Masters or a Doctorate, I think," Casey said. "And maybe I can become the next representative for the district. I hear there could be an opening in the future," Casey beamed knowingly.

"Five years is a good amount of time," Genna agreed and smiled back. "And, if it's settled, then let's head back to my place to decide where we'll meet. I have cosmos and a giant globe that we can spin," Genna offered, grinning with nostalgia.

"Ready, everyone?" Adoma asked as they settled the bill.

They departed the restaurant as happy as they were a decade

ago, the night of their initial promise. But, this time, Adoma, Genna, Casey, and Mya left adorned in symbols of their unity. These last ten years had been remarkable. Life events had brought them wisdom, and through it all, they learned to love each other deeper than before.

As they strode away hand-in-hand, Adoma felt the sun on her face and tilted her head upward to absorb its rays. Adoma gleamed at this heavenly moment. She loved her best friends and she loved the sun. They both bestowed her with clarity, warmth, and light.

A Note from the Author

I believe that no child or adult should die from a mosquito bite - but hundreds of thousands do. The staggering number of annual deaths caused by malaria, a preventable and curable illness, breaks my heart.

I'm called to raise awareness about important issues like malaria through my art. I do so through writing, and have collaborated with Malaria No More to donate 20% of the proceeds of *Tenth Year in the Sun* to support their work, particularly malaria education and prevention programs in West Africa.

Thank you very much for purchasing *Tenth Year in the Sun* and supporting this important work.

malaria
NO MORE

Malaria No More is a nonprofit organization based in the U.S. that envisions a world where no child dies from a mosquito bite. The organization's mission is to use innovative partnerships and focused advocacy to elevate malaria on the global health agenda, create political will, and mobilize the global resources required to achieve malaria eradication within a generation.

To support Malaria No More directly, please visit their website www.malarianomore.org.

Adoma - West Africa

2) Casey - high school / college
nympho

* (1) Genna - elem / neighborhood

3) Mya - East Africa

67095770R10179

Made in the USA
Lexington, KY
02 September 2017